MW01134589

THE SECRET WAR OF 1834

B. B. LECLERE

outskirts
press

PREFACE

All people throughout history have considered themselves
at the cutting edge of accomplishment. We look back at
our predecessors and scoff at how primitive their methods
were, just as our descendants will look back and scoff at us.
Progress is made by those few with the courage to push
beyond what is known and dare to try the untried ideas.
It is around these brave pioneers that this story revolves.

MEDICINE OF 1834

In the first half of the 1800s, medical practice was still based more on philosophy than science, focusing on the four humors; blood, yellow bile, black bile, and phlegm. This theory is credited to Hypocrites, circa 460 BCE–370 BCE. There was very little change made in this practice over time. The established doctors defended what they had been taught and rejected new thinking.

Options for treating maladies were limited. One was a form of herbology, practiced almost exclusively by Indian doctors. There was also hydropathy, a practice that dated back to Egyptian and Roman times. The therapeutic use of water had seen a resurgence in England and Germany in the 1700s. In addition to the supposed healing power of water was a focus on better hygiene, the washing of the hands and face, to ward off ailments that were thought to be catching, or contagious.

A group called the Thomasonians fought the long-established restrictions, working to win doctors the right to try other means of finding relief and cures for their patients. In the meantime, there were a few doctors who went to the unregulated frontier to search for answers.

WAR TACTICS OF 1834

The weapons of war also had not changed for over two hundred years; the staple weapon was the flintlock. A cumbersome item by today's standards that took twenty to fifty seconds to reload. The smooth bore barrel and round shot meant that accuracy was poor. Successful ignition of the charge was about 70 percent.

The methods of war had remained unchanged for even longer. Brightly colored uniforms, fife and drum playing the march, with soldiers advancing in a great line were still held as the norm; the objective was to have the opponent break and run in fear or to surrender. Guerrilla warfare was a new and, some thought, uncivilized method of war first seen when battling the Native Americans and was not yet accepted by those who thought themselves more cultured and refined.

Both of these were fairly effective modes of combat ... provided the other side was doing roughly the same thing. Though, with a foe using an entirely different mode of fighting, people had to adapt. However, when men are faced with utter savagery, how drastically their definition of war changes.

1:

IN CHICAGO

The sun hung bright and low in the clear, early-morning sky as Dr. Deggory Periwinkle bade his wife and son goodbye and made his way out of his stately home, a handsome two-story affair of whitewashed clay brick with three large windows across the front. Chicago had only been founded two years before Deggory arrived, before the popularity of the frontier city had taken off.

As he walked down the packed earth streets, he greeted the farmers and shopkeepers who made up the town and his clients. At the bridge he was hailed by James Kinzie, the proprietor of Wolf Tavern, and William Walters, the landlord.

"Good morning, Deggory!"

"Good morning, James! Good morning, William! What has the two of you up and working so early?"

"We had to clean the place back up," James replied, mopping sweat from his brow. "We had another scrap here last night. They broke a few chairs, a table, and some glasses. They will most likely be needing your services when they sleep it off."

"Sorry about your pub getting messed up, fellows."

"It's not a big problem," William chimed in. "A little bad news for my business is a little good news for yours."

"True enough. I will probably see you this evening."

Deggory continued to exchange, "Good mornings" as he walked to his medical practice in the middle of town. The only other physician in Chicago, a Dr. Thaddius Wolcott, catered almost exclusively (and rather obstinately, Deggory felt) to the soldiers in Fort Dearborn and dealing with cholera that was running rampant through "his troops," as he called them, so Dr. Periwinkle had his own growing population of clients, and he did not miss the ostentatious finery of Boston at all …

The only remnant of his fine upbringing was that he bore himself with a slight air of haughty pride. He also possessed a sharp mind, having graduated in 1820 from Columbia College in New York. His intelligence was evident when his brown eyes locked onto a patient or problem needing attention, and he was a man not content to give up on any case or condition.

That was why Dr. Periwinkle had brought his young wife, Margaret, and five-year-old son, Joshamy, from the sophistication of his New York practice to the comparative wilds of Chicago, in the hopes of finding a cure for the tuberculosis that was eroding his family's life. Both Margaret and his young boy had nearly died several times from consumption, as it was more commonly called, and he felt a tremendous burden of guilt and shame constantly gnawing at him as he repeatedly failed to cure them.

He was Dr. Deggory Periwinkle, by God! A learned man of medicine taught by the finest professors and tutors money could buy. Yet this disease stood, knocking at his door and intending to rob him of the family he had always dreamed of having.

One starlit night, not long after Maggie had joined her husband in Chicago, she lay awake gripped in fevers and sweats and horrific, blood-speckled coughing fits.

"Deggory," she whispered as he pressed a damp cloth to her heated brow, "you are an accomplished physician and scientist. You possess an innovative mind that many others in your field are profoundly lacking. Moreover, you are my husband, and I have no doubt that you will be the one to realize the cure for this plague. I believe in you."

Deggory gazed deeply into her sea-blue eyes and brushed a wisp of her blond hair behind her ear. "Maggie, my love, I fear the man I would become without you. My life started the day I met you in school, when we were not more than children." He continued, his own voice slipping into a thin whisper, "I knew when I saw you that you were my future. To lose you, or the son you blessed me with, would break me." He held her closely and pressed his lips ever so softly against the back of her hand. She had become so thin and fragile these last few years, and he couldn't help but treat her like a porcelain doll.

Maggie brushed away the tear that hung on his cheek, "You are a far stronger man than you believe yourself to be, Dr. Deggory Periwinkle. Should the worst occur, you will persist, and you will prevail."

Dr. Periwinkle had made it his life's work to find a cure.

After failing to gain any progress or support in New York or Boston, he was now sure the best chance for an answer lay out here near the unexplored American wilderness; it involved a mixture of modern European medicine and Indian herbal lore.

He had made a good friend and ally in Howakan, the medicine man from the Winnebago tribe north of Chicago. Still, he lived in doubt of his ability to find an answer in time to save them.

Shaking himself from his dark musings, Dr. Periwinkle made his way down Randolph Street. Reaching his office, he discovered that his first patient of the day, a young Master Clayton Williams, who'd had himself a bit of a cough, was already waiting for him, with his mother worrying over him as a hen does her chick. Clayton, it soon appeared, was fortunate in that all he had was a simple cough and not the start of something more insidious. Too many townsfolk and soldiers over at Fort Dearborn were coming down with consumption, cholera, or any number of terribly fatal illnesses that he could still do little to remedy. After young Mr. Williams was given some honey and lemon, he and his smothering mother left.

Dr. Periwinkle had barely had time to peruse his notes from his latest laboratory experiments before he was obliged to treat Ferdinand Peck and Chauncey Bowen for scrapes and bruises sustained in the tussle at the bar. These two were the best of friends but would get into a bout of fisticuffs on an almost weekly basis. However, Mr. Bowen had very nearly lost an eye this time, and Dr. Periwinkle had needed to take great care in sewing the skin of his brow shut. Mr. Peck had only minor injuries that simply needed topical ointments and bandaging.

Dr. Periwinkle was losing patience with these two being so careless with their well-being. "Have you two gone back to pay James and William for the things you damaged in their business?"

"What?"

"You broke a table, some chairs, and more. You had better get up there and make things right."

"Yes, sir!"

Following not twenty minutes behind them was Mrs. Amelia Featherstone, who'd developed an infected tooth that needed pulling, and as the local barber was away on business for the next month, her needs fell to him. Dr. Periwinkle had needed to call on the assistance of Mrs. Featherstone's teenaged son to hold her head still while Dr. Periwinkle lanced the gum and extracted the infected molar. She'd requested a chloroform cloth before her extraction so was never in any real distress; however, pulling a molar required leverage, so assistance was appreciated.

As he walked the two of them to the door, he was confronted by Mato Hota, a strapping man from the Winnebago Indian tribe to the north. He was quite tall, muscular, and lighter of skin, hair, and eye than most of the Natives. He was dressed for long travel, his tribe's village being several days' journey to the north. Mato Hota was single-minded on his mission.

"Good morning, Dr. Periwinkle. I need you to give me the cure for my people that you and Howakan have been working on. I cannot wait. Time is running out for my little sister."

Time was running out for his wife and son as well. He fought back the dark thoughts and turned away from Mato Hota, hiding his shame at not yet having a cure to give, "I am still working on that, but it is not yet ready."

Mato was crestfallen. "Dr. Periwinkle, Howakan thought you might have something … "

"I am sorry," Dr. Periwinkle interrupted, fiddling with the now dried chloroform cloth he'd used with Mrs. Featherstone. "Tell Howakan that I am working with the new herbs, phosphors, and fungus he sent me. I shall get word to him with information when I can."

"But, Doctor?"

"I have NOTHING I can give you!"

Visibly dejected, Mato Hota turned and stooped through the door and away from the office, shutting the door a little harder than necessary and unknowingly adding another layer of guilt over the doctor like a stifling blanket. Deggory took a deep breath and a long swallow from his hip flask before opening the door again.

Edwin Potter then came in, leaning heavily on his farm hand. Dr. Periwinkle took a moment to reorganize after Mrs. Featherstone's procedure before addressing Mr. Potter.

"Hey, Doc," Edwin said in a shaky voice. "I lost my grip while I was cutting back some weeds. Sliced my leg open pretty bad."

"I will have to clean that out and sew it up. Do you want something for the pain?"

"Just a dash of whisky if you would, Doctor."

"You did the right thing by wrapping it up. If it happens again, wash it out as well."

"I hope I *never* do this again."

"Good plan. Say, Edwin, are they still planning on putting together a fall festival?"

"Yes, they're working on it; you should bring your wife and boy."

Deggory did not respond.

Finally, Deggory's last patient of the day came in. Little Aaron Milchrist had broken both bones in his lower leg falling from an apple tree, and Dr. Periwinkle spent a hard-fought hour setting the bones correctly and splinting the eight-year-old's limb. Aaron had fainted at the start of the setting, directly after his sip of morphium, so wasn't too unduly distressed during the procedure. His mother, however, had nearly became unhinged.

He bound the splint with wet leather that would shrink and constrict the leg as it dried. Dr. Periwinkle then advised Mrs. Milchrist, who'd carried her son to the office in a wheelbarrow, to leave the casting on Aaron's leg for eight weeks or until he was fully healed. He also recommended that they head down to the woodsmith's to have a crutch fashioned for the boy.

⸺◉⸺

Then, after he'd finally closed his practice for the day, Dr. Periwinkle was up in his laboratory, carefully examining the rat, mouse, and rabbit specimens in wooden cages lined up along the left wall of his laboratory. All nine of the rodents (three of each) had been injected with the blood of consumption patients; he'd then given them variations of what he'd hoped would be a cure to this disease. It was with great disappointment that he made notations in his ledger: nine more test subjects, nine more failures. Two rabbits and a rat were dead, one mouse was near enough, the other two mice and the remaining rabbit seemed unchanged, and the last two rats … He leaned closer to the specimen cages. These rats were much thinner than they should have been. The fur was falling out in large clumps, and the exposed skin had a strange coloration, reminiscent of moldy bread. He made a notation in the ledger,

The day is Wednesday, the 20th of May 1834. Specimens 282 and 285: Day 7 under serum; show extreme negative reactions; discontinue all tests of serum 68.

He filled in the unusual reactions these rodents were exhibiting then flipped closed the leather-bound ledger, tossed it negligently onto his desk, and carefully capped his fountain pen before placing it gently in a drawer, having had one too many spillages of his ink onto shirt or trouser to set about that task with any half measure. Dropping heavily into his chair, he removed his spectacles and tossed them carelessly upon the ledger. Scrubbing his face with his hands, he stared at nothing for a moment, letting his frustration subside before standing, redonning his spectacles, and moving back to his blackboard and the notations and formulas thereon. He had just lifted the chalk to the surface when there came a knock on the door, and his manservant entered.

"Milord, the Lady Periwinkle requests you return in time

for dinner; she bade me inform you that she is 'insisting that you return home to your family and leave the rodents for another day,' sir."

The manservant, James Sutton, gave an apologetic half bow to his employer. James was on the shorter side for a man, with a lithe but muscular build, thin at the waist and wide at the shoulder. He had closely cropped powder-white hair that stood out in shocking contrast to his dark African skin tone. He was adorned in his usual uniform attire of tan cotton breeches, white linen shirt and socks, a red vest, a black frock coat, and black buckled shoes.

James was hired on to assist Deggory in his daily life, both at home and at work. When Deggory would get so wrapped up in patients or experimentations, he'd lose all track of time. This day was an excellent example as, Deggory realized with a start, he'd missed his midday meal.

James's wife, Annie, had originally been hired on to assist Maggie with the housework, as Maggie wanted to do the raising of Joshamy herself, contrary to the custom of the day. Now, though, Annie looked after both Maggie and Joshamy, ensuring they weren't overexerted, as consumption was aggravated by even minor activity.

Through the years, the Suttons had come to mean much more to the Periwinkles than that of mere servants. They came to be members of the family in their own right and were highly respected in the small community of Chicago as well.

"Yes, I don't doubt that she is, Jim. She's always been against my experimentations on animals, even those seen as vermin." He laughed, gesturing with the chalk to the caged creatures. "Thank you for the message; you may inform the Lady and my son that I will arrive home shortly."

Deggory placed the chalk back in the tray on the blackboard, brushed the dust from his fingers, and shrugged off his white lab coat. After hanging it on the coat rack by the door, he moved to his tailcoat, gloves, top hat, and ledger. After stowing the ledger in the satchel he wore over his shoulder and donning his accoutrements, he doused the lamps and made his way down the stairs, through his practice, and out the door. Lifting the small lantern by the doorway off its hook, after locking the door securely behind him, he headed down the street.

As he made his way toward home, he felt the too-familiar burden of guilt settle around him again. "Another day and still no answer." He dreaded carrying this dark mood home once again, to an already suffering wife and child and adding to their burdens.

As he reached the bridge, he was hailed by Jake Cummings, a barrel-chested family man who owned a farm just to the west of town.

"Hello, Doctor! That tonic you gave my boy did the trick; he is definitely on the mend. Please, let me buy you a drink over here." Jake implored him, gesturing across the bridge to the currently bustling Wolf Tavern Pub.

"You know, I think that just might be the tonic for me, Jake," Deggory replied with a jovial smile. "Lead on, my good man, but I cannot tarry for too long."

The two of them talked about the coming fall and the harvest it would bring. They pondered whether the festival would actually happen this year and enjoyed talking of nothing in particular as they sheltered from the misting rain on the pub's porch. As a cool breeze came up the river, they also took a moment to appreciate the peaceful beauty of their thriving town.

Wolf Tavern was positioned just at the fork where the North Branch and South Branch of the river met and flowed out to the sea as the Chicago River.

The two men cordially returned the wave of a distant Indian paddling his way downriver to the coast and talked for a short while longer. Jake was expecting a good harvest; the year thus far had been going quite well for them, especially with his son now back to work, coming out of the sickness he'd had for the better part of the past fortnight.

Deggory, however, did not share much about his personal life; he never really did. Privately, he thought of his wife, whose health was declining yet again. Consumption was one of those insidious illnesses that would seem to be cured, only to return with a vengeance at some later date.

He turned the conversation. "The great growth in population that Chicago is having should be a boon for both our businesses."

They had just decided that the rain was here to stay and were preparing to leave the glow of the tavern lamps, when they paused to watch the new steamship, *The Prince Eugene*, cast off lines, sound its whistle, and make its way out down the river.

Deggory turned away from the river, gave Jake's hand a hearty shake, and headed home, Mr. Sutton turning to do the same after throwing a cheery goodbye to the doctor. As he had done countless times before, Deggory decided to put away the failures and frustrations of the day with his experimentations and tried to focus more on his day-to-day concerns at home.

He couldn't help but smile as he saw the single lamp burning in the window, something his dear Margaret had always done to help him find his way home. Her father had been a merchant mariner, and she'd held on to the tradition of her mother. Truth be told, Deggory didn't really want her to stop. It had once been a quaint reminder of her love for him each night, when their lives were carefree, before the illness leached into their lives. Now it was a beacon of hope in the night for him, telling him that his wife and son were still here, still with him, and he had been gifted yet another day to attempt to cure them.

2:

THE CATALYST

The dirt roads of Chicago were growing dim as the evening waned, throwing ink-black shadows among the brilliant-red beams of the sun setting behind the buildings. A shadowed pair of eyes peered out of the darkness of an alley as the sound of Dr. Periwinkle's footsteps faded away. A tall Indian, the Dakota Sioux warrior Mato Hota, who'd visited the good doctor just a few hours earlier, stepped out and moved swiftly across to the door of the practice. After a futile tug on the door, he tilted his head back and set his gaze on the laboratory window of the second floor. It was quite a simple matter for him to scale the crenulated corner wall and lift himself onto the windowsill. It took him but a moment to dig his fingers under the wooden frame and pry up the window. He dropped silently into the gloomy laboratory and peered around.

He could not wait for the doctor to finish completing a cure for the disease his tribe had contracted. His people needed an answer now, even if it was not yet perfect. He knew they didn't have the time to wait; he had to find something to help his family. Unfortunately, he didn't see anything in this strange, dark room that looked like it would help.

While his eyes slowly began to adjust to the darkness, an odd squeaking caught his ears as he stared through the gloom at the foreign instrumentation and equipment. Whipping around, he discovered nine small wooden cages in a row on a tall counter.

As he stepped closer to the line of filled cages he scoffed under his breath, "These crazy, backward white men do strange things when searching for medicines."

It looked like four of these wretched animals were dying in their pens. Three others look sickly as well, though not as bad. And the last two … The last two were rats; it was one of these two that made the odd noise.

He leaned in; the pitiful creature was huddled in on it-self, trembling violently. Most of its fur was lying about the cage in matted clumps along with its tail, both ears, the left foreleg, and part of its nose. Mato sat on his haunches and brought his face level with the trapped rat; he could see the thing foaming at the mouth.

"You poor thing. You are in terrible shape. And, as if your other problems were not enough, you look like you are af-flicted with rabies."

The creature shuddered and lifted its head before, quite literally, sneezing explosively in the Indian's face. As it did, a fine greenish mist pervaded Mato's senses, and he reared back and toppled onto his butt. His feet reflexively kicked out, striking and breaking the table leg and sending the cages, and the animals within them, crashing to the floor. Some of the cages burst open, and the animals who weren't already dead bolted into the darkness.

The green mist almost instantly clouded Mato's mind; it had a disgusting odor of decay and mold that had him coughing into the crook of his arm, trying in vain to keep silent and not paint the floor with that morning's meal.

Mato gagged and retched; he clamped one hand tightly to his mouth, and through sheer force of will, the Indian warrior was able to regain his composure. Scrambling his free hand wildly across the floor, he snatched up a cork-ed bottle filled with some sort of viscous fluid along with a small syringe. Rising shakily to his feet, Mato stumbled toward the window; in his befuddlement, he knocked over a standing rack full of glass jars and vials containing vari-ous fluids, powders, and he knew not what. Barely giving the mess of glass, wood, and detritus a second glance, he climbed through the window and out into the night.

He nearly fell off the side of the building twice in his attempt to get down, and once he was back in the Chicago street, he realized he hadn't any idea which way the river was. He prided himself on his sense of direction, as a war-rior and a hunter both, and was angry and confused that he was unable to recall such a simple thing as where he'd left the canoe he came in on.

He skulked around in the building rain and the darkening streets and alleys for what seemed like hours before finally finding the canoe and physically stumbling into the river as he pushed away from the bank in the direction he was pret-ty sure led home. The rain that had been threatening all day started to fall in earnest as Mato finally got his canoe properly moving. The steady rhythm of pushing on the paddle seemed to help him focus.

As he turned at the fork, he glanced up, in an almost habitual fashion, and waved at some men having drinks in front of the Wolf Tavern. He set his mind to covering as much distance as he could the first night. He found it difficult to keep a thought steady in his head, as though there was a fog in his mind preventing him from thinking clearly as a true fog prevents one from seeing clearly. He kept up a mumbled mantra to keep himself on course and as focused as he could.

"Get home with help. Get home with help. Get home with help."

An hour later, he seemed to be leaving the heavier rain behind; however, the clearing sky did not help clear his increasingly muddled mind. He kept trying to think of his tribe and his mission, but nothing seemed to help. He kept faltering with the paddle, once almost losing it altogether to the dark waters. His arms and legs felt stiff and weighed down. Then the rain returned, and he could tell it was here to stay.

Stopping to wait it out was not an option. "Get home with help."

So, on and on he pushed, out into Lake Michigan and up the coast, stopping only as needed to bail out the gathering rainwater from his canoe.

Eventually his head started to clear somewhat, though it still felt ... heavy, weighted, as if it were filled with wet sand. He decided to pull up and make camp on a beach head just south of the Milwaukee River inlet; it was sometime around midnight, he thought, though that was a pure guess on his part. His dreams during those few hours of sleep he managed were fractured and terrifying, wild flashes of blood and screams that he couldn't find a source for. They left him feeling as if he'd not slept at all, and the coming of the morning had him feeling no better. So, with mild trepidation, he turned up the Milwaukee River, deciding to stop at the nearby trading post so he could get some dry provisions for the remaining two days of his journey, and possibly some ale to clear the stuffing from his head.

Mr. Ezra Clark was the proprietor of the *Post*; he was also a traveling trader in the off season when customers couldn't get to him. He was equipping a couple of families at the moment, who were heading out for a day of fishing, when Mato walked in.

Even though the brave had been making good time, he was finding it unexpectedly difficult to maintain his patience. He caught himself sizing up the family members like he, or they, were going to attack. He turned resolutely and stared out the window, forcing his mind back into line as the words of their conversation echoed in his head.

"Mr. Clark, do you have any parasols?"

"Mother, could I have some rock candy?"

"What do you have in the way of live bait, sir?"

"*Mother!* I want some *candy!*"

After what seemed to be an exorbitant length of time, Mato got his turn, and he quickly picked out his provisions.

"Thank you, Mr. Clark. I wish you the best of health. I look forward to seeing you soon," Mato mumbled. He reached to politely shake the man's hand. Ezra, who had known Mato

Hota since he was a boy, pulled him to give him a solid pat on the back. As he was being embraced, Mato Hota noticed that his old friend smelled like … fresh meat! He turned and quickly left, though he had the bizarre urge to do something far worse. He focused his attention on the ground in front of him as he headed rapidly back to his canoe.

He pushed out the freshly laden vessel and paddled up the Menomonee River, headed for his tribe's day camp and what he hoped would be a couple solid hours of sleep. Calmer weather made for an easy day up the river and into the camp. Even though it was after dark when he got there, the near-full moon provided enough light to stow his canoe and prepare for the long hike tomorrow.

He was just getting the fire going well and getting warmed up when he felt within himself an alarming change … He felt an intensity rising from deep within him, and the burgeoning anxiety quickly became unbearable. This was beyond hunger; it was beyond thirst. This was beyond anything he had ever imagined. What happened next was like it was happening to someone else. He could see it, he could feel it, but he could not control it. He had a want, a *need*; it was immediate and inconceivably intense, and nothing else mattered.

He started dashing about the campsite, upending his belongings and scattering things to and fro … He didn't know what it was he was searching for, but the wanton *need* was growing. Then he heard a fish breaking the surface of the river. He leaped into the frigid water and sprang on the fish like a wild animal, flailing about in the murk for a moment before he caught it. He didn't move to cook it—he didn't even clean it; he just ate it there and then, squatting in the muddied water. The cold, slimy chunks of fish meat, blood, and scale slid down his throat in whole pieces he ate so quickly. As he crouched, hunched over the dripping remains of the fish, his flaming skin began to cool; he'd not even realized he was so hot. He slowly began to return to himself again and to realize what he'd done.

Mato Hota cautiously stood up and mechanically started cleaning up himself and the shambles he had made of the camp. No longer feeling the undeniable urges that had overtaken him, the only thing he felt now was confusion … and a deep shame over the *creature* he had briefly become. He could not understand what that change had been or where it had come from. One moment he was starting to feel himself again, warming up and preparing to eat the dried fruits and nuts he'd purchased from Mr. Clark; then it was all a haze. His vision had blurred, his heart had begun hammering painfully, and he had been filled with a frenzied *energy*. He couldn't control himself as he'd dashed about his campsite, and when he heard the splash of the fish, all the bizarre things happening to his body seemed to find a focus. In an instant, his entire world became that fish, and nothing else mattered. He *had* to get that fish, and he had to do it *immediately*. Mato wasn't sure if it was the catching of the fish or the eating of it that calmed him back down and allowed him to regain his senses; he was simply grateful that he had been able to regain control at all.

The rest of the night passed with no return of whatever living nightmare that had been. He woke with what felt like a massive hangover and gaps in his memory. He decided to never tell anyone of what had happened. He was still surprised at his earlier, unthinkable behavior and was, even now, unsure as to just what had come over him. He checked first to be sure that the medicine for the tribe had fared well and then packed everything he needed for the long walk to the village.

Although the village was only a day's walk away, that one day seemed to last forever. He finally arrived home just after sunset and was greeted with no small measure of excitement and optimism; Howakan, the medicine man, quickly made his way through the hugging tribe members. In meeting Mato Hota's gaze, however, the medicine man viewed the brave with sudden concern.

"Mato, are you feeling well? Did you get a cure?"

"I don't know," Mato Hota replied, providing a single answer to both questions. "I got this," he mumbled as he fumbled in his carry pouch and produced the bottle of greenish-yellow fluid.

"Did he say it would work?"

"He … didn't say. I … I … stole it … " stammered Mato, staring listlessly at the ground; the fog was returning, and it took all of his waning willpower to focus on his words.

Howakan jerked in shock and peered up at Mato's sallow, detached face. This was not something he thought the man he knew would ever contemplate doing. A sudden shriek had him turning to look back at his people. Many were now celebrating and weeping with joy at the sight of the bottle in Howakan's hand. He studied this scene for a long moment, pondering what he should do. When he turned to ask another question, Mato was gone, vanishing as swiftly and silently as smoke in the wind.

Seeing the people of his tribe happily chatting around the fire like this was something Mato had not seen for a while, though he desperately wished to, he knew he was not going to join them. He stood hidden in the shadows of the trees at the edge of the forest. He had seen the other members of his tribe who were sick with consumption, and he was sure that his new affliction was something else entirely.

They don't have what I have; they are still themselves. I do not have the same sickness. I am no longer myself. This is different ... I ... am different ... I am ... changed.

Mato stood up. He could feel the wanton need beginning to overtake him again. He watched his people gathered by the fire, and he felt himself tensing; he felt his body readying itself for the attack. With a supreme effort, he turned and ran, crashing into the forest, vowing to get as far from home as he could and to never return.

His village spent the evening in celebration, singing the praises of Dr. Periwinkle; though they were as yet unaware if this elixir would cure them, they had, at least for the moment, hope again for the first time in a long time.

3:

THE CONFLAGRATION

Deggory was awoken sometime in the wee hours of the morning by a muffled pounding at his front door. He could hear James, his manservant, answer it. He could not make out the words, but he heard a man speaking with a less than cordial tone, followed by raised voices, and the sound of James hastening up the stairs. With only the briefest of knocks James flung open Deggory's bedroom door and rushed in.

"Dr. Periwinkle, sir!" James exclaimed. "The man at the door says your office is on fire! The whole building's gone up in flames!"

Deggory had a brief moment of absolute astonishment and incredulity, dimly aware of Maggie sitting up blearily in her own bed before he practically leaped from his bed-clothes and hurried to dress in some semblance of proper attire. Half a moment later he was speeding out the front door, James hot on his heels, heading for the bright glow he could see emanating from the direction of his practice.

Reaching the street where his practice was located, the doctor saw that many of the townsfolk from the surrounding area had formed a bucket line and were ferrying water from the river to the blaze, in an attempt to quell the conflagration. He could tell at a glance, however, that the building was a complete loss.

Deggory and James were soon found by Chicago's mortician, Orsemus Morrison, who had set an eye toward becoming a constable for the blossoming town. Mr. Morrison was a giant of a man, weighing nearly three hundred pounds, and though he was a rather peaceful fellow, he was also fearless and fair minded.

"Any thoughts on how this was started, Dr. Periwinkle?" Orsemus asked, getting right to the point.

Deggory shook his head, his eyes still riveted to the burning building. "No, Mr. Morrison, everything was quiet when I left it this evening … Everything, all my work, my experiments! Oh, no!" Deggory's face grew as clouded as the smoke-filled sky.

As the flames lessened, ceding victory to the bucket line, the doctor noticed something amiss. "Mr. Morrison, I did not leave that window open," he said, pointing to the second-floor aperture.

The mortician gazed at the window and nodded, thinking carefully. "Could any of the chemicals you were working with cause a fire, if combined incorrectly?"

Deggory nodded. "Yes, quite a few. But I'm always careful to keep them separated. I assure you I did not cause this."

Orsemus waved away Periwinkle's assurances. "I have already spoken with some people here who had observed you take a pint or two at the tavern and then head home some time ago, so I am already of the belief that you are not a suspect in this, Doctor. My hypothesis is that someone broke into your practice through that window. Are you in the habit of keeping money in your office?"

"No, sir. I always take it home or put it in the bank."

Orsemus rubbed the stubble on his chin with his huge hand. "They may not have known that, or possibly, they meant to steal medicines or equipment. It might have been kids getting into mischief, and they either accidentally dropped something or purposefully combined things just to see what reaction it would cause. If we find a body once the fire is out, we'll be able to postulate more on the happenings here, but I have very little reason to believe that this fire was your doing."

Deggory nodded in mild relief that he was not to be prosecuted for this crime; truth be told he was still in a state of shock over all this. Just a scant few hours ago, he was doing his research in this very building. Now as he watched the bucket line quench the last few smoldering embers, he realized that any hope he had for curing his wife and child may well have been quenched with them. All his research was now gone, his medicines, the Indian herbs, the animals, nothing remained save for his ledger. He had failed for the final time, and he couldn't see being able to rebuild, repair, and replace everything he'd lost with enough time to still be able to cure his family. He felt sickened with a growing fear that all was now lost.

4:

THE DEADLY PRINCE

In the still, dark quiet of the Chicago River bank at sun-down, the steamship *The Prince Eugene* was moored at the dock and sat serenely in the black water. She was bound for New York, a fourteen-day trip in the best condi-tions, and these days it was not the best conditions. As the deckhands loaded the cargo on board, they failed to notice the decrepit form of the afflicted rat scamper its way up the mooring line. The doomed rodent was well hidden by the time the sailors' gaze roamed in that direction.

The next morning, as the crew was making headway down the river, the cook was sorting through his supplies when he came across a horrid sight. He was fairly certain it was a rat, or had been at one time or another. The fur on this godforsaken creature had nearly all fallen out; the exposed skin was tight against its painfully emaciated form. The last two-thirds of its tail were missing, as well as its left ear and a goodly portion of the skin around where the ear once was. It was huddled behind a bag of corncobs, shivering and shaking as though racked with cold, though the hold they were in was quite warm.

The cook shifted to reach down with his rolling pin, to put the wretched thing out of its misery, and the rat caught sight of him. With a keening screech that set his teeth on edge, the foul beast leaped at him. He instinctively threw his arms up in front of his face, and the rodent landed on his forearms, latching on with its needle-like claws and sinking its sharp little teeth deep into his left hand. The cook let out a bellow of pain and rage and flung the abomination to the floor before raising his boot and stomping the life out of the beast. He took in a deep breath through the nose, raking his free hand shakily through his hair, then straightened his waistcoat one-handed as he cradled his injured appendage to his chest. He fished a handkerchief clumsily from his left pants pocket with his right hand as he looked down at the rodent, noting that he'd only managed to crush the hind end of the creature. He raised his foot again before stomping on the remains of skin and bones once more, for good measure. He then gingerly reached down and lifted the mashed corpse with his hankie, to better see what had attacked him. He had just raised the thing to eye level when the creature burst in his face and filled the area about his head and shoulders with a fine greenish mist. He reared back in renewed horror, dropping the rat even as he registered the rotten, moldy odor of the mist. Coughing and retching into his hands, he abandoned the hold in search of the surgeon, and a stiff drink.

Later that night, lying in his bunk, after having completed his duties by serving a fine meal to all the well-to-do, the cook was not feeling at all well. His brow felt feverish, and he was having difficulty breathing. He was so nauseous that he'd attempted to empty his stomach more times than he cared to recall. He feared he would not make it through the full voyage as he curled deeper in on himself involuntarily, his trembling frame racked with deep, agonizing coughs. His thoughts were muddled and confused, but he prayed that he would survive to see his wife and children at this journey's end. As the steamer plowed over some rolling waves, the wind sent a blast of moist, steamy air shooting through his open porthole. He groaned as the now icy droplets contacted his flaming skin; it felt very like having needles shoved into his flesh, not a welcome sensation at the best of times, made doubly worse by whatever affliction this miserable creature had given him, and he slammed the swing plate of the porthole closed with his clenched fist.

Two decks above, the gentry were enjoying the band's lively tunes and fine brandy as they took in the night air and laughed at each other's bad jokes.

"I made my fortune in footwear; how about you?"

"Spirits, sir, the finest in rums from the Caribbean, according to some."

"Oh my, did you bring any with you? Perhaps we could work out a deal—shoes for booze, my good man!"

"Ha-ha, spirits for soles, eh! That's quite good, what!"

He clapped a hand to the other's shoulder, and they shared a hearty chuckle, making their way down the deck of the ship to mingle with the other well-to-do of society who had joined them on their journey.

A pair of high-class ladies stood by the railing, giggling

and blushing to each other behind the spread of their lace fans as they watched the two gentlemen moving toward them. The bolder of the two stepped away from her companion just a bit and, leaning ever so slightly forward, inhaled deeply, putting on prominent display her best assets.

Her performance was soured by the expression of disgust she suddenly wore. "What is that smell?" she exclaimed as she placed a lace-covered hand daintily to her nose and straightened back up.

The men faltered in their steps, confusion and affront warring on their faces, before they too caught the odor, a putrescence they could not place, and had no desire to hang about and try. They gallantly turned to the two ladies and, offering their arms, led them away from the malodorous area, not noticing the growing cloud of greenish mist rising over the gunwale. The ladies were already giggling cutely at the joke one of the men had told, all thoughts of the offending location flown from their flighty minds.

———— ((◉)) ————

The morning fog was just burning off the upper regions when it happened. As she came in, the bow dug into the sand and slid up almost silently onto to coast. The steamship *The Prince Eugene* did so in such a peaceful, unassuming manner that it belied the terror she was bringing. As soon as the ship had fully run herself aground and shuddered to a stop, they came clamoring across the gunwale like a bizarre pack of two-legged dogs. Some were screeching and clawing at nothing, as if they were trying to rip chunks out of the very air. Some were making disturbing, guttural noises and seemingly belching out some kind of greenish-tinted mist. Most were still dressed in the refinery of their once proudly held stations. All of them were now nothing more, and nothing less, than raging, rabid monsters.

5:

THE MACKINAC INCIDENT

The few families of the Crow tribe who lived on the island had gone down to the beach to let their children play in the sand. They never stood a chance. They had watched the ship come ashore, at first believing it was just a ship passing, as ships did on a regular basis. Their concern started when it was clear that the ship was off course. When the ship finally ran aground, the adults of the tribe went up to her immediately to offer aide, those offers quickly dying on their lips at what greeted them. The once-dignified passengers of the ship set upon the families like a pack of wild animals. The ill-fated Crow were unprepared for a fight and certainly unprepared for whatever this was. The adults tried to protect the children as best they could, shielding them with their own bodies, shoving them down the beach to run away as they braced to meet this astonishingly unusual and vicious foe.

One poor woman, a cradleboard strapped to her back, bolted for the trees, her fingers digging painfully into the leather straps of the board in a desperate means of keeping her infant child safe. She reached the nearest tree and grabbed ahold of it just as her skirt was yanked from behind. She screamed and whipped the cradleboard from her back and flung it further into the trees. The creature attacking her was once the more demure of the two high-class ladies. Now she shrieked at the young mother, ripping and clawing at the pitiable woman's back as she wrapped her arms tighter around the trunk. Suddenly, she felt an almighty lurch as she was yanked away from the tree, her nails scraping through the bark. As she was thrown to the ground, she caught sight of a man where she had thrown her child, or what once was a man, dressed in dapper finery, the now bloodied blanket that had been wrapped around her baby being torn apart in his claw-like hands. Her wail of anguish drew the attention of the other creatures, and she was quickly set upon from all sides. The attack was so sudden and so savage that there was no escape to be had by anyone; and almost the entirety of the Crow families died painfully and terribly on that now blood-soaked beach.

Only one teenaged boy, who had gone wandering into the woods earlier, had escaped the attack. He watched, stunned into paralysis, as the whole thing happened in mere minutes. He stood in shoulder-high bushes, frozen, throughout the whole ordeal. He was barely able to even process what he was seeing. He was in such shock he felt he was watching someone else watch the carnage, as if it weren't he, himself, witnessing this horror. So, he helplessly bore witness as these men and women fed upon his family. He watched as his aunt futilely threw her newborn, cradleboard and all, into the woods several dozen yards from him, and as one of the attackers found the babe before the boy could even contemplate trying to rescue his cousin. He could tell that if he was seen by these monsters, he too would be killed, and quickly.

When they finally stopped, stood, and looked around, he could see that they were covered in blood and gore and yet were still looking for more. They then ran off, though they didn't really run so much as scramble, some on all fours, like animals. Most of them headed south, while a small few headed to the north. None came deeper into the woods, where he was still rooted in place, for which he was indescribably relieved. The traditional clothing that had served his people so well for so many generations had served him well today. His buckskin shirt and pants with the fringed leather combined with the feathers in his hair all helped to distort the edges of the thin fifteen-year-old boy and show no man-shaped profile in the woods. He stood for some time after, still trying to process what had just happened, what he had just seen.

Somehow through the tempest now raging in his head, a clear thought came through, almost like someone else's voice: "The others! Warn the others!"

He backtracked into the woods, turned south toward the fort, and ran. He ran as fast and as hard as he could. His two long braids were streaming out behind him. Raw panic gave him more speed and endurance than he thought he had. He didn't slow down until he was at the fort, and seeing the north blockhouse through the trees, he suddenly stopped and crouched down behind a decaying log.

"What if those things are here already? What if I'm too late?" He moved forward to kneel behind a bush and, trying to get his breathing under control, he watched the fort and the people there.

Everything appeared normal around the fort, as the soldiers were talking and walking as they should, so, gathering his courage and half running to warn them and half running for safety, he charged through the entrance shouting, "Help! Help!! HELP!!"

One of the soldiers from the gate caught him in his arms as he came through. "What is it, lad? What is it?"

Emotion and reality finally caught up with him, and he burst into tears and gibberish, clinging to the straps of the man's uniform. The soldier carefully extricated himself, took the boy by the shoulders, and shook him gently. "Look at me, boyo. Look me in the face!"

The shaking helped bring him back to himself, though did nothing to calm his wild fear. The young Indian looked up at the soldier and managed to blurt out, "We've been attacked! On the beach, we've been attacked!"

Soldiers dotted across the open parade grounds turned to look at them. A higher-ranking soldier came quickly over from the barracks. "I'm Sergeant Chambers; what's your name, boy?"

The boy looked up at the sergeant in bewilderment at the seeming randomness of the question. The soldier was a huge man with a kind face and auburn sideburns.

The question helped the boy get himself back under control, and he took a breath, "Nektosha. Sir ... my name is Nektosha ... The ship ran aground up at Griffin Point. You see, our parents dragged us down there so the little ones could play and … my … my parents … They… " Nektosha's legs gave out, and he crumpled to the ground.

"Come on, son—get it together! Now, focus! Tell me what happened," Sergeant Chambers demanded, hauling the boy to his feet.

"Y-yes, sir, the ship ran aground while I was in the woods. I came back to see what the noise was, and they came crawling over the side of the ship, and they killed everyone!" Nektosha started to shudder involuntarily. "Then, sir, they started to eat them."

"What? Who ate what? What are you saying?" The sergeant took his arm to steady him.

"The people from the boat were *eating* the people on the beach! M-M-My family… Oh, my *family*! But they weren't acting like *people*; they crawled from the boat, not like people, really. They were … they were … I don't even know!"

Nektosha seemed to come to his senses with a realization. "We have to go! They're coming this way! We have to run!!"

Sergeant Chambers looked the young man over and decided that he was serious, and even if not all of this wild story was correct, something was definitely amiss. So, he took the boy to see his superior, Commander Schoolcraft. The stationed officers were taking lunch with their families in the still-unfinished officers' quarters just passed the north blockhouse. There they found all of the officers, women, and children just being served a magnificent meal in celebration of the near completion of the new living space.

Sergeant Chambers felt that Commander Schoolcraft was using any excuse he could conjure up to have lavish meals and celebrations.

The sergeant hesitated briefly then approached the gathering, "Sir, I have a matter that needs your immediate attention."

"We are busy here, Sergeant," The commander said as he nodded a thank you to his server.

"There has been an attack, sir." At this, the commander reluctantly stood and gestured for the sergeant to follow him out of hearing range of the other officers.

"Yes?" he asked, his napkin still tucked into his unbuttoned shirtfront.

Sergeant Chambers quickly relayed the incredulous story he'd just heard to his commander. Commander Schoolcraft took a long moment to study Nektosha, as well as his sergeant.

"Well, even if this isn't entirely accurate, we should at least investigate the matter."

"My thoughts as well, sir," said Chambers.

Commander Schoolcraft took a deep breath and gave a forlorn look at his robust lunch. "Sergeant, you take a few guards and secure the fort. The officers and I will make ready to go out and dispatch this ... threat. Send someone to the barracks to tell the soldiers to form ranks, armed and ready for action in the yard."

"Yes, sir," replied the sergeant with a salute.

He then turned to the soldier from the gate who had followed them over and instructed him to relay the orders to the troops. Sergeant Chambers, with Nektosha following, headed farther down the wall to the southwest blockhouse. He assigned a few of the guards to secure the perimeter, telling the others to prepare and assemble. Sergeant Chambers and Nektosha had just made it down the wall to the northwest blockhouse when all hell broke loose.

It was the ghastly noises that first got their attention. Then the screaming, not just the women and children— the soldiers were screaming as well. They came flooding through the gate in a single formless mass. The men were still preparing their equipment and had no idea how to handle this completely different threat. The officers who were still eating and discussing troop allocation were the first attacked. Chambers watched helplessly as Commander Schoolcraft vanished under a wave of desiccated bodies, his forgotten napkin still dangling from his collar. As for the troops, some tried to load their muskets, some tried to fix bayonets, some froze, others ran; the result was complete and utter chaos.

Sergeant Chambers took all of this in at a glance. He turned to the handful of guards at the blockhouse and gave a one-word order: "Run!"

They all went up to the second floor of the blockhouse and one by one started squeezing through the outward-facing canon port. One of the guards was too large about the middle and just couldn't fit.

Sergeant Chambers clapped a hand to his shoulder. "Private Jenkins, try to make it to the southern gate, maybe the docks."

Jenkins froze. "The storehouse gate! Yes, sir." The portly man nearly fell down the stairs in his haste to beat the attackers to his new destination.

Once everyone made it to the ground, Chambers looked to his remaining guards and the boy who'd basically saved their lives. He gestured silently to the others to follow and began making his way through the woods surrounding the fort.

As they gained a goodly distance from the horrors behind them, and the sounds of screaming faded to a distant wailing cord, Chambers spoke softly over his shoulder. "This is Nektosha." He gestured to the boy. "These guys are Corporal William Benson, Private Benjamin Jacobs, and Private Douglas Smith." Everyone nodded at each other. "Now, I'm going to go get my family; you can all go for cover if you want."

He glanced at Nektosha, who immediately replied, "Oh, I'm staying with you!" The young brave then moved to walk by the big sergeant's shoulder as if in conformation.

Private Smith piped up. "I'm with you too, sir." The other two nodded in agreement.

"Sophie said that they were going to decorate the mission church for the spring festival," Chambers explained, already beginning to move at a faster pace.

Without any further discussion, they all took off at a run, headed southwest for the church.

When they finally reached the church, their nerves frayed from reacting to every little sound within the darkening trees, Sergeant Chambers threw the door open and, spying his family unharmed, cried out, "Oh, thank God!" before running over to his wife and two children, who were sweeping the floor of the church, and scooping his daughter into his arms.

Sophie startled and looked up. "Jack! You scared the wits out of me."

"You have no idea! We are under attack, and the fort has been overrun by … " He stopped, deciding to spare her and the children the gory details. "We have to go! Right now!"

"You heard him. Drop what you're doing and go!" Sophie ordered their children. She saw the look in her husband's face and tried not to panic. Neither ten-year-old Thomas nor eight-year-old Victoria questioned the orders; they just quickly gathered their things and headed for the door.

When they got outside, Corporal Benson asked, "Where are we going to go?" There was a moment of blank staring.

Nektosha spoke up. "We could go to Fort Holmes. It's deserted and overgrown, but we can hide out there."

"Good idea," said Sergeant Chambers.

The eight of them headed north to the interior of the island. They moved more slowly and cautiously now, keeping in the trees for cover. They went around the parade grounds and came up to Skull Cave. Sergeant Chambers looked into the darkness, assessing that it was too small to adequately hold all of them.

"That's where we bury our dead," said Nektosha. "The fort is just over there."

Fort Holmes was not big at all, being basically an outpost, with an earth-and-timber perimeter wall and a single gate. There was one building inside, a blockhouse design with the second story looking like it had been placed on top of the first at a forty-five-degree angle.

No one needed to be told what to do. Everyone went about the business of clearing out the interior space and using the debris to make a barrier of sorts in the gateway, as the gate itself was long gone. Sophie and the kids had headed into the building. As they moved into the dark interior, they scared a cat that screeched and bolted out across the yard. This caused a full-on panic. Again, chaos ensued. Private Smith got tangled in the branches he was arranging and fell into them, ensnaring himself. Private Jacobs, having never let go of his weapon, fired a shot, splintering a corner of the building. Sergeant Chambers and Corporal Benson scrambled to ready their weapons; Benson fumbled and dropped his in his haste. When the soldiers finally calmed down, they realized their young Indian savior was missing.

After a brief search for the boy, poor Nektosha was found hiding behind the blockhouse. He had wedged himself between a stack of rotted firewood and the wall of the building. He was nearly catatonic in his distress. Once everyone had figured out what had happened, they tried gamely to laugh it off. "A cat?! Ha-ha." But there was no real humor in their voices. Sergeant Chambers finally ordered everyone to get inside the relative safety of the building.

When they were all fully ensconced in the upstairs room, Chambers addressed his men. "What happened just now was actually an eye-opener in more ways than one. If that cat had been the enemy, we would all be dead right now. So, we need to establish some rules for our own safety. First of all, no one goes anywhere without an armed escort. Which brings up the second rule, we soldiers must keep ourselves ready for a fight at all times with muskets loaded and bayonets fixed. We must try to keep those who are trained to fight circled around those that aren't. I don't think we will

be able to hold up here for long. We have to assume that—"
He froze. "Did you hear that?" He moved quickly and quietly
to the window.

The response from the soldiers this time was much better; their training kicked in, and in an instant, they had fixed
their bayonets and taken up positions at the top of the stairs
and the sides of the windows. Then everyone heard the
cause for alarm. The branches at the gate were being moved
and broken, and they could hear muttering and cursing.

Sergeant Chambers looked back from the window and
said in a loud whisper, "Here!"

Four muskets were quickly pointed at the source of the
commotion.

"Hold!" the sergeant yelled half to his men, half to the
man at the gate.

"What in blazes is going on?" the unknown man shouted back, moving only to raise his hands in the air.

Chambers studied the man and looked over at Nektosha,
who shook his head and said, "I do not think he is one of
them; he is not acting like they did."

The sergeant nodded and hollered down to the man,
"State you name and intention."

"I'm John Tucker. I'm a trapper. I heard a shot and a commotion. I came to see if everything was all right. This place
is supposed to be abandoned, after all."

After a moment, Sergeant Chambers shouted back,
"Well, 'all right' is not a term I would use right now. You had
better come on up; we should talk."

The trapper took a moment to patch the gap in the
branches and joined the others in the building. To spare

Nektosha's nerves, Chambers briefed everyone on the full nature (as much as he knew it) of the ship crashing and the massacre on the beach, as well as the attack on the fort. The full outcome of the fort attack was not yet certain, but they did know that it was bad. John and Sophie looked at them both like they were crazy. Then the soldiers spoke up, confirming what they had seen, and John and Sophie were left thinking it was *they* who were going crazy.

"Whatever they are, they are too many and too ... unknown, for a group like this to take on. I think the best we can do is to get away and bring reinforcements. However, to get to the docks, we have to go back through the fort, so we'll have to figure something out. Jesus, I thought this island seemed small before. Going back to Nektosha's village doesn't sound good either, as that is where this all started."

"We could take my boat," offered John. Everyone paused and turned to look at John.

"You have a boat?" asked Chambers.

"Well, it's mine now," said John defensively. "It was abandoned after the war. She's anchored over thataway by Arch Rock."

"Well, let's do that!" said Sophie, noticeably shaken after hearing for the first time what they were up against. She'd pulled her children to her bosom and looked to not be letting go of them any time soon, not that they looked to be wanting her to, as little Victoria was softly crying and Thomas was white as a sheet.

The group gathered themselves and their belongings together, the soldiers making sure their weapons were loaded and primed. John had an old, rusty pistol that he readied as well, and they headed as quietly as they could out through the gate. They formed into a tight group, Sophie, the children, and Nektosha in the center, and moved at a slow jog the relatively short distance to the western coast of the island. There, tied to a tree next to Arch Rock, was John's ten-foot birchbark canoe.

"This?!" asked Sophie incredulously.

"No, that," answered John, and he pointed at the two-masted gunboat about fifty yards off the coast.

"Will it hold us all OK?" asked Chambers.

"Oh, she's watertight all right. They took the guns and stuff, but they left her in pretty much working order, and I've made some repairs and adjustments myself. She's built to hold anywhere from twelve to twenty-four, but she'll run just fine with us few. I named her *The Badger*. The canoe, though, won't carry all of us at once, so we will have to make a couple of trips."

Nektosha came out of his stupor enough to recognize the canoe. "Oh! You got this from my tribe!"

John nodded with a smile. "Sure did. Traded twelve excellent fox pelts for it too."

Nektosha nodded back, a small smile playing on his lips. "My older brother got one of the skins because he harvested the birchbark on his own for the first time. Another went to Ska-Cha for painting it. I was hoping that she and I would ... That maybe we could be ... " He paused, remembering the slaughter on the beach. He moved to the prow of the canoe where a small arrowhead was painted with the spruce-gum-and-tallow mixture the two of them had used to seal the canoe watertight, "She painted this here," he whispered as he touched the symbol. "This canoe was built by my family and my friends."

John threw an arm around the boy's shoulders kindly, ignoring their slight shaking, "They're still with you, boy. They're here with you in the crafts you made together, and they're here with you in the heart and mind of the boy they loved. Remember them as they were when you built this canoe together and do their memories proud."

Nektosha lost his battle against the coming tears and turned into the embrace of the trapper, sobbing into his chest.

The sound of a falling branch had everyone looking back into the woods and Nektosha's sobs stuttering to a halt. They were suddenly very aware of every noise the birds and beasts were making as they moved through the trees and undergrowth.

"All right," said Chambers, "Corporal Benson, you go on the first trip with Sophie and the kids; stay on the ship while John comes back for the rest of us." John told them where and how to sit, and Chambers and Nektosha pushed the canoe from the beach.

The wait on shore was intolerable. They wanted to take cover, but they also did not want to get closer to the trees and the deepening shadows therein. At last, John returned. Chambers, Nektosha, Jacobs, and Smith joined John in the small boat. Under normal circumstances, putting this many men in this small a boat would be just foolhardy. There was nothing *normal* about today. With their craft just barely afloat, and every muscle of the five men taut as bowstrings, the only movement was John's paddle slowly slicing through the water as they made their way to his small ship.

6:

FLIGHT OF THE BADGER

After what felt like ages, they finally reunited at John's boat. They quickly got on board, John hauling his canoe up to rest over the sternrail of *The Badger* and lashing it in place. He now paid the small craft a great deal more respect, in deference to its departed crafters. Everyone then found themselves standing in a huddle on the main deck.

"Thank you"—Sophie was the first to speak up after a long bout of staring at each other—"for getting us off that island. I don't know what it was that attacked the fort, but I am forever grateful to you for sparing my children that fate."

"Yup, yup, glad to help. Well, of course, you probably saved me as well. Welcome aboard *The Badger*!" he exclaimed with great pride. "I found her beached near Saginaw Bay. It had looked like her stern was blown clean off, so I reckon they gave her up as ruined. I figured to just use her for temporary shelter at first, but when I got to looking at her, I realized that just the top of the transom was gone. So, I spent the next few months doing the repairs and trading my furs for sail cloth and rigging and such. Once I got her set back up good and proper, my hunting and trapping business was much easier, and life has been pretty good ever since."

Again, everyone fell to silent staring, no one really knowing what to say.

"All right, so what do we do now?" Nektosha asked in a thin voice, peering blankly back at shore.

Everyone instinctively looked at the sergeant. "We need to get some help and come back here better prepared. We don't really know what this is. We only know what happened to the fort and to the Indians." He paused, with an apologizing glance at Nektosha. "It could be some new tick of the Black Hawk tribe, or the British. Or it could be something else entirely. We just don't know what that was. Nektosha, did you get a good look at the attackers?"

"No, sir, not very good. They were some ways off, and I was looking through the trees and branches. They just seemed to be normal people, aside from … what they did."

"I didn't truly see much either," admitted Chambers. "When I realized the ferocity of the attack, I was more concerned with escape."

"Good thing, too," said Corporal Benson.

"Well, the question remains, where do you want to go now?" John asked as he went to the bow and checked the tension on the anchor line. He had cleverly set the rigging with longer lines so that most of the sails and braces could be handled from the helm, allowing *The Badger* to be more easily operated by one man.

"I think the nearest fort would be in Detroit," said Chambers.

"They have a good docking situation there," offered John, motioning to the soldiers to help him pull up the anchor line. When John had finished showing the men how to raise and stow the anchor, he headed to the helm and started dropping the sails and spinning the wheel, shooting glances in every direction to check the reactions to his efforts.

Sophie, Nektosha, and the kids moved to the center of *The Badger* to get out of the way. Chambers, who had been at the bow with the men as they hauled in the anchor, looked back and asked, "Hey, John, can we sail by the docks?" Pointing to the southern coast of the island, he said, "Maybe we can get a better look at the enemy."

"Yeah," said John, "I want to see what's going on myself."

The scene at the fort and harbor was eerily still and quiet. Even though the moon had come out, they could not see much from sea level, and the natural points that extended to form the harbor prevented them from getting very close. At Chambers's request, they sailed up the west coast of the island to see where the attack on the Indian families had happened. The scene they discovered there was the stuff of nightmares. The steamship hid a good portion of the carnage until they'd come around her. Chambers noted that the name of the vessel was *The Prince Eugene*. The bodies of the Crow families had been torn open and ripped apart. Gulls, vultures, and other carrion eaters were already picking at the remains and wheeling in the sky. Nektosha moved to the far side of *The Badger* and grabbed the rail in shaking, white-fisted grips. Sophie quickly joined him, putting her arm around his shoulders. There was, however, nothing larger than a fox moving here, either, though there was an unnatural quiet over the area. Even the wheeling birds were silent in their flights.

"All right," said John, somewhat disappointed, "let's get away from here." Everyone mumbled their agreement, and John spun the wheel, and as he moved to grab the lines, he told the men to drop more sail.

"How long will it take us to get there?" Chambers asked John.

"We should be there just a couple of days if the winds stay like this," John said as he looked into the setting moon.

"Well we should be sure to approach by day—we don't know if Detroit's been attacked or not."

John agreed solemnly as he steered *The Badger*, and her new crew sailed out toward the middle of Lake Huron.

Chambers looked at the ragtag group and called out, "Everyone had better try to get some sleep—we don't know what's ahead of us."

Sophie turned to John. "Would it be all right if I put Thomas and Victoria out of the weather in your cabin for the night?"

"Of course." He replied kindly, "There are a few extra wool blankets in the hold."

The night was quiet and clear, but there was not much sleeping to be had. Sophie stayed with the children while Nektosha and the men gathered by the helm, pondering what they might find in Detroit, and what they might do with this situation or that. Eventually the rolling and soft creaking of *The Badger* had its effect, and most on board managed to get at least a few solid hours of sleep.

Jacobs relieved John at the wheel for a while, having been told, "Just keep those two stars over that yardarm, and we should do fine," by a waning John.

Early in the morning of the next day Sophie found Nektosha sitting on the deck staring blankly over the bow. He seemed so lost in his thoughts that she approached carefully so as not to startle him. "Nektosha, are you going to be all right? You have been through a lot. I cannot even imagine."

Nektosha stared into the wind and waves for a moment before he replied, "I still can hardly think of it all. I have to stop from time to time and make myself not think of it. It was not just *my* family—it was all of the families who had come to live there. We had become our own people. We were making a great village together. Some of us, like me, were trained by the missionaries; some were trained in the ways of our ancestors. It was all working so well. I had even met Ska-Cha. She is ... She was ... wonderful."

Sophie interrupted him. "Loss is the hardest of all things to deal with. I lost my father and brother in the war. I was just a mess for a while. What has happened to you is beyond my ability to grasp. We do not have the time to heal. That's not the right word ... to recover. Everything has changed, and we have no idea how much. I just want you to know that, if you ever need to talk, or just a hug, I am here for you." She embraced him for a moment and gently tucked a strand of hair behind his ear as she surveyed his face. She could see a torrent of emotions being held at bay by this courageous boy. She turned to look in on Thomas and Victoria hoping that she had been able to help.

They kept *The Badger* away from the docks until it was almost full daylight and people could be clearly seen moving around in a normal fashion. John brought his craft in and smoothly along the dock at the end of the wharf. He had Smith and Jacobs wrap the lines and hold them until he could go down and tie them off properly.

"I have to check in with the dockmaster," he told Chambers as he tied off the bow line.

"Well," Chambers began, not really wanting to part with John but knowing he had no right to ask the man to stay, "thank you very much for saving us and everything. I cannot really ask any more of you. What do I owe you?" he asked, reaching into his pouch.

"If it's all right with you, I'd like to stay with you for a bit, to see what this business is all about," John said.

"That would be most excellent indeed," Chambers replied, relieved.

The sergeant then turned to address the rest of the party. "Corporal Benson, you and Smith stay here with Sophie and the kids and watch the boat. John and I will head to the fort."

Nektosha spoke up. "I'm staying with you, sir," and again, stitched himself to the sergeant's side.

"All right, fair enough," the sergeant replied.

As the sergeant, the trapper, and the Indian walked to the fort, they all kept looking down each of the side streets and into open doorways just to be sure everything was normal.

When they reached the fort, they found a single guard

at the gate. The sergeant approached, came to attention, saluted, and said, "I am Sergeant Jack Chambers from Fort Mackinac. I need to see the commander."

The guard also came to attention, returned the salute, then relaxed his posture, and said, "I'm sorry, Sergeant—the commander is not here. He has gone to check on our men who are away tending to the other forts, and most of the company is gone with him—those that were not already sent to shore up defenses at the forts. We must defend the frontier," he added, clearly mocking some officer. He shot a glance at Nektosha, who stepped shyly behind Sergeant Chambers. "They say that there may be another uprising."

"Understood," Chambers replied. "Is there anyone here I can speak to?"

The guard shrugged and answered, "You can go see Major Shepard; he is running things while everyone is away."

"All right, thank you, soldier," the sergeant replied. They exchanged salutes, and Chambers, John, and Nektosha passed into the fort.

The guard was right—the place was nearly deserted. They found the command office and knocked on the door.

"Come in" came the tired reply. The three visitors entered and found the major sitting at a desk covered in piles of disorganized paperwork. Sergeant Chambers advanced, saluted, and waited.

Major Shepard looked up. "Oh, right, sorry about that." He stood up and returned the salute. "At ease, Sergeant. What's on your mind?" he asked as he sat back down.

"There has been an incident at Mackinac, sir; there has been an attack," Sergeant Chambers told him.

"What?! What sort of an attack?" Major Shepard demanded, standing up again.

Sergeant Chambers began his report. "The supply ship *The Prince Eugene* was headed in to Mackinac Island, and it ran aground on the northern part of the island. The people on the ship jumped over the railings and began attacking the Indian families, sir, in a most savage manner."

"What do you mean, 'savage manner'?"

Sergeant Chambers had been hoping to avoid the incredible details, but he was obligated to be forthcoming to a superior officer. "They were, well ... eating the Indians, sir."

"Hold it," interrupted the major, shaking his head. "Who put you up to this?"

"No, sir, I am quite serious," the sergeant replied.

The major put up a hand to stop him. "Cannibals!? Really? Look, even if I believed you, which I don't, there is nothing that we can really do. As you can plainly see, everyone is gone. With the cutbacks, they never replaced all of the men lost in the Black Hawk War. Then we got hit hard with cholera, and it about wiped us out. What few men we do have in the area are spread so thin ... Ours went out to resupply the other forts and aren't expected back for a week or more. I will file your report, which I am required to do, with the commander if and when he returns."

"But, sir," Chambers began.

"You are dismissed, Sergeant!"

Chambers turned dejectedly to the door, where the other two were waiting, and gave a shrug.

"Hold on," said the major. "Just in case there is something to this, I will send a rider out and get word to the commander. Will that be sufficient?"

Sergeant Chambers came to attention, saluted, and said, "Thank you, sir." The officer returned his salute and then returned to his mountain of paperwork.

Outside the office, John turned to Chambers. "Wow, that is not what I expected at all."

"That is what I *should* have expected," the sergeant replied gravely. "I didn't bring this up earlier because I didn't want everyone worrying too much, especially Sophie and the kids. We barely had enough men to hold proper watches at Mackinac. I don't know why I hoped for anything different here. If we can't get a regiment together and wipe them out, we need to at least try to contain the situation ourselves."

"What do you mean?" asked Nektosha.

Chambers paused to choose his words for a moment before he replied, "They are on an island, right? We just have to prevent their leaving it. Did anyone see how many boats were at the docks?"

John shook his head. "I didn't even check. My attention was on the fort. I was looking for this horde of … well, whatever all of you saw."

"I didn't think to check that either," added Nektosha.

Chambers gazed off at nothing for a moment, then he abruptly charged back into the office. "Sir!"

"What?!" replied the major, startled and annoyed as a stack of papers tipped precariously. With a scowl, the major slapped a hand to the top of the pile, preventing its toppling.

"Can you put the word out to isolate the island? Stop anyone else from going there?" Sergeant Chambers asked although his questions this time sounded more like orders.

The officer gave a hesitant nod, moving the stack of papers to his lap. "Well, yes, we can do that."

"Lamp oil?" the sergeant continued, an idea forming in his mind. "Do you have any lamp oil and lanterns?"

"Nothing to spare," the officer replied with a shake of his head. "Everything extra has been used; we are barely getting by here."

Sergeant Chambers snapped to attention and gave the officer a sharp salute. "Thank you for getting the word out, sir." The major returned his salute then looked absently down at the papers in his lap as the three once again left the office.

As they crossed the fort grounds toward the gate, John asked, "So, you mean to burn all the boats, trapping them there?"

Chambers nodded. "That is what I'm thinking, unless you have a better idea."

"Not hardly. I know a guy in town—we should be able to get some oil and lamps from him," John said, angling his course slightly to lead them to his contact.

They had walked a few blocks in silence before Nektosha spoke up. "What if they already left, sir? What if they already sailed off Mackinac Island?"

"I've been thinking about that," Chambers said. "That was not an organized military attack, not like any I've ever seen. That was like a mob, a pack of wild dogs, or something, but with no clear leadership. I'm hoping they haven't thought about leaving the island yet."

There was another long silence, as everyone considered the possibilities of this new and unknown foe. John broke the silence this time. "We had better lay in some extra provisions on *The Badger*. We don't really know what may be in store for us."

"Good thinking," said Chambers, as he reached into his pouch and produced a handful of banknotes. "I did pretty well at the card table this past week, so I can contribute my fair share," he added.

When they reached the shops, their spirits had lifted again. Having somewhat of a plan in place, knowing they were doing something *themselves* about their situation, helped boost morale more than could be believed. Instead of just running away and calling for help, they were now going on the offensive. John's friend ran a large general store with everything from hardware, to hunting supplies, to bolts of cloth. John headed straight to the pot belly stove in the middle of the store, where he found the owner chatting to his customers. Chambers and Nektosha started wandering among the merchandise, looking at this and that. Chambers eventually browsed his way back to where John was talking to a small, older gentleman in a brightly colored waistcoat and silk cravat.

John turned as he approached. "Sergeant Jack Chambers, this is Mr. Fogg."

"Nice to meet you," Chambers said, taking up the offered handshake. "How much oil can we get?"

Mr. Fogg's eyebrow went up at this. "Well, I sell it by the five-gallon cask, or by the barrel, which equates to about fifty gallons."

Chambers and John looked at each other for a second, considering the task ahead. "Five casks?" John suggested.

Chambers nodded thoughtfully. John turned back to Mr. Fogg and asked him if he could have them delivered to his ship.

"Of course, John. Will there be anything else?" Mr. Fogg asked.

"Lamps," said John, "pottery lamps, if you have them."

"This way," said Mr. Fogg, who nodded at Chambers as the two of them headed off.

After bartering with Mr. Fogg, Chambers was looking to get going. He glanced around to find that Nektosha was not by his side, which was most unusual. A quick scan of the shop found him over by the dry goods area. When he approached, he found the boy gazing longingly at a barrel full of unstrung longbows and fingering the wood and string of one of them.

"Do you know how to shoot one of those?" Chambers asked.

"Yes, sir, my father taught me. I'm pretty good at it, so he says ... so he said," Nektosha answered, dropping his gaze to the floor.

Chambers thought through the awkward silence for a moment and considered that the boy needed some form of comfort and security. For that matter, they all did. He looked back to the young Indian. "Well, then, pick one out."

"Really, sir?" Nektosha asked, as wide-eyed as a child given a new toy.

"Absolutely," the sergeant replied. "Get a few dozen arrows as well. Based on what we have seen, we will need every advantage we can muster."

Sergeant Jack Chambers stood back and considered

Nektosha in a new light. He did not, at the moment, look like the frightened boy who had run up to him at the fort. He showed a glimpse of self-confidence that Chambers had not seen in him before. However, in a flash, the young man was gone and the boy was back. Chambers decided to leave well enough alone and moved off to the racks of munitions. It had also occurred to him that he should get more ammunition for him and his men. He quickly collected several boxes of shot, a few packs of flints, and some powder, and took them to where John and Mr. Fogg were talking. He told them to add these to the list and that he was going to *The Badger* to see if those aboard needed anything from the shop before they sailed out.

He and Nektosha hurried to the dock, and he told Sophie and the soldiers about the conversation at the fort and about the new plan. Then he asked if any of them needed to go shopping. He almost instantly found he and Nektosha were left standing on *The Badger*, and Sophie, the kids, and the soldiers were headed up to the shop, and Sophie now had most of his remaining money.

"We *are* in a hurry," he yelled as they disappeared into the crowds on the street, Sophie throwing a wave of acknowledgment and dismissal over her shoulder.

Mr. Fogg had a wagon at the dock within the hour, everyone helped get the supplies loaded aboard, and the lines were cast off. John stood at the helm and directed Jacobs and Smith to drop the sails and stow the lines, and *The Badger* headed north. As they got underway, Sophie and the kids got to work stowing all the provisions and supplies. The boat had a surprising amount of space below the main deck. Storage, no doubt, for the munitions the boat no longer carried and now used for large stacks of furs that John had gathered. Thomas and Victoria were able to stand and walk around easily while the adults had to crouch, so they helped get things organized below. Chambers enlisted Nektosha to help him securely tie a large cookpot between the rear mast and the rails, which was filled with firewood and lit. A slightly smaller pot was rigged just over that, so they could cook safely on the boat. Soon enough, Sophie had prepared an excellent dinner of a hearty buffalo stew, accompanied by bread and cheese.

As they were finishing their meal, Sergeant Chambers addressed the crew. "I think it's best to attack under the cover of darkness. Our mission is fairly straightforward; we take the canoe into the harbor with some whale oil and clay lanterns. We light the lanterns and throw them onto the boats, where they'll shatter and spread the flaming oil over the deck. Then we move back and watch to be sure the boats are fully destroyed."

Corporal Benson interjected, "Shouldn't we get the supply ship to the north first, since that's the way they came in?"

Sergeant Chambers looker over and nodded. "Good point, Corporal. We will go after the supply ship first."

It was around midnight when they spotted the island. They were not used to seeing it like this; it was so dark. No lights in the watchtowers, no lamps in the windows; it was difficult to be sure what was what. They sailed up the western coast of the island, looking through the darkness to see any signs of life. They couldn't really see anything, but they could hear something. Strange moaning, odd screeches, and what sounded like a woman screaming in the distance. As the transport ship came into view, the sergeant got the final preparations in order.

"It will be myself, Benson, and Smith going out," he said. "We will need one iron lamp lit and five clay lamps filled but unlit."

Nektosha spoke up immediately. "I'm staying with you, sir."

Chambers put his hand on his shoulder and looked him in the eyes. "I need you here to help watch over *The Badger* and my family. Can you do that for me?"

Chambers watched Nektosha's face turn back into the frightened boy for a moment, then he visibly steeled himself and said, "Yes, sir, I can do that."

"Thank you," John said earnestly, then headed off to get the canoe organized. That was when the misty rain began, along with a considerable amount of gusty winds. The clouds and fog settled over the area like a thick blanket, making the darkness feel complete.

Smith was situated in the front of the canoe with his musket in hand, Benson was in the middle minding the box of lamps, and Chambers was paddling in the stern. The others stood on the deck of *The Badger* and watched. John guided her out into the hazy distance. They watched as the canoe faded into the consuming dark of the night. From *The Badger* they could only see the flicker of the flame as they lit the first lamp. They watched the tiny flame move in a small arc back and then a long arc forward as Benson launched the lamp toward the doomed *Prince Eugene*; it disappeared short of the steamboat. Throwing something from a small boat in these winds and waves was proving to be even more difficult than they thought. They could hear that there was urgent conversation on the small boat, but they couldn't make out any words. They saw another small flame appear in the mist. It too moved back, then forward, and disappeared.

Little Thomas's voice rang out, seeming too loud in the darkness. "Did they miss again? Did it not work? What is happening?"

Sophie shushed him, "Wait."

Then, slowly, a red glow appeared. It got bigger, brighter, and they began to make out the lines of the ship. They stared as Benson launched another, and another, and another, each landing on a different part of the ship. They were transfixed, as the ship's details became clearer and clearer in the growing firelight. There was a loud bang at their feet. All of them jumped; poor Victoria shrieked. It was the canoe bumping into the side of *The Badger*.

Chambers whispered, "Now we wait to be sure that's the ship burning and not just the oil."

When the flames grew to encompass it, they could hear a frantic rustling in the nearby woods. But whomever, or whatever, it was would not break the cover of the trees. John called to move the boats away just to be sure. By the time Chambers, Benson, and Smith got back onboard and let out some line so the canoe would trail properly behind, it was clear that the ship was fully engulfed in flames. They could smell burning wood and paint along with the sweet smell of the whale oil. The ship had sailed its last voyage.

John turned *The Badger* to the south and headed toward the harbor.

He brought *The Badger* just inside the edge of the harbor. "I can hold her in here for now, but the wind is picking up. There may be a storm coming in. I do not want her getting beached here."

Chambers surveyed the shadowed harbor. There were four boats at the dock: two small fishing boats and two larger boats that he knew had been there for some time. They set the canoe up the same way, Smith in the front, Benson in the middle, this time with more filled lamps. Chambers was in the rear. They approached the smaller boats first, and Corporal Benson hit the first one with ease; three oil bombs were sufficient for the smaller boat. With difficulty, due to the pitching winds, they maneuvered the canoe over to the second fishing boat. The water was getting quite choppy now, so on the first two shots, Benson missed.

"Hold it steady!" he hollered.

"I am! Try throwing better!" Smith snarked back.

The wind and mist were picking up, and Chambers and Smith were struggling to keep the canoe under control. Benson lit another lamp and, taking his time, found his mark. With another well-placed shot, the second boat was soon burning nicely as well.

Chambers wrestled the wobbly canoe over to try to hold it next to the smaller of the two ships. Smith even had to help, using the butt of his musket as an impromptu paddle. Soon they were alongside their third target, and Benson lit and launched the first lamp, which hit a few yards down the length of the ship. It was when he was lighting the second lamp that it happened. All of a sudden, they heard two sounds; one was a high-pitched gurgling screech that sounded not at all human, nor sounded like any wild beast, but sounded like something else entirely. The other sound was the unmistakable scream of a man. A *man* was screaming. He was screaming in shock and terror. It took Chambers a moment to realize that it was Smith doing the screaming. The canoe had drifted too close to the ship, and a pair of long, spindly arms had reached over the rail, grabbing Smith's musket, and was pulling it, and him, up and out of the small boat.

"Don't let it tip!" Chambers commanded.

"I'm trying!" Benson replied, fear lacing his voice.

The shift in weight left Benson and Chambers unable to do anything but to crouch down and work to keep balance. The macabre figure was lifting Private Smith up toward the rail of the other boat, his arm caught fast in the taut strap of his musket, his feet desperately hooked around the seat he'd just occupied. It was pulling him closer and closer to itself; its strength was nearly unbelievable. The figure was absolutely appalling—it looked like something that had died long ago and been left to dry under a desert sun, and the noises it made were like nothing anyone had ever heard. It appeared to be gaining the advantage, and it raised its desiccated face to the sky and arched its back to leverage Smith fully from the boat; then suddenly it stopped. A feathered shaft was now protruding from the center of its throat. The thing immediately went limp. With the upward force removed, Smiths's arm was freed from the musket strap, which left the gun to fall into the water with a splash that that was barely heard through the increasing rain and wind. Smith fell limply back into the boat with a moan that was part relief, part horror at what he'd just escaped. All eyes turned to *The Badger* to find Nektosha standing at the rail with his bow in hand and another arrow already set, his braids whipping in the wind, and his face set in firm determination.

7:

THE INDIAN PROGRESSION

E zra Clark had been a trader nearly his entire life; he'd been a drunkard for half that. His father had been a trader and a drunkard as well, and as soon as Ezra had freed himself of his mother's petticoats, he'd taken up the family business and the family's shameful habit. He had a small trade outpost where the Menomonee River branched off the Great Lake Mishigami and a path he followed almost as religiously as he followed the bottle. The loyal buyers who were dotted along that path were worth well more that the random passersby he might find for days of travel in any direction, and the steady flow of travelers to his outpost kept him well stocked in spirits. For all his intemperate ways, Clark was attentive to his profession, creating a set routine for his route, his outpost, and his traps during his travels. He had several traps spaced out along the trail at the intervals where he'd be spending more than a single night in a location. While bunked down, he'd check and reset his traps for bear, rabbit, deer, skunk, wolf, and other assorted creatures so as to sell their furs as well as, for some, their meat, organs, and bones. Those he didn't sell or trade on his path were cured and turned into baubles or ornaments to be displayed, along with his traded goods, in his outpost upon his return.

His habit was also what returned him to the bottle after drunken brawls with friend and stranger alike, hours and days blacked from memory and mornings waking feeling as though his head had been cleaved in two. However, this morning's pain was something new, something he'd never felt before. It was akin to some fever or influenza, with his head feeling stuffed with cotton, his mouth drier than a cracked creek bed after a drought, and his skin aflame. What was disturbing was the other ailments that were unknown to him. He couldn't seem to get his bearings. On a trail he'd traveled, quite literally, thousands of times before, he was constantly getting turned around, stumbling about like a Londoner fresh off the ship. There were also the odd patches appearing in various places on his skin, his right hand predominantly, though there were others scattered about on his left arm. Weird spots of what looked like, if he didn't know any better, the blue-green mold that grows on bread or cheese that was left too long. His eyes also felt dry and itchy, as if trail dust had blown into them. Finally, there was the problem with his breathing; he just *couldn't* catch his breath, and any attempts at deep breathing left him gasping and coughing, feeling as though a swallow of his best whisky had chosen the path to his lungs rather than his stomach. Clark headed back to his outpost, but he felt if this went on too much longer, he'd have to seek the care of the physician in Howard Township at the tip of Green Bay, a good four days' walk away, and he hated to break his routine.

———=»((◍))«=———

Howakan, the medicine man of Mato Hota's village, sat by the fire, smoking his pipe, and let his gaze rove over the people of his tribe. His was an unusual tribe as, due to their war with the Pawnee, nearly all of their warriors had been killed in a devastating sneak attack two winters ago. He, Mato, and a handful of others were the only men left in a village that was now very distrustful of outsiders. They'd secluded themselves from their neighboring tribes and, consequently, were a very small community comprising fewer than fifty individuals, most of them women, and nearly all of them had been sick. They depended on established integration with warriors from other nearby Sioux tribes and the occasional trusted trader to maintain their numbers. The Indian Removal Act had sent some from other tribes to join theirs, but most of them went farther west. Now, with so many of them ill, none of their contacts would touch their women. Their necessary apprehensiveness toward bringing in outsiders meant that their tribe had been on the brink of annihilation for several seasons.

Howakan turned as he heard footsteps approaching. Shasta, the chief of the tribe and Howakan's longtime friend and confidant, made his way over to join the man. The chief was nearing sixty years of age, and those sixty years had been wrought with hard-won battles against man and sickness alike. Shasta lowered himself gingerly onto the offered other half of the mat Howakan was on, and the two sat together in silence for a long while, watching the fire, before Howakan spoke his fears aloud.

"Seventeen of the forty-two people left in our tribe have taken ill, and three more are showing signs," he reported. "I had attempted, unsuccessfully, mind you, to cure our people until I had nearly dropped from exhaustion—before Mato had finally returned with his miracle in a bottle."

Taking a long pull of his pipe, he pondered on the cure Mato had brought them and the warrior's strange disappearance the same night. He finally turned to look at Chief Shasta. "Mato had seemed strange and unwell; his skin appeared unusually dry, even cracked in places and oddly colored. Not actually pale, more … gray, and patchy, as if his body was losing color, not blood, I suppose. He also seemed changed as a person, acting not himself." Howakan paused, still shocked over this revelation. "He admitted to stealing the medicine from Dr. Periwinkle. This leaves me with great worry that the medicine is not what we need, that it will do us no good." He shook his head. "As to his strange affliction, I am still unsure of what it could be; it is certainly not anything we've seen before. It was a curious affliction that I, as a medicine man, am anxious to examine closer. However, something deep within me is telling me that I don't want to get anywhere near whatever this is."

Shasta agreed. "True, from what you say, this is not like the sicknesses the colonists have brought upon us before." They both gazed into the fire for a while.

Howakan continued, "I've never before seen anything like it, and what brief glimpses I got from Mato both horrified and fascinated me."

Settling more comfortably on his buffalo skin mat, Howakan contemplated the happenings of the past few days. He remembered a white trader named Ezra Clark, a man whose monthly arrival was as dependable as the sun rising each day, had passed through their land with his wares. He, too, had refused the company of any of their women, though they had made good trades for coffee, sugar, grains, furs, and new dried meats as well as bowls, plates, and other objects made of metal.

The trader, though, had also seemed unwell. Not as severe in appearance as Mato, possibly due to his lighter complexion, but he too had the same odd pallor, the same parched skin. Howakan knew the man enjoyed his drink a bit more than he should; however, whatever was ailing the stout man did not seem related to the drink. He worried that this was some new disease set to ravage the land, and he prayed that it would pass over his tribe; they'd had more than their share of sickness and were ill suited to handle more.

Over the following few days, however, Howakan came to realize that the mysterious malady that had befallen Mato and the trader was indeed touching his tribe. Curiously, it was the six who had not previously taken ill were were now showing dryness of skin and that odd gray blotchy pallor that he really couldn't explain. It almost looked as if these people had rolled in ash, but the color had a vague blue or green hue that was rather reminiscent of mold or fungus.

The patches of discolored skin would start as what appeared to be an abrasion, as if the individual had scraped their skin too hard over rocks. However, this "rash" would just get deeper into the skin and take on this perplexing color and rotting odor. It almost seemed that the skin was starting to decay and harden before the body had actually died. Howakan, Chief Shasta, and the few elders remaining in the tribe held a counsel, to discuss what was to be done about this new plague.

Howakan started his six afflicted tribe members on herbs and ingredients known to help with legions and skin wounds—pastes and serums to be spread on the affected skin. Nothing seemed to work as it should, though he wasn't really surprised; these medicines were not truly meant for … whatever this was. One remedy that he abandoned almost immediately was a spiritual cleanse in a closed tent, with fire and incense burning filling the tent with thick, cleansing smoke. He'd barely gotten through the first part of his chant when he noticed the rash visibly growing before his eyes and the disposition of his tribesman grew suddenly, *savage*. He'd known this man since birth—indeed, he'd attended the child and performed rites over him and his mother right after she'd returned from her birthing hut. But the man staring viciously at him in this suddenly tiny tent was not the man he'd watched grow through the years. There was a bestial gleam in the man's red-rimmed eyes, a savagery in his expression that did not belong. Howakan was a learned man, a respected elder in the tribe, and thus carried himself with dignity and poise at all times. That day however, he bolted out of that tent like a scolded child, and it took him hours to calm his shaking hands and feverish heartbeat. The young man had gone darting into the woods much like Mato Hota had done, and nothing had been seen of him since.

Now, Howakan's attempted remedies were performed with another warrior present, as he dearly wished to never feel that kind of primal fear again. The look that man had given him had awakened something deep within Howakan that set his nerves on edge and had his instincts *screaming* to get away from him.

After much meditation on the event, he realized that if the dry heat of the closed-off tent had accelerated the affliction, moisture could possibly slow or reverse it. This, it turned out, seemed to be another mistake. Howakan had gotten just a few yards from the afflicted man before the wretched soul had seen the herbal water in his bowl and gone absolutely *mad* with rage. Howakan beat a hasty retreat and retired to his hut to meditate on the problem, telling the remainders of the tribe to take that time to perform dances and chants to cleanse and heal the spirits of their ill.

Howakan had tried, methodically at first, then with more and more desperation, to save his five remaining tribesmen. He failed. Over the next fortnight, one by one, the three women and two men grew more and more savage, needing to be restrained, first within the huts and finally within deep pits they'd had to dig. Watching these people, men and women he had known all their lives, turn into raging animals, clawing at the earth and stone attempting to get out and do who knows what to the rest of the tribe, filled Howakan with a powerful sadness and impotence. Nothing had worked. He'd tried literally everything he could think of, and *nothing* had worked. They'd had to cover the pits over with animal hide when the first of them had … exploded. She'd given a great, wailing screech, and then her chest had burst open like a dropped melon, and this … odd powder had come out of her. Howakan knew instinctively that getting that dust on them was a bad idea, so he'd had the pits covered over. They also decided to move their village.

Many tribes were nomadic, and though theirs hadn't been, they would have to adapt. He and the rest of the tribe performed their last dance and chant around the pits, singing and hollering their prayers for the souls of these four remaining tribesmen, until they'd all given their screeching wail and gone quiet. The tribe grew silent as they filled each pit with dirt. They couldn't lay them to rest as was their custom; that required removing the bodies from the pits, and they all felt it was terribly unsafe to do so.

They then gathered all of their belongings and moved off, hopefully away from all the diseases saturating the land, heading east at first, then turning south to follow the banks of the Great Lake. Howakan had decided to move them to the terminus of the Menomonee River, where they had a day camp. From there sent a runner down the river and along the banks of the Lake Mishigami to Chicago, where his colonist doctor friend lived. It was the same man Mato Hota had … stolen … from, Dr. Deggory Periwinkle. This bizarre affliction was far beyond Howakan's understanding, and he knew he would need the consultation of his colonist counterpart and friend.

They reached the camp in about five days, the trek

having taken much longer than normal due to the extra precautions and the slower pace of some of the tribe. Howakan dispatched his runner to Chicago without delay, grateful that, even in his befuddled state, Mato Hota had stored the canoe where it belonged. It was on the seventh night after they'd set out, two since arriving at the day camp, that one of the older women came to him, shaking like a leaf in a gale and crying enough to fill a bowl. She didn't say a word to him, just lifted her skirt to reveal a patchy greenish rash on her knee. Howakan felt his heart jolt painfully, feeling as if he'd just been hit in the chest. They hadn't escaped it. He knew, logically, that there was absolutely nothing he could do for this woman, and looking into her eyes, he could tell she knew it too.

"I must return to the village," she whispered. "I can already feel the oddness creeping into my thoughts, as a fog creeps through the forest. I will return to the village, and I will barricade myself in my hut."

"Keep yourself dampened for as long as you can," Howakan admonished. "From what we saw with the others, heat and dryness spreads it faster, so do your best to avoid them until you can't stand the water. Take care on your journey back to the village and hold on to hope there may be an answer, that you may be able to survive it."

She nodded and moved off to collect her meager belongings before moving off into the gathering darkness of the night.

The runner, a young lad just barely into his adult years named Tamaha, traveled the same path his tribe always took when going to Chicago, the same Mato had taken, canoeing down the Menomonee River to the Great Lake Mishigami. Then down the lake, following the banks, until, after four days of paddling and camping in the wilds, he arrived in Chicago. He had a moment of confusion, as the location he was given for Dr. Periwinkle's practice was a cleared area with building materials scattered about. It looked as though someone was preparing to construct a building; however, there was nothing here that could remotely be called a doctor's office at the moment. After some asking around, with his limited knowledge of the colonists' language, he discovered that the original building had burned down and the debris cleared just over a month ago. He was, therefore, directed to the local barber's shop, where Dr. Periwinkle had set up a temporary office to see to patients.

Dr. Deggory Periwinkle looked, even the young brave could see, to be a shadow of the man he should be. He was slumped over in a chair, his fine clothing rumpled, his hair mussed, and his face unshaven, ironic given that he was sitting in a barber's chair. When the doctor faced him, presumably to see who had entered, Tamaha could see from the redness in his eyes and the heaviness of his movements that the doctor was either very inebriated or had very recently been so. The state of the doctor left Tamaha with little hope as to the success of his venture, yet still he pressed on.

"Dr, Periwinkle," Tamaha began, "we are needing your help. There is new … sickness. Causing … um … bruise?" Tamaha cursed under his breath at his previous disinterest in learning the colonists' tongue. "Not bruise, wrong word. There is … rash … on the skins … "

Tamaha stuttered to a halt as Dr. Periwinkle flung his hand up through the air, as though he were trying to bat away a troublesome fly, "I haven't the time for new sicknesses, don't you see!" he exclaimed drunkenly. "I've got far too much to do right now; my office is gone, my research is gone, everything is in RUINS!" He took a deep, shuddering breath and seemed to sink further within himself and the chair.

"I am … apologize, Dr. Periwinkle," Tamaha said, stammering over his words. "We are bad needing your help. My people are *dying*!"

Dr. Periwinkle flung both hands through the air this time, stumbling to his feet, and startling Tamaha into silence again. "No! I can't be bothered with this now! I haven't the *time* for you people!" He tripped over his own feet and crashed to the ground. After a moment, he began to snore.

Tamaha stared at the man, now sleeping flat on his face on the barber's floor. This man, this drunkard, was their final hope? The Indian felt anger rising within himself. The doctor hadn't the time for *their people*? Well, he'd be sure to pass that message along to his people! At that thought, his anger ebbed away into despair. His tribe was going to die. After all they'd survived—the war with the Pawnee, the various diseases the colonists had brought, the droughts and freezes that plagued this land—they were finally to be brought down by this ravaging affliction, and they would again have to face it alone. Tamaha turned away from the broken man on the floor and headed down the road and out of town. If he was quick at the trader's, he'd be able to head up the Great Lake before the day was too far along and make good time back to *his people*.

8:

AT THE TRADING POST

Tamaha decided that he did not want to be in Chicago anymore. He would trade with their friend near home. He reached the trader's at the joining of the Mishigami Lake and the Menomonee River to find the interior of the building in a shambles. This was the same trader who had passed through his village over a month ago and, now that he thought on it, that man had shown signs of this new sickness too, though they hadn't known just what it was, and just what it *did* at the time. If this man had burst open as those in his tribe had, who was he to buy supplies from? However, if he hadn't, if he, like those six, had gone feral … Tamaha gazed warily around the shop, his canoe paddle the only defense he had available, yet he *needed* the supplies.

He stepped slowly over the scattered beaded necklaces, boxes of ammunition, and bundles of feathers on the floor at the entryway and moved as silently as he could over to the packs of dried herbs, fruits, and meats in troughs along the back wall. He set his paddle down and pulled open his pack. He told himself that he'd leave the copper coins the trader preferred on the counter for what he was taking and had almost finished filling his pack with provisions when he heard a sudden thump followed by shuffling from behind the stacks of furs near the back of the building. The noise startled him so much that he accidentally knocked over his canoe paddle from where he'd leaned it against the wall. It hit the ground with a sound like a falling tree, and the shuffling stilled suddenly. Tamaha held his breath as he stared at the furs, slowly reaching down to retrieve his paddle. He'd just managed to grasp the handle when a form shambled out from behind the furs.

It was the trader—Tamaha could tell that much—but the man was badly damaged. His right hand and large portions of the muscles in his left arm were missing, though that wasn't the worst of it. Cradled in the crook of his right arm, as one might cradle a babe, was the detached leg of a young woman, judging by the silk stocking that dangled from the foot, riddled with gouges. As the trader stepped into the light streaming from the windows, Tamaha could see that the gouges were made by the trader, that he'd *bitten* chunks out of the leg.

"Wentiko," he whispered without conscious thought, calling up the name of **an Ojibway evil spirit**.

The trader's eyes snapped to him, and an unearthly shriek erupted from the man. He moved swiftly, though stiffly, and lifted the severed leg in the air like a club. Tamaha could feel the bile rising in his throat. The smell of gore was overwhelming, as this man-beast, this Wentiko, advanced on him. With great effort, he swallowed the bile down, snatched up his loaded pack and his paddle, and bolted for the outpost door, stumbling over the beads on the floor and knocking over a barrel holding several scythes in his haste. From the flat of his back, he snatched up one of the scythes and held it out above himself, using it more as a shield than a weapon. He screwed his eyes tightly shut and braced himself. It felt as if a mountain had crushed down on him as the man fell atop him. After a moment, he realized the man was no longer moving, and opened his eyes, giving a small shriek upon discovering the man's ghastly face mere inches from his own, and he pushed him off and to the floor beside him. Picking himself and his belongings up from the ground, he turned to leave, and paused, spying a collection of flint and steel strikers by the door.

⸺⸺●⟨◐⟩●⸺⸺

He sprinted down the path to the river, crackles and snaps of the burning building echoing in his ears. He scrambled back to his canoe, tossing his overfull pack into the bottom of it, and shoved it into the river with all his might, slipping and stumbling in the muddy riverbed before leaping into his seat and plunging the paddle into the water.

The remaining journey was an arduous one. He pushed himself harder and further than he should have, emotions warring in his chest: anger at the doctor, fear for his people, and horror at what he'd seen and done at the trader's. As a result, upon his arrival back at day camp, he had no energy or will left to him to wake Howakan to give his report and fell asleep nearly as soon as he'd arrived. It was well into the following morning that he was able to rouse himself and take stock of his tribe. The first thing he noticed was that eight more people were missing; he learned that the affliction had indeed followed them, and those who had been touched by it had returned to their old village, to keep the others safe.

He told his story to Howakan as he sat himself dejectedly by the fire, all his previous animosity toward the doctor now vanished in light of this new information. He still found himself shaking badly when telling of what he'd found in the trader's outpost and how he'd handled the situation, and Howakan offered him some valerian tea to ease his nerves.

Upon learning what Dr. Periwinkle had said, Howakan was terribly incensed, his face a thundercloud of rage and betrayal as he sat with the tribe around the fire. He and this colonist doctor had been partners in medicine for several years now, and to throw it all away because he wanted to wallow in self-pity was not something Howakan could readily understand. Yes, the man had lost his practice and progress, but he still had his wife and child! He still had his own life, for that matter, though he now seemed content to drown himself in spirits. Howakan had lost *dozens*. Men he'd known as small children and watched grow into proud providers for the tribe, only to be cut down in the cowardly Pawnee sneak attack. Women he'd know and cared for, for decades, so ravaged by the effects of cholera that they begged for death hours before it finally claimed them. Babes he'd swaddled and done all he could to ease their passing as they coughed up what little blood they could, with consumption racking their tiny bodies. Howakan held little sympathy for the colonist doctor, who'd lost a building and a few notes. Yes, it was a setback, but in Howakan's experience, Dr. Periwinkle had lost very little and was giving up far too easily.

The other news from Tamaha took the fight right out of Howakan. The trader had indeed been struck by this new illness and, apparently, had survived when his limbs had burst rather than his chest, as those from his tribe had done. Howakan paled when he thought of those he'd sent back to the village, whose afflictions were centered on limbs and not torsos. If those afflicted of his tribe had their wounds burst on their limbs, then they could survive it, as the trader had. Would they, too, become beasts that killed and *ate* people? Were they, even now, roaming the wilds, killing and *eating* all they found? Tamaha's referring to them as Wentiko seemed very appropriate in light of what had become of the trader. A man-eating demon was what he had become.

Howakan was still lost in thought when a warrior seated a few places down from him spoke his name. "Howakan, I need you to kill me."

All conversation in the camp stopped. Howakan blinked at the man for a moment and shook himself into alertness.

"Now is not the time to be losing hope, my friend. We must remain strong and firm as the mountain."

The warrior shook he head and held out his arm where a pale-blue fuzzy rash could be seen. "It has touched me, as well. I cannot go through that horrid existence. I will not! If you cannot do it, I will find a way to do it myself." He took a shuddering breath, lowering his arm. "Just as the others who were touched before me, I can feel a fog of oddness, of *wrongness*, creeping over my mind, and it scares me. More than the Pawnee did, more than any other disease or illness our tribe has been touched by. After hearing what became of the trader, this affliction *scares* me."

Howakan stared gravely at the man, another he'd watched grow from babe to child to warrior, who was now asking for death—so much death in his tribe—and Howakan found himself speaking before he'd even understood what he was going to say. "If this is your true desire, my friend, I shall aid your passage into the afterlife."

The warrior nodded and turned to stare into the fire, his face a mask of stone, his eyes a sea of swirling emotions. "Thank you, Howakan."

Howakan wasn't really sure how to respond; this situation was not something he felt right saying, "You're welcome," to.

He decided to do it that night, after everyone had gone to bed—no need for the others to suffer through the knowledge of it happening, though he had realistic expectations of anyone getting any real sleep. He had some opium that he used as a painkiller, and he knew that too much put the recipient into a sleep before they died; it was the most painless way he had available to him to end someone's life, though just the thought left a bitter taste in his mouth. He knew that there were times when putting a man out of his misery was preferable to prolonged suffering. However, he'd never had a man who outwardly looked so healthy make the request before, and it went against everything he was as a man of healing to willingly end this man's life.

Howakan spent the next day in deep meditation, trying to reconcile within himself what he'd done. Yes, the man had asked, even begged, for Howakan to prevent his suffering before it began ... Still. Howakan meditated and found solace in the understanding that he'd not delivered death to this man but release. The following day he emerged from his contemplation to a realization: the others who had returned to the village now had no such chance for release. They were forced, *by him*, whispered a small voice in the back of his mind, to endure the horror and agony of this affliction until it ultimately killed them or turned them into beasts. As soon as Howakan was fully aware of these ramifications, he hastened from his hut to the remaining twenty-seven tribesmen. He had to pause for a moment to let the sudden wave of sorrow pass over him. Their once-great people, at one time numbering in the several hundreds, were now just under thirty men, women, and children. Their tribe was slowly dying, and it seemed there was nothing he could do to stop it.

Shaking himself from his musings, Howakan spoke to his tribe. "My meditation revealed to me that the changes caused by this sickness are far worse than a release granted by a friend. We gave those eight who returned to the village no offer of any such release. Therefore, I need three volunteers to return to the village and give those still alive there a peaceful transition to the afterlife."

In the end, four of his tribe members volunteered to return to the village. Howakan praised them for their bravery and sent them without delay. It was odd, but he prayed that the ten he'd sent back to the village were dead. To be subjected to the living hell that the luckless trader had suffered through ...

9:

THE HERO OF DETROIT

"We have another ship to take care of!" Sergeant Jack Chambers urged as he paddled the near-foundering canoe backward furiously from the now burning ship.

John's voice carried over the increasing wind. "Get back here! It's getting too rough for the canoe!"

With no disagreement, but with great effort, Chambers managed to get the little boat turned around and back to the relative safety of *The Badger*. With some difficulty, they timed the rising and falling of the two boats and got back on board the larger vessel; it required all of them hauling mightily on the canoe to pull it aboard.

"How are we going to destroy the other ship?" Benson asked.

"I don't dare take *The Badger* any closer!" John said.

Everyone nodded in agreement as they darted nervous glances back at the site of the recent altercation. Private Smith was still visibly shaken up and disturbed.

"I have an idea," Sophie offered as she turned and headed into the cabin.

She returned with one of John's wool blankets. "How about if we cut this up and tie strips to arrows, soak them in whale oil, then light them, and let Nektosha shoot them at the last boat."

After a brief silence, everyone spoke at once.

"Yes, that could work."

"It's worth a try."

"That last boat *is* made of wood."

"Let's do that."

It took only a few moments to prepare the arrows, and Nektosha only missed twice due to the increasing gusting winds and the pitching and rolling of *The Badger*. Soon enough, the last target was lit in several places. They had no choice but to stay and watch the boats burn.

John had told them, "Leaving the harbor in this storm is just not an option."

They dropped the anchors off each end of the ship near the east end of the harbor, set watch shifts, and secured *The Badger* to ride out the storm. There was no doubt that everyone wanted to be as far away from the island as quickly as possible, but it was also clear that leaving the shelter of the harbor was foolhardy. That did not ease anyone's discomfort, which was compounded by the howling of the wind mixing with the howling, and other macabre sounds, from the island. They all stood holding the rail for a time, pitching up and down with the salt spray hitting their faces, watching the fires in the harbor, wondering if they got all of the boats and wondering what was in store next.

It was still dark when the storm let up, and John and the soldiers set to work pulling up the anchors and letting out a portion of the sails. They were not far from the harbor when the weather and choppy waters settled down enough for everyone to feel some relief and attempt to get some sleep.

By the time most of the group got up and moving about in the morning, Sophie and the kids had a good breakfast ready to go. They had the most troubled night of the group; this was their first time seeing one of these things. As they all sat around the deck, Sergeant Chambers surveyed the group with a new appreciation.

"For all that we had to deal with, I believe we all dealt with it very well."

There were mumbles of agreement over mouthfuls of food.

"We should head back to Detroit," he continued, "to find out if there is any word back on our request for troops. This time just me and the soldiers will go to the fort; maybe that will improve our reception."

"Yes, sir," answered Corporal Benson.

Sophie added, "I would like to get some dry clothes for the children and myself; we got pretty soaked through in the storm last night."

Chambers nodded slowly. "Good point. We will do some shopping after we find out the answers from the fort. Is that all right with everyone?"

"Yes, of course," Sophie replied as she adjusted the wool blanket that Victoria had around her shoulders.

John spoke up and offered to cover the expenses with

some of the furs he had on board. "No need for you to cover everything," he said with a nod to the breakfast pot.

It was midmorning when *The Badger* approached the dock. After careful examination, they found that Detroit was just as they had left it. People were peacefully moving about, blissfully unaware of the horrors that were just north of them. Sergeant Chambers and the three soldiers adjusted their still-damp uniforms and headed out for the fort. Again, the sergeant was looking into the side streets and doorways, hoping not to see any signs of trouble but no less ready for it. A door slammed beside them, and all four muskets were trained on the spot in an instant. This startled several of the townsfolk, who suddenly decided they wanted to go in a different direction and disappeared into various side streets. The soldiers offered no apologies; they shouldered their weapons and continued their walk up the street with their faces set in stone-like determination.

They arrived at the gate to find the same guard at his post. Sergeant Chambers stepped forward, and he and the guard exchanged salutes.

"Good morning, Private. Permission to pass?"

The guard, still at attention, replied, "Yes, Sergeant, welcome back," before relaxing a bit and nodding at the other soldiers, as they all dropped their salutes as well.

Chambers's men followed him as he went directly to the commander's office. He could see that the storm had taken a toll here too. Several men were nailing replacement shingles onto various buildings around the fort. Sergeant Chambers approached and knocked on the door. There was no answer. He knocked again and still no answer. He opened the door slightly and peered in. Seeing the room unoccupied, he then pulled his head back, shut the door, and started looking around the fort. He spied the major adjusting his clothes as he was leaving the outhouse. He studied the soldiers as he walked across the yard; then, recognizing Sergeant Chambers, he nodded and approached. They all snapped to attention and exchanged salutes.

"Come on in, men."

They entered and pulled the heavy door closed behind them, as the major added wood to the fire.

When they all were all in and settled, he continued, "I haven't heard back from my runner yet. He most likely took shelter from the storm the other night. Did you guys get caught up in that mess?"

"That and more," Chambers answered. "Let me tell you how things went for us."

The men were offered chairs and hot coffee by the acting commander, the former of which they drew up around the desk as Chambers relayed the report of the actions taken at Mackinac Island.

⎯⎯⎯«(◦)»⎯⎯⎯

John and Nektosha were checking the sails and lines for any damage they may have taken from the storm. Sophie, Victoria, and Thomas were sorting through the clothes and blankets, hanging things up to dry along rails, when they realized there was trouble. They heard a noise they had heard once before. A sound that made all of them freeze in place.

A sound that caused their skin to tingle and their chests to tighten. It was in the distance and somewhat faint, but there was no mistaking it for anything else. The baleful howl accompanied by the maniacal screeching.

John looked at Nektosha and, in a hoarse whisper, spat out, "Weapons!"

John grabbed his musket and a machete while Nektosha got his bow and arrows. Sophie ordered the kids to get down in the hold, secure the hatch as best as they could, and then hide under the furs.

She then stood on top of the hatch and, looking at John, said, "I need a weapon."

Without hesitation, John handed her his pistol and a long skinning knife.

They then stood, and watched, and listened. The sounds were still there; they were still distant, but it was clear that they were getting closer.

"Somebody has to warn the town!" Sophie said in a loud whisper.

She looked at John and Nektosha, who had both stepped forward, and told them, "You two stay here and protect the children. I'll go get the word out."

"Do you want me to come with you?" Nektosha asked.

"No," she answered, "you two being here is the best chance we have to keep Thomas and Victoria safe!"

"Yes, ma'am!" Nektosha replied, giving her a reassuring nod, which was mimicked by John.

They could see that she was pale and trembling and had a tear on her cheek when she simply looked at them in fare-well. She didn't try to talk. She knew she would lose her composure and possibly her nerve. She just turned and left, striding toward town and the peril approaching from the north.

John and Nektosha watched her walk, then run, into the town. She was already casting about, looking for the best course of action.

John looked to Nektosha. "How about you climb up onto the yardarm and see if you can tell what is going on?"

Nektosha quickly agreed, glad that there was something he could do rather than stand and wait. It took very little time for him to get himself situated with his bow and quiver ready, standing on the yardarm.

"I can see her!" he called down to the trapper, "She is going door to door. She is yelling at the shop owners and homeowners both. Some are following her, and some are running away."

"Good," John answered. "Can you see any sign of those things yet?"

"No, sir." Nektosha answered with a shake of his head.

John then turned and lifted the hatch to ask the kids if they were all right.

After hearing a muffled, "We're fine," from the darkness, he resecured the hatch, checked his weapons, took a deep breath, and waited.

⸻ ◈ ⸻

As Sophie started to run up the dock, she formulated a plan. She knew she would not be able to get to everyone in time. She also knew, logically, that she would not be much good trying to fight these things herself. So, she fixed a quick speech in her head.

When she got the first door, which was a warehouse, she ran in and blurted, "We're under attack! Get some kind of weapons and come with me, and someone needs to go into town and get more help!"

The men inside paused for a moment and just looked at her.

"NOW!" she yelled, using the same tone she used on her children when ordering them to bed.

The men were scrambling to comply before the echo stopped. She continued this for a couple of blocks, and soon she had a good-size militia trailing along behind her. A minute or two more and some of those who had run for help were starting to return with more townsfolk.

Among one of these groups were several dandies in expensive suits, the shortest of whom stepped forward and said in an authoritative tone, "What's the meaning of all this?"

Sophie stopped for a moment then said, "Listen," holding up a finger.

Even among the buildings and people it could be heard, the wailing and screeching. Sophie had to hold her breath to keep herself under control.

"They are coming! If we are not ready, we *will* die." She fixed the man to his spot with a hard stare.

"Right!" said the man. "Sean, get the rest of the men. Jeremy, you go to the fort."

When she heard him say, "the fort," Sophie's knees nearly buckled.

"We have got to do this," she told herself.

"What do we do?" asked a man holding a large pickaxe.

"Well ... " Sophie began, realizing that she hadn't gotten that far in her plan.

As she spoke, she reflexively looked back to *The Badger*, where she had been when this all started. There she saw Nektosha standing in the rigging, and when he saw her, he pointed to indicate a spot between and to the north of their locations. Listening for a second, she was able to confirm the message.

"This way!" she shouted, pointing with the long knife.

The growing mob moved with her as she zigzagged her way diagonally through the blocks, some of the crowd taking parallel streets and alleys to keep the pace.

When she finally saw it, she froze. There it was, a chaotic mass of bodies with hands and arms reaching forward at odd angles. The only thing she could think to do was what she did.

Remembering the instructions she had been given, she pointed John's pistol at the thing in the middle of the mass, pulled the hammer to full cock, and pulled the trigger. The pistol erupted in her hand like thunder and lightning, with a deafening crack and a cloud of smoke. As she struggled to keep her balance from the recoil, she saw one of the monster's head explode. The recoil had sent her hand high over her head, and she left it there in shock for a moment.

It was her first time firing a gun, and the force of it stunned her; her hand went briefly numb and her ears rang. She had not hit the one she was aiming for, but it did not matter. At the sound of the pistol, the makeshift militia leaped into action. They rushed past her, and in their fury, she found herself jostled out of the fray and off to the side.

When she found herself with a moment for clear thought, she looked down at John's pistol and spoke quietly to herself, "I wish I had thought to get stuff to reload this, although I haven't the faintest idea how to do it."

She then heard a clamor coming from the other direction.

"What now?!" she thought as she pressed herself to a nearby wall.

She held the knife up in front of her chest. Around the corner came an impressive number of soldiers running in formation. Lowering the knife to her side, she stepped out, causing the troops to pause for a moment, and she searched for her husband.

She spotted him almost immediately, standing at the front, "Jack! Oh, Jack, there they are!" she yelled when she saw him, pointing with the knife toward the battle.

She then charged up and put her arms around him.

"Sophie! Are you all right? Are the children all right?"

"The children ... " she gasped, "yes, they're fine. They're hiding on the boat, with John and Nektosha."

"Good! All right, you take care of them, and we will take care of this."

She nodded. With tears in her eyes, she stretched up and kissed the large sergeant on the jaw. She then turned and began to run down toward the merchant dock, where *The Badger* was tied up.

Major Shepard broke the moment. "Right, men, they appear to have them bottled up here. Our best bet is to take the flanks, to contain, and to finish them off. Chambers, you take these ten men around that side. I will take those ten with me around this side. The rest of you, shore up the middle. Don't let any of them out alive!! Brigade, ready?!"

"Ready, sir!" came the booming reply from the troops.

With great efficiency, the soldiers divided into three groups and headed for the fray. Sergeant Chambers led his men at a run; they went two blocks over and cut in to the left.

"Keep an eye out for strays," he shouted over his shoulder.

When they got to the site of the attack, the scene was appalling. The people of Detroit had done as well as could be expected against the ravaging horror that set upon them that day. Unfortunately, a great many already lay dead in the streets.

"Ready, and FIRE!" Chambers heard Shepard shout from across the way.

He echoed the same cry as did a voice from the center. The muskets thundered and boomed, and the air filled with acrid smoke and other smells more cloying, and swamp like. Many of the vile beast-men fell, but not as many as Chambers expected. Typically, a volley like this would have sent any enemy retreating, but not these things.

"Ready bayonets, and charge!" Sergeant Chambers bellowed.

He heard his words repeated from the other two squads. They lowered their bayonets and advanced on the horrific opponent.

Sophie had made it to the edge of town and was at the docks when she heard John cry out, "Hey!"

She immediately thought he was going to say something about the children and strained to see if anything was amiss on the ship.

"Behind you!"

She looked back to see two of those inhuman abominations scrambling toward her. She let out an involuntary scream as she turned back to run to the ship. She flinched as she saw two figures coming from this direction. It was John and Nektosha! She dived down and between them as they passed her. Nektosha's arrow was promptly planted in the eye of one, as John shot the other in the upper chest. The one that John shot barely acknowledged the normally fatal wound and kept coming. Its arm was now gone, and it seemed unfazed. John let out a yelp and swung the butt of his musket around, catching the crazed thing in the temple with a sickening crack. Then that one, like the other, fell off the dock and splashed into the harbor.

Sophie was in a fit by this time; all that she wanted to do was to see her Thomas and Victoria and to know that they were not harmed. She struggled for a moment to free her legs from her tangled petticoats and stand back up.

"Thank you!" Her voice was trembling. "Thank you! But I ... " She was looking to the boat.

"They are fine." John cut her off. "Go! They're still in the hold."

She was on the ship in an instant and pulling at the hatch. She was greeted by two wide-eyed and beautiful children. She kneeled down and drew them into her embrace, and for a moment, tears streamed from her eyes as visions of what could have been played out in her mind.

They waited, guarding the ship in great uncertainty, for what seemed like a very long time. The sounds of the fighting died down fairly soon after Sophie's return, but they could not tell what was going on.

Even when Nektosha climbed up the mast, he said, "I can't see any movement. I can't tell if it's over or if they all just moved to where I can't see" was all he could report.

They didn't want to leave the boat and children unattended, but what if those in the town needed help? Were they all mortally injured? Were they all even still alive? After many long minutes of torturing themselves with these questions. Sergeant Jack Chambers rounded a corner and came walking up the dock. His uniform was dappled with blood stains on one side, and he seemed to be walking with a bit of a limp.

"Oh dear!" Sophie exclaimed as she hurried to meet her husband on the dock. "Are you hurt? Did they get you?" she asked, squeezing his arms and chest and reaching up to cup his face with her trembling hands.

"I'm fine, dear. I just got a little banged up. This blood is just a smack on the nose. One of our guys was swinging a garden rake of all things!"

"What about the others?" Sophie asked.

"Jacobs didn't make it," Chambers said solemnly. "He was on the other side. I saw one of them grab him, then the rake hit me, and I couldn't see anything for a moment. I tried to look for him afterward, but I was unable to tell what was what. It was brutal. Benson is fine, but I haven't seen Smith. Sophie, they want to see you in the town hall."

"What? Me? Why?" Sophie was surprised and confused. "They don't think that this was my fault, do they? Surely they don't think *I* caused all of this."

Chambers chuckled. "No, I don't think you are in any trouble, but they still want to see you."

As they entered the town hall, the man at the front was saying, " ... So, until we are sure things have settled, the military will be on the streets day and night."

He spotted the couple in the back of the hall. "There she is now."

Hundreds of faces turned to look at Sophie, an unsettling situation even after a day like today.

"Would you come forward, please." The man extended his hand and waved her in.

Sophie grabbed Jack's arm and dragged him with her, their every step echoing in the otherwise silent hall.

"Our town suffered huge losses today," he began when they finally reached the speaking platform. "Today our Detroit faced a challenge unlike any other, and that challenge took its toll. Of that there can be no mistake. We shall be grieving our losses for many days to come. One other thing is certain, that toll and those losses would have been immeasurably greater if it were not for you, Sophie Chambers."

The hall erupted into thunderous applause. Jack Chambers could feel his wife tremble and weaken at his side. He put his arm around her waist to support her.

The man continued, "We cannot repay you, but we can at least say thank you."

"Thank you," Sophie replied in a meek voice. "I just wanted to … " She did not have the words.

"We should go," Jack told the man in the top hat, who looked at both of them.

Seeing Sophie racked with conflicting emotions, he nodded softly. "I understand. We shall talk later."

"Thank you," said Jack and Sophie in unison, and they turned, walked through the applauding crowd, and left.

10:

THE COUNCIL

Howakan waited three days before informing Chief Shasta and the few remaining elders of the worries he'd been having.

"We need to go back to the village. Those three we sent to take care of our people afflicted by the Wentiko have not returned from their mission. I fear that they were unsuccessful."

Chief Shasta paced before the fire, worry etching deep lines into his face.

"Yes," Shasta agreed, his eyes staring into the moving shadows of the swaying trees surrounding them, "we cannot be assured these Wentiko were taken care of, and we cannot leave them there to wreak more havoc on the tribes and towns nearby—they must not." Were there Wentiko prowling in the darkness, beyond the touch of firelight? He felt a cold sweat form on his back.

Chief Shasta nodded to himself, turning to face Howakan. "We will leave at first light. Our women will have to become our warriors now; our men are too few. I will explain all of this to them now."

Howakan watched his chief leave the tent, ruminating over the affects the past several years had had on the leader of his tribe. He had been a bear of a man: strong, tall, and brave. Now, as he strode slowly away from the firelight, Howakan could see the damage that had been wrought. His form was beaten, diminished. The years had definitely pulled a heavy price from the old Indian, and Howakan mourned the man he was. Howakan rose and turned to gather new supplies for the journey to the village.

This, he knew, was going to be a difficult task.

—————«(O)»—————

The journey to the village was an arduous one, made all the worse for the discovery of one of their tribesmen halfway back. It had once been an old woman. She had fashioned a gag out of a torn strip of her skirt and a branch, had forced it into her mouth, and tied it tight. She had then apparently used her belt to bind her hands together around a tree—she had been so determined to not hurt anyone. Her leg had finally burst, just above the knee, and the creature she now was was moaning from the kneeling position it had been forced into. Chief Shasta had the rest of the tribe move off before dispatching her himself. He sat for several moments with her afterward in silent prayer and contemplation.

The tribe finally arrived on the outskirts of the village to a scene of horror and devastation. The remaining contents of the village were scattered and broken about the area as though a few buffalo had rampaged through it. Several of the huts were demolished; one looked as if it had been burned to the ground. Their lead warriors slowly creeped into the village, examining the detritus and searching for the Wentiko and keeping alert to any movement among the shadows.

"Howakan!"

The medicine man whipped his head around at the call, seeing one of the now-warrior women waving him over from the remains of the charred hut.

"There was someone in here," she explained, pointing to the blackened husk of a man, judging by the size of it.

Howakan dropped to one knee, using a torn bit of cloth to cover his nose and mouth from the putrid odor emanating from the corpse. This body seemed to have gone through a prolonged period of rot before the fire, and the smell was indescribable. Howakan used the butt of his club to sift through the ashes and debris, which only served to increase the potency of the stench and revealed nothing to explain what had happened to cause this.

<hr>

There was no warning. There was no battle cry. The branches and bushes just past the clearing suddenly started snapping and whipping in a frantic explosion of activity.

"It's an attack!" cried one of the warriors. "There is

one here ... a Wentiko!"

One of the crazed men crashed through into the clearing. Two of the muskets exploded into action, and the foul creature was pierced through the thigh and the cheek.

"Raahaieaaeeee!" it cried out.

It stumbled, but it did not fall. It continued its wild advance to the group of panicked defenders now clustered in a rough circle in the center of the village, where they had once gathered for celebrations and stories.

"Get away, stop, STOP!!" Tamaha cried out as he recognized the face of what used to be a friend.

It did not even falter. "HEEEYAWWAAAAEEE!" came the high-pitched sickening cry as it closed the distance between them.

Instinct kicked in. He dropped back into his well-learned fighting stance and swung the butt of his musket around to deliver a crushing blow to the skull of the Wentiko. It spun to the ground and was still. There was no time for relief. Tamaha looked up to see two more brawls were already happening. Howakan was pushing himself forcefully between the chief and pair of the Wentiko, and another single beast was tangling with a group of his people on the other side.

"Calm yourself; you can do this," Tamaha whispered to himself. However, before he could even take the needed breath, a Wentiko staggered through the smoke and mist and latched itself to Chief Shasta's back, bearing him to the ground.

Tamaha charged past Howakan and thrust the butt of his musket into the eyes of the Wentiko dismounting it from his chief. His momentum carried him across the falling foe, and he found himself standing on its chest hammering the gun-stock into its face, his rage and fury overtaking him. When the primal storm cleared itself from his head, he turned to help Howakan. There was no longer a need, as Howakan had driven a spear completely through the chest of the other Wentiko. The chief was behind him on one knee with his head down.

"Chief!" Tamaha said in a loud whisper.

"I am not hurt."

A quick glance at Howakan showed that he was breathing heavily and distraught, but he also looked unharmed. Tamaha turned to the other fight. It too was over; the other group had pummeled the thing beyond any recognition as ever having been human. The quiet that followed was almost as terrifying as the chaotic noise of the battle. No one dared to move they all took turns staring at each other and into the woods. It was a long time before anyone spoke or moved.

"I think that is all for now," Howakan said, taking the chief by the arm and pulling him to his feet.

The chief spoke with a strength that few had ever heard him use. "We cannot stay here; we are too vulnerable. They have cover, and we do not; they could be staring at us from the trees even now. We should go to the lakeside—we do know that they do not like water—and at least we will only have to watch in one direction."

With that, he moved with the deftness of the warrior he once was through the clearing, picking up weapons along the way and guiding the remains of his tribe to the banks of Lake Winnebago. In a slow run, they followed the mean-derings of the Fox River that marked the north end of their village down to the lake; there they found a small peninsula where they stopped. It was only when they arrived unhin-dered that they felt safe enough to check themselves for wounds or signs of the affliction, finding themselves now two fewer in number.

"We cannot take any more chances," Howakan an-nounced, visibly shaken at their losses, "We must strip down and scrub all of our skin and hair in the lake. We must do the same for our clothes and anything else we have. I will also now be checking everyone every day for any signs of this affliction. Are we all agreed?"

The chief immediately spoke up. "Clearly, he is right in this; it must be done."

Everyone set to stripping off their garments without complaint, or much of any other conversation, the horrors of recent happenings still too vivid in their minds.

"Drink lots of water. We will forage tomorrow, as safely as we are able. We have nothing to fish with now, and I don't want to risk a fire, so we shall not have a meal tonight," Chief Shasta added as they were all bathing and washing.

When they were all cleaned, checked, and dressed, they gathered in a tight circle at the extreme tip of their small peninsula, where Chief Shasta and Howakan had been talk-ing as they were checking the bodies and possessions of their fellow tribesmen and women.

The chief addressed his tribe, diminished as it was. "We cannot now go home—there is not a home to go to—and we cannot expect to defend ourselves for long as we are now. We have decided to go to Chicago. We may band to-gether with the white men for defense. We don't know how many of these Wentiko there are or where they will strike next. We will follow the river to Lake Michigan and follow the banks of the lake down to Chicago. We will sleep here and leave at first light."

Tamaha stepped forward. "I don't think I will be sleeping tonight. Ca,n we not leave here now?"

Chief Shasta looked at all of the scared faces and said "Yes, we can make it around to the other side of Lake Winnebago by morning. Stay together, walk softly, and keep your eyes and ears open."

Their moccasins made almost no noise as they made their way around the southern end of Lake Winnebago. The first rays of sun gave some traces of optimism through the tribe, and the pace quickened as they headed east along the trail toward the trading post. They gave the smoldering ruin a wide berth and continued following the river to Lake Michigan. It was not until they reached the great lake that they stopped long enough to think about eating. Tamaha and a few others went out to hunt. They managed to get a few squirrels, some mushrooms, and some wild onions. They cooked these in a small fire that they put out as soon as possible, and they ate and slept in shifts on the beach. They walked south for three more days before finally reach-ing Chicago and counted themselves fortunate that they ar-rived unmolested.

11:

SOMETHING MUST BE DONE

As Jack and Sophie walked down the street, they found themselves holding hands, something they hadn't done for some time. They were walking down the docks and waving at the children when they heard irregular footsteps approaching from behind them. The husband and wife spun around, ready to fight with startling speed, to find Benson hurrying to catch up. He was limping and doing a poor job of trying not to show it.

"Sergeant," he called out when they made eye contact, "they are having a meeting in the morning. They want us all there. They have also offered us rooms and baths tonight at the hotel."

Jack and Sophie looked at their children and realized just how nice it would be to have a hot bath and clean sheets. They also noted the beleaguered looks on the faces of Nektosha and John.

"Yes, that sounds like a wonderful idea," Sophie replied.

"Can we get someone to guard over *The Badger* for us?"

John asked as he started moving to secure the dock lines.

Corporal Benson answered, "I doubt that will be a problem. They say dinner will be in about an hour."

"Won't that be nice," Sophie said as a warm smile took over Jack's face.

He watched as Sophie was already starting to fuss over the children "to make them somewhat presentable." Nektosha found himself being sorted out some as well. He even held still while she mopped over his face with the wet rag she'd used on her own children. Dinner turned out to be a wonderful thing indeed. After seeing the number of guards patrolling the streets and edges of Detroit, they all felt at ease enough to sit and eat in the fine comfort of the hotel dining room. They had not realized how hungry they actually were. As they were eating, a woman approached who had clearly been crying.

"Thank you again for your help yesterday. Because of you, I still have my son … " She put her kerchief over her face for a moment then continued, "If you want your clothes laundered, just leave them outside your rooms. We have some nightshirts waiting for you."

The next morning Chambers was up before the sun. He found their clothes cleaned and folded outside the door.

He saw a guard walking through the hall who called out to him, "The trapper and the Indian asked me to tell you that they couldn't get no sleep here, so they went back to the boat around midnight. They said they would come back for their things when they was dry."

"Thank you," John replied.

He understood very well their plight. He hadn't slept as

well as he thought would either. Every creaking floorboard, every gust of wind had to be rationalized in his head before he could relax again. They all met up again for breakfast in the hotel dining room, including Corporal Benson, who joined them.

As he was pouring himself a cup of hot coffee, he told them, "They will be meeting at ten in the town hall, and they want you in attendance, Sergeant."

"I think we all should go," Chambers suggested. Everyone paused and then agreed.

The counsel hall was very different on this visit; it was quiet and almost empty. All the way at the front there were a few people scattered among the first few rows and a few more standing around chatting to one another on the speaking platform. The man with the top hat was there, as well as Major Shepard and a few others.

"Good morning, Sergeant. Please join us," Mayor Trobridge said as he gestured to the assembly of tables and chairs on the platform.

Chambers turned and nodded at the rest who went to sit behind the others waiting to hear the meeting. As the assembly was still assembling, Sergeant Chambers stepped up to take his place on the platform, and the mayor approached him.

"Now that I have been briefed on yesterday's events, I would like to offer my thanks to you and your men as well, Sergeant."

"Yes ... well ... certainly, sir." Chambers replied, not quite sure how to properly address a mayor.

When they separated, Sergeant Chambers found his

way over to Major Shepard. He broke out of the conversation he was in. "Good morning, Chambers—how are you and yours doing?"

"I'm fine, sir. We lost Jacobs in the skirmish, and I haven't seen Private Smith. Have you heard anything of him?"

"He showed up in the fort last night. He was pretty shaken up but not hurt," Shepard told him.

Chambers heaved a sigh of relief. "Thank you, sir."

"Seats, please!" the governor called out. "Let's come to order, please."

Murmured conversations were replaced with chair legs scraping and people jostling. In a moment, everyone was in position around the table.

"Let's get started, shall we?" Governor Porter began. "It will take some time to fully realize the losses of yesterday's happenings. Many farmers have already come to us with reports of major losses of livestock in a similarly horrific fashion. The death toll in Detroit is expected to exceed five hundred souls." He paused for a moment to control his emotions before proceeding. "What attacked us yesterday was not something we have seen before. I want to thank all who stood with us against this awful attack."

Light applause filled the hall. The governor paused for this; then he continued, "We must now decide what to do next. We cannot assume that this enemy has been defeated and run off. These twisted human abominations attacked like animals, and we have to assume that they will attack again. We have some of our doctors examining the bodies, so we can get a better idea of what we are dealing with. The next question is clear. Where did they come from?" He looked at Sergeant Chambers. "I understand that you saw them first on Mackinac Island. Is that correct?"

"Yes, sir," Chambers answered.

"Major Shepard told me that you think they there arrived by ship."

"Yes, sir." Chambers answered again. He then glanced over at Nektosha, who shook his head and held up his hands. Clearly, he was even more uncomfortable in this kind of situation than Chambers.

"It ... It ... was a supply ship, sir," Chambers continued, returning his attention to the table of important men. "A supply ship that crashed onto the island. We went back and destroyed the boats on the island to try to contain them."

"Apparently, they got out," said a bespectacled man with an odd accent. He shuffled some papers in front of him and continued, "Did you get the name of the vessel upon which they arrived?"

"I ... " Chambers hesitated, suddenly noticing that he was sweating, "well, no, sir. It was dark when we saw it, and I wasn't thinking ... "

"That much is obvious," the man interrupted.

"That is enough of that!" The governor overrode the conversation. "The sergeant is not on trial here; we have all suffered losses."

The chided man gave his papers a smoothing they didn't need and resumed. "Can you tell me when the vessel crashed and on what part of the island?"

"She crashed at Griffin Point at the northeast part of the island. As for when, well, it must have been the fourth. Yes, we had just gotten paid a couple days before that, so it must have been the fourth."

The man with the glasses glared at him for a long, awkward moment. He then grunted and looked down at his papers. "The only vessel due into Mackinac around that time would have been *The Prince Eugene*. She sailed out from Chicago four days prior."

There was a gasp from a woman at the left side of the room, who then ran out crying, "Oh no ... Oh NO!"

Major Shepard spoke up at this point. "Having seen the crazed lunatics up close, I cannot picture them managing any kind of boat."

"Well, they clearly got *The Prince Eugene* to Mackinac," the bespectacled man interjected.

After a moment of silence, another man spoke up. "Yes, but it crashed. Perhaps they snuck onboard and killed the captain and crew midvoyage."

There was another long silence. Mayor Trobridge was the one to break the silence this time. "That makes more sense than anything else right now. This means that we should assume that these things came overland from the Chicago area. We need to secure this city against any further attacks from land or sea."

The bespectacled man spoke up again. "We need to suspend all shipping in the region until we get control over this."

"I agree," replied the governor.

Major Shepard called out over the rising chatter, "We need to get word to Washington. We are going to need more men."

"Yes, yes," confirmed the mayor.

"Is someone going to go check on Chicago?" rose the quivering question from the back of the room. It was the woman who had run out earlier. "I have family there. Some of them were to be traveling on the ship."

Major Shepard responded distractedly, "If we can, ma'am. First we need to be sure Chicago isn't coming for us."

He instantly regretted his choice of words. The woman slowly turned and left again. There was another profound silence in the room.

The governor looked at the bespectacled man and asked, "Can you shut down the shipping?"

"Yes," he replied, "we can blockade the river just south of town and send out patrols to check on anything that is perhaps already north of us."

Governor Porter then looked over at Major Shepard, who was clearly deep in thought, and waited.

"Yes," Shepard finally answered, "I think I have enough men left to secure the city. I will need to call upon the town militia. I am going to ask you to go to Washington for reinforcements."

Chambers jumped in his chair a little when he realized that he was the one being pointed at. "Me?" he said.

The major's answer was clear. "Yes. That little boat you have will do just fine. I will need all the men from here to hold the town, and we already know that these things came at us through the woods."

Chambers looked over at Sophie and the others, who immediately started whispering vigorously with each other.

Sooner than he expected, they all looked up at him, and

Sophie said, "Yes. We can do that."

Chambers almost choked up with pride and repeated, "Yes, sir! We can do that, sir."

After the meeting, Chambers again met up with Shepard. "Sir, could I take Benson and Smith with me?"

The major shook his head. "Benson is a good man. I would like to keep him here, but I won't; he can go with you. Smith, however ... I'm not sure how much of an asset he will be to any one right now. He is pretty badly shaken up."

Chambers mulled this over. "I'd like to talk to him, if I may, sir, at least to see how he is doing."

"You will find him in the barracks," Shepard said. "I didn't want to put him on guard post until he had a chance to sleep it off."

When Chambers got to the fort, he found Smith in the barracks in a chair with his head down, rocking slowly back and forth. He stopped for a moment, staring at the private, deciding what to do. He finally grabbed a chair and sat facing him.

"Hey, Smith," he said softly.

Smith stopped rocking and looked up at his sergeant. The man blurted out, almost sobbing, "I ran, Sergeant! I ... I saw them, and I ran ... "

"Well, of course!" Chambers said, a little too loudly. "Of course you ran! I have seen those things! They're terrifying!"

This was clearly not the reaction Smith was expecting. He didn't know what to do with this. He finally raised his red, tear-streaked face and looked Sergeant Chambers in the face.

All he could say was "So ... I ... "

"So … You are human," Chambers said. "Look, just between you and me, the only reason I stood my ground in my first battle is because I was just as scared of what they were going to me if I ran as what the enemy would do if I didn't."

"So, you don't think I'm a coward?" Smith asked

"No, Douglas, I don't think you're a coward. In fact, I asked Major Shepard to let you come with me to Washington to get reinforcements."

"But what if we see them again, and what if I … ?" He choked on his next words.

"You have faced the enemy now, and you have faced your fears. I believe that you are now a better soldier for it."

Private Smith sat up straight in his chair. "Really? Thank you! We are going to Washington? We are leaving Detroit?"

Chambers chuckled. "Yes, we are leaving tomorrow, so get up and ready."

12:

TO WASHINGTON

P rovisions from the fort were more forthcoming this time. They got some fresh uniforms along with extra muskets, powder, and ammo as well as lots of food, water, and other necessities. They were also given two sealed envelopes, one with orders to be delivered to Major General Macomb in Washington and one for the harbormaster in Buffalo. They were also given some money for canal tolls and other expenses. The dockmaster had also arranged for some men to fit *The Badger* up with some better sails and got donations of timber nails and oakum for repairs on the way if needed.

The mayor pulled Sergeant Chambers aside on the dock as they were loading and preparing *The Badger*. "The importance of the success of this mission cannot be overstated," he said. "Make no delays and get us as much help as you can. I fear that if there is another attack like the one we have endured, we will likely be over run, and all would be lost."

Chambers turned to help and hasten the preparations. Even still, they all worked late into the night.

———))(((•)))((———

It was just after dawn the next day when *The Badger* sailed out, headed to the south down the Detroit River, toward Lake Erie. Sophie, Thomas, and Victoria had set up hammocks in John's cabin while Benson, Smith, and Nektosha got the cooking kettle set back up and Chambers went over the navigation charts with John. They all felt better being back on *The Badger* and somewhat removed from the horrors that were lurking on land. This feeling improved even more when they passed out of the Detroit River and John turned *The Badger* toward the east and into the open expanse of Lake Erie.

"The wind is coming good and steady from the west," John said as he motioned Smith to come take the helm.

"Just maintain our course by using distant landmarks to take sightings and keep us headed down the middle."

Smith liked this a lot and felt well suited to working on a boat. It gave his troubled mind somewhere else to dwell.

Then John announced that he and Nektosha "had some plans for improvements in mind for *The Badger*, the first of which is a pair of platforms, or crow's nests, above the yard-arm," which held the top of the main sails. This launched an inordinately long conversation about adding weight aloft and ballast bellow. Soon enough, the project was commenced. They also added some lines between the two platforms, to serve as a catwalk. They arrived in Buffalo late on the second day. The city was thrumming with activity.

Benson spoke up. "That's all of the immigrants headed westward, searching out freedom and a new frontier. They are all hoping for a brighter future."

There was a pained pause as they all realized what a problem the quarantine information they were about to deliver would cause.

"Well, let's hope we can help to make that a possibility for later, but we have to stop them for now. We stop only long enough to deliver the orders to the harbormaster and get fresh water, and then we move on," Sergeant Chambers said; he was already adjusting his uniform and donning his hat. "Corporal Benson, I need you, Sophie, and Nektosha to see to watching and preparing *The Badger*. I will take Smith into town to check the papers and posters to see if there is any word about those things here or news of what's happening back to the west. We should plan to cast off in an hour or less."

There must have been a steamer or two about to board. Heading into town was like swimming upstream through a sea of humanity, and all were dressed in their finest. It seemed like everyone around them was talking at once, with all of them smelling too strongly of the latest French perfumes and powders. Once they got past the more congested area, finding a few posters and buying a newspaper was easy; keeping Private Smith out of the bars was not.

"I just want to check to see what people are talking about." It was quickly quite clear that no news of what they had endured had reached Buffalo.

When they got back to *The Badger*, everything was ready to go.

John was the first to give his news. "I have arranged for a tugboat to take us to the start of the canal. I'm not familiar with this area, and I don't want to waste time fighting the wind and current." They could already see billows of smoke as the tug chugged around the end of the nearby passenger steamer.

The passage through the Erie Canal took only a few days even though they had to traverse eighty-four locks along the way. There were men with teams of oxen pulling the boats and barges and keeping traffic flowing. After sailing south down the Hudson River, they were collectively over-whelmed by the sight of New York City. The sheer number of people and activity was beyond anyone's expectations.

John announced, "We won't be stopping here—there is no reason to, and we don't dare take the time. Washington is just two days south."

"I would really like to get off of the boat, even if for a moment," Sophie said, clearly frazzled and disappointed.

"John is right. We cannot afford the time," Chambers said a little too loudly. He too was running short on patience.

Fort Washington was an imposing sight in its own right. There certainly seemed to be no shortage of soldiers here. Several of them helped to get *The Badger* secured.

Chambers told them, "I have orders for General Macomb. Is he available? This is most urgent."

"I'm sorry, Sergeant; he's at a meeting in the capital. We think he's going down to Florida to fight the Indians." The soldier leveled an uncomfortable glare at Nektosha.

"That will be all, Private!" Chambers commanded, breaking the glare.

When the private and his comrades had departed, Chambers turned to the others. "This is maddening! To push to get here so quickly and now to have to wait a day because he has some meeting ... "

"Maybe we could go to the capital and catch him there?" Benson offered.

"Well, that's a bad idea," John interjected. "It's bad enough that we have to get one man to understand this mess, but those politicians ... "

Chambers shouted over him, "So now you are in charge ... ?"

Smith spoke up, louder still. "Well, he should be allowed to speak, shouldn't he?"

Sophie stepped in the middle. "Enough! Clearly the tension is getting to all of us. We've been cooped up on that musty boat for two weeks solid."

They all fell quiet, then one by one they turned and walked in different directions like spokes on a broken wagon wheel.

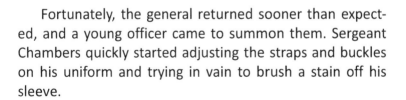

Fortunately, the general returned sooner than expected, and a young officer came to summon them. Sergeant Chambers quickly started adjusting the straps and buckles on his uniform and trying in vain to brush a stain off his sleeve.

He then looked to Benson and Smith. "We're about to meet General Macomb, men—get presentable."

They engaged in the same futile ritual.

He then turned to the others. "I'm going to ask all of you to wait here. We don't know what kind of reaction we will get."

They all nodded quietly and inched slightly closer to *The Badger*.

Sergeant Chambers, Corporal Benson, and Private Smith were escorted up to and into General Macomb's office. They walked in, lined up, and saluted.

The general saluted in return and said, "At ease, men. You have some information for me?"

"Yes, sir," Chambers barked, and he hurriedly produced the sealed packet from Major Shepard, almost dropping it in his haste.

The general looked the trio over again, broke the wax seal, and started reading. The soldiers watched the general's demeanor change visibly as he absorbed the information.

"This is amazing … really … " At last he finished staring at the document and looked again at the men standing before him, this time with a different regard.

"And you have seen this … these … My God … " He looked at the letter again. "You were there?"

"Yes, sir."

"Is it just you three that came here?"

"No, sir, the others are down with *The Badger*. Um, the boat. Er, *The Badger* is the boat, sir."

The general held up a hand to stop Chambers. "I'd like to ask some questions. Take a seat, men." He looked past them to one of the two young officers posted by the door. "Bring the others up and have some chairs brought in for them as well."

"Yes, sir!" he replied with a salute, then turned and left.

"It says here that you were there in Detroit and that you engaged them on Mackinac as well."

"Yes, sir." Chambers stiffened as he spoke.

"Relax, Sergeant, I'm just trying to clarify the situation here. How many would you say there were in Detroit?"

"A lot, sir. It was hard to tell—they weren't in formation or anything. I would say several dozens, sir." Chambers looked to Benson for confirmation and received a nod for a reply.

General Macomb pondered for a moment. "I've ordered some tea; would you like some tea? Or coffee?"

"Some tea would be great," Smith said.

This fetched a quick glare from Chambers that startled him. The general motioned to the second guard at the door, who turned and motioned, and a soldier brought in a full tea service. Soon the young officer returned with John, Nektosha, Sophie, and the children.

When everyone was greeted and settled, the general continued. "You say there was no organization?"

Chambers answered, now noticeably more at ease. "They attacked more like packs of wild animals."

"And there was no second wave? Once you defeated the first attack, there were no others?"

John answered this time. "There were a couple that attacked us at the dock, but we got them." He slapped Nektosha on the shoulder, causing Nektosha's eyes to get quite big; then he nodded vigorously at John then the general and at John again.

"I see," said the general. He paused and thought before he continued. "This is an unexpected threat.

I am very familiar with this area. I oversaw the building of these defenses. We have very few troops at our disposal at the moment. Most have gone west to establish relationships with the Native populations.

"I can, however, ready a full company of regulars and fifty dragoons. We will endeavor to recruit volunteers along the way. It will take a couple days to ready the troops and provisions for the march. Thank you all very much for your efforts in getting this information to me. Where will you be if I have any more questions?"

"Oh," said Chambers, looking at Sophie and the children.

"We'll be at *The Badger*," John said, slapping Nektosha on the shoulder again.

"Yes, yes," Nektosha agreed.

"We'll see if we can find a hotel nearby," Chambers said, motioning to his family.

"And you two can stay in the barracks," General Macomb told Benson and Smith.

It was early the next day when the general summoned everyone back to his office.

He wasted no time getting to the point. "This is Captain Dave Hunter. He will be leading the company. He had been stationed in Chicago and so is familiar with the region."

The captain shook everyone's hand in turn. "General Macomb has briefed me on the situation, and the details sound appalling. The fact that you men have encountered this particular enemy and are still standing ready to fight is reason enough for me to be impressed. I intend to get more details from you as we march."

The general said, "You will march out at first light tomorrow. Sergeant Chambers, you and your men will be marching with Captain Hunter. We may need your experience if you encounter any attacks along the way. Mrs. Chambers, you and your children can stay here in the fort until this matter is settled. We have some officer housing available for you. That will leave the trapper and the Indian to take your vessel back to Detroit if that is your intention. I can send a soldier or two with you if you think more deckhands will be required."

John and Nektosha glanced at each other, and John replied, "No need; we can handle her." Nektosha nodded in agreement.

The general continued, "Fine, then. Mrs. Chambers, my assistant will show you and your children to your quarters. Chambers, Benson, and Smith, report to the quartermaster to get properly equipped, then be on the green ready to march out at sunrise."

When they gathered back together outside, Chambers was surprised to see Sophie in tears. He took her in his arms and held her for a moment.

"Jack, I'm scared," she sobbed.

"You'll be fine, honey. You'll be in this fort, with all these soldiers ... "

She pounded his chest with her hand. "I am not scared for me, silly!" She was laughing and crying at the same time now and pulling on the straps of his uniform. "I'm scared for you! What if you get hurt? Those *things* are horrible! After seeing you come back all bloody last time, this is different!"

"I'll be careful, honey. I know what we are dealing with now. I know what to look for. No vicious garden rake is going to get me again."

She laughed again, and they held on to each other tightly for a time. When they released each other, they saw that everyone was still gathered around talking to one another.

Sergeant Chambers called out, "Let's get everything situated and meet back here for a good dinner, before we split up."

The rays of the morning sun beamed through gaps in the clouds, sending spots of brilliant light wandering across the field of soldiers, glinting off their uniform buttons and weapons.

Sophie found a place on the fort wall where she, Thomas, and Victoria could watch the troops getting organized and falling into ranks. They could also look over and see John and Nektosha letting out the sails and casting off the lines of *The Badger* to begin their journey.

She kneeled down and held her children close. "It's going to be all right. Please, God, let it be all right."

"Ready! Forward, march!" came the cry from the field, and the sounds of the drums and fifes filled the air, as the soldiers marched away.

It was early November when *The Badger* reached the harbor at Buffalo. The temperature had been dropping quickly, and snowfalls were already becoming more regular. John and Nektosha wasted no time stopping. Instead, they sailed straight out into Lake Erie, bound for Detroit. Their crossing of the great lake was much more difficult this time; frequent headwinds and rough waters made the trip slower and downright perilous at times.

Nektosha later admitted, "There were three times that I thought we were going to die, and one time that I was just sure of it."

They did, however, reach Detroit in fine enough shape, and after surveying the docks and finding people waving them in and otherwise walking around and working as normal, they brought *The Badger* in and threw the lines to the waiting dockhands, who deftly secured her to the dock. They had not eaten a good meal for days, so once secured, they then set out for the tavern for "some news and some brews," as John called it.

They noticed a lot of changes right away. There were soldiers and armed townsfolk everywhere; the streets looked unused and grown over; and there were barrels of tar burning, billowing, foul-smelling black smoke at many of the intersections. They decided the hot meal would have to wait, so they diverted and headed straight to the fort.

Captain Hunter questioned Sergeant Chambers about their foe and about the trapper, the Indian, and the soldiers

Jack had been fighting with as they led the force through the towns and cities on the road northwest. They did not have time to stop and wait for long, so the number of men they were able to get to join their militia was not what they had hoped. They were only able to add thirty-seven volunteers to the force; adding this to the company of one hundred infantry and fifty dragoons, they were still short of the two hundred men the captain had hoped to have in his command for this expedition. The plan was to get to Detroit, assess the situation, regroup, and march out to find and destroy the rest of the threat. It was a disappointment to not fill his ranks, though it was not an altogether unexpected one. After all, "the best laid schemes of mice and men go oft awry," as that Robert Burns fellow once said.

They were just south of Detroit, and had just crossed the Lafayette Bridge, when they heard it.

13:

THE BATTLE AT LAFAYETTE BRIDGE

Chambers stopped first. "I hear them; I know that sound." He pointed forward and left into the woods at the other side of a small field.

Captain Hunter called for the company to halt. "Form three ranks; prepare for volley shot. Horsemen, take the flanks. Volunteers, fall in behind the third rank!"

The soldiers moved quickly and fell into place like parts of a machine, the front rank of muskets pointed uniformly downrange in the direction of the cacophony of hellish noise that was approaching.

The captain called out, "Wait for it … Waaiit for it … " Then he muttered under his breath, "We've got piteous poor light on this cloudy morning and very little clear space between us and that damned dense forest line. It's too difficult to tell what is happening in the shadows. I knew things were going to be different, but this is highly irregular. I don't like it."

The screeching and wailing echoing through the trees

were making things much worse. The men were getting uneasy and skittish.

Captain Hunter called out in a careful tone, "Hold the line. Hold the line. Mind our flanks."

The next moments passed like hours; the soldiers were sweating in the cool Michigan mist. The mass of twisted forms burst through like a wave. It was shocking even though they knew it was coming. The sight and savagery of them was even more horrific than the sounds.

"First rank, fire!"

The sound of muskets echoed across the small field like crackling thunder. A few of the abhorrent, barely human savages fell, but most did not. Open terror spread across many of the soldiers' faces as they got their first real look at the monsters they had been training for months to fight, but these handpicked men barely faltered in their well-practiced routine.

"Second rank, fire!"

The men in the front rank had already taken a knee and were efficiently reloading their muskets, many of which did not fire in the moist air. Those still had to be reprimed. The second volley exploded in kind, and those men didn't bother to kneel to ready their weapons. They could see that there would be no time to do so.

The third rank was bringing their muskets to bear between the heads of those in front and firing on the approaching horde when time ran out. Unlike the other enemies they had faced, these monsters did not pause to fire any guns, and they did not flinch as a hail of lead balls ripped through their ranks. In fact, very few of them fell at all; even those that had massive wounds still ran at them.

The men performed admirably in the face of this horror. Their bayonets already set, the ranks shifted into a tight phalanx formation, and they finally had some success in stopping the front of the surging charge.

Captain Hunter called out orders as he cut down one of the horrors with his sword, "ADVANCE! Drive them back! Do not let them pin us to the river!"

The wall of soldiers began to push forward. The mounted units came up the flanks to close the sides of the box and compress the enemy. It turned out that it was their own horses that did the worst harm. The army's very own battle-trained horses fell into a state of raw panic at the sight and smell of the enemy. The horses' wide-eyed terror was so utterly complete that they were beyond any hope of control. Many of them turned and trampled the very men fighting beside them. The men were barely able to control their fear of the enemy before them; the unexpected attack of their own massive warhorses was just too much for most men to bear. Cavalrymen were being thrown from their mounts, some landing *on* the infantrymen.

Many of the volunteers finally panicked, broke ranks, and fled back across the bridge, and a good many U.S. Regulars ran as well, many scattering into the woods. Those that remained fought hand to hand with bayonet and sword. The screams from the soldiers were at times louder than the screaming cries of the creatures. All of this, combined with the heavy musket smoke made worse by a sudden musty fog, made the chaos absolute and almost too much to bear.

Sergeant Chambers himself was almost lost when an

afflicted he had bayoneted through the chest refused to die. It was wildly reaching down the length of his musket. It had ahold of a short, stout stick and swung for his head. It knocked off his hat with a vicious swing that would have knocked his head from his shoulders, had it been just an inch lower. The swing left the creature off balance, and the sergeant took the chance to pull his bayonet back, so he could try again. He put all of his force and weight into one grand shove to create some space between them. He had never been this close to a "live" one before, and he did not like it at all.

As the beast rocked back, the sergeant jerked on his gun-stock and plunged the bayonet into the nose of his foe. His momentum and adrenaline carried him forward to topple over the thing, and he ended up with his weapon pointed straight down, pinning its crushed head to the dirt.

An involuntary battle cry burst out from somewhere deep within him: "Hyaaa!"

As the noise of the battle came surging back to his ears, he put his foot on the chest of what was once a gentleman farmer and recovered his weapon from its face.

Casting quickly about, he saw Smith drive his bayonet into the throat of a particularly large creature and pull fiercely across. The things neck gushed an eruption of blood and flesh, and it fell in a heap.

Chambers saw that, behind Smith, one of the cavalrymen was killing his own horse, and several others in the distance were riding wildly out from the battle, fleeing in various directions.

He heard a strangled, snarling sound behind him and

turned to see a very small boy of an afflicted charging him with a large kitchen knife in hand. He struck a solid hit to its head with the brass plate on the butt of his musket. It stumbled backward and fell; the sergeant spun his weapon and put his bayonet deep into the center of its forehead. He could not keep the thought out of his head that this was probably the young son of the farmer that he had just killed, and a brief flash of his own son's face passed across his mind's eye.

He shook his head and turned quickly to survey the situation. He saw several soldiers breathing heavily and looking around as he was. The few fights that were still happening were too far away for him to be of any help.

When at last it was finished, fewer than fifty infantry and only a dozen horsemen were still standing, most of them without their horses. The few horses were in a state of wide-eyed panic, and their riders' attention was fully occupied in keeping them under control. Even the general was visibly shaken by the ordeal.

Amid the cries of the wounded, Chambers heard the heart-wrenching sound of Private Smith desperately screaming, "No! *No!* You're going to be all right! Hey! Look at me! Breath now! *You are going to be all right!!*"

Chambers ran quickly over to discover Smith pulling a belt down tight around the stump that had formerly been Corporal Benson's left forearm but was now little more than a rag of flesh and splintered bone; an afflicted woman with a sword through its head lay beside them. Benson was thrashing in pain and fear, his eyes wide and hollow. Chambers turned at once to help hold Benson still, as Smith pulled a musket charge from his pouch and emptied the gunpowder from the paper-wrapped charge onto the wound.

Chambers and Smith locked eyes for a brief second, and the private asked, hesitantly, "One more?"

"Yeah."

Though his hands were trembling, he deftly poured another charge over the wound, then grabbed a flint and striker and quickly lit the powder before he could think too long on what he was doing. One more shrieking cry pierced the air that morning before Benson, blessedly, passed out. When they looked up, Captain Hunter was already ordering the troops to quit the field and to prepare for a quick march back to Detroit. There was still a trace of panic in his face. They found some relatively clean cloth on the nearby corpse of a militiaman and bound Benson's wound as well as they were able.

The troops tied the few surviving wounded to what horses they still had and then moved out at a gruelingly rapid pace back toward Detroit. They were met at the edge of town by several of the Detroit guardsmen, who helped them get the soldiers back to the fort and the wounded to the hospital.

14:

DEATH ON A PALE HORSE

There always were those soldiers who turn and bolt at the onset of the battle. This time it was the horses themselves that bolted, whether the riders wanted to or not. They fared no better for their retreat. They could be seen being overtaken and brought down by the marauding packs of demonic creatures.

Cavalryman Lewis Durdon was hunkered down low astride his galloping horse, a gelding the color of misty starlight called Quicksilver.

Man and horse were both wide-eyed with panic. However, their retreat was too late for the soldier to escape fully unscathed. His leg was seriously wounded and begged his attention. The wound was just above the knee, and the blood was flowing freely into his boot. He needed to bind the wound, quickly. He felt sure that he would pass out if he did not.

Durdon cast his awareness around himself to discover that he and Quiksilver were now quite alone and that they were trotting unhindered along a narrow path through a wood. With the trees so close on either side, he couldn't properly tend to his wound or examine his horse for injuries while remaining astride him. Not wanting Quicksilver to drop out from under him any more than he wanted to drop off of him, he found a small clearing, reined him in, and dismounted carefully. Leaning forward against Quicksilver's neck, he rotated on his belly, so his feet were dangling off one side; then he slowly slid down to the ground onto his good leg. Gingerly, he shifted his weight to his injured leg, holding tight to the saddle should his leg not hold him. However, other than more shooting pain, he was able to stand. He could tell that his knee would be useless soon, as the swelling was already affecting the mobility of the joint. So, he used the sash worn under his belt as a bandage. He wrapped it around his leg several times and tied it off snugly. He was able to staunch the bleeding and maintain fair mobility. He then turned and started examining his horse.

Lewis Durdon had always been a man who liked to talk, though it often got him in trouble with his superiors. He was one of those folk who would prattle on about anything for hours on end and sound as if he really cared about what he was talking about, even if it was something as inane as discovering a tick on his horse. His gift of gab was not hindered by his injury or by his feelings of guilt and shame at his desertion. It was likewise unhindered by the lack of someone to talk to, as he'd been talking to his horse right from the moment he'd gotten him. So, it was no surprise that he spoke now as he turned his attention over to Quicksilver.

"I tell you, old boy, that there was like to frighten three

years off my life. Never have I ever been so scared, not even when I was eight and came across that bear down by the creek near Uncle Ketch's place. This fear was down into my *bones*, it was. This bite I got is hurting something awful too, I tell ya. It feels like there's a hot coal in my leg, and make no mistake. I'd best make sure you ain't got yourself an injury too. Hold still for me for just a moment." Quicksilver lowered his head and nudged Durden's forehead with his nose. "There's a good horse."

Limping back a few steps, he cast his gaze through the trees, looking for any sign of movement, before turning his focus to the well-being of his steed. Beneath the stiff, silvery-gray hair on Quicksilver's flank, just behind the saddle, was a series of long surface scratches. The skin was raised in welts but, thankfully, not broken. Durdon wasted no further time in clambering back into the saddle, taking extreme care not to aggravate his injury, and heading off down the trail again, chattering away to his steed.

"Well, Quicksilver, you sure are a damn sight luckier than I am, that there is for certain. Though I suppose that shouldn't really surprise me. A man's fingernails would never, ever pierce horseflesh, mark my word. He could be all sorts of insane, but it don't make no difference—horseflesh is just too tough for a man's nails to get through. I only wish the same was true of my own flesh. Course I got me a bite, not a scratch, and I suppose a man could possibly *bite* through horseflesh, if'n he ever got the opportunity to. It ought not be much harder than biting through a tough piece of jerky."

Quicksilver chomped the bit and yanked on the reins

slightly, causing Durdon to jerk in his saddle and glance wor-
riedly at the back of Quicksilver's head. "You understand,
Quicksilver, that I'm just postulating here. I'd never think of
doing such a thing to you, even for experimentational pur-
poses. It just wouldn't be right, you know, a man eating on
his own horse. But, I *suppose*, if'n a man had the opportunity, and the drive to do it, I *suppose* he could bite through
horseflesh."

<hr />

The next three days were a succession of fevered de-
lirium and forced movement. His leg ached with a white-hot
pain that made it difficult to focus, and his skin was developing strange patches of discoloration, not just around the
wound as he'd seen happen with untreated injuries before,
but all over his body, with no apparent rhyme or reason. He
also felt oddly muddled, as if he'd been in another bar fight
and taken a strong blow to the head. He'd already eaten
through the rations he had available; having been preparing for the half day's ride from Lafayette to Detroit, he'd not
packed any sort of proper provisions for the journey he now
found himself on. Having had nothing for two days, his need
for water and food was growing desperate, and it seemed,
the need was taking over.

He came to a field dotted with the white forms of sheep,
and his need reared up in him, powerful and inescapable.
He very nearly leaped from his horse to chase down the
woolen creatures before forcibly gaining control of himself

and slinging his rifle out from over his shoulder. Loading and priming the weapon was a quick and easy process, something he'd done countless times in his life—he could do this in his sleep. Sighting along the barrel, he spotted an older lamb, not quite a yearling, that was slightly apart from the rest of the herd. Drawing on the reins of his horse a little tighter, Durdon slowly exhaled before squeezing the trigger. The shot rang out, seeming louder than a cannon blast, and the herd startled and bolted. His lamb, however, dropped where it stood, and Durdon whooped out loud from his saddle.

"Would you look at that, Quicksilver! One shot! Wait till I tell Pa that I felled a lamb in one shot from fifty paces, fifty paces if it's a foot, and I got him in one shot! Hoo-wee! That there's a bit of good fortune at last. I was sorely in need of some luck, I tell ya. This damned leg is paining me something terrible, and I can't seem to get my thoughts in order. Feels like I've been drinking too much or fighting too much ... or both. One too many wallops across the noggin, and make no mistake. But this lamb is gonna do me just right. Once I get some good meat in me, I'll be on the mend, just you wait and see. I just gotta get my busted self outta this saddle and get ahold of that blasted lamb, first."

After guiding Quicksilver over to the downed creature, Durdon took tight hold of the horn of his saddle. His injured leg would no longer straighten and was stuck in a half-bent position, necessitating his having to lean over and manually pull the stirrup off his boot, then ease himself as gently as he could to the ground. He still had to pause for a moment and breathe when his injury sent such a sharp stab of pain shooting up his spine that his vision went briefly white.

"Good*ness*, Quicksilver, this is surely the worst pain I've ever been in, and that's the truth. It feels like my whole body is aching with the pain of my leg. With each beat of my heart, I can feel this pulse of pain all over. This blasted *thirst* just won't quit, neither. I reckon you have to be getting rather parched too. We done already emptied my canteen and my reserve skin of water. But where there's sheep, there's water—we just gotta figure out where their watering hole is. Let me get this blasted lamb up onto ya, and we can find ourselves a lake, or river, or whatever it is these walking mutton drink from."

The stiffness of the joint made it relatively easy to keep off the ground once he was down there but also made it doubly difficult to get on and off his horse. He held tight to the stirrup and leaned down on his good leg. Grabbing the lamb by the foreleg and bracing himself, he yanked it straight up, hard and fast, making the carcass arc through the air over his head, to land directly on the withers of Quicksilver, just in front of the saddle. Pleased that his wrangling and roping skills as a ranch hand weren't forgotten, he laboriously remounted his horse, having to jump with his good leg up onto his belly on the saddle and shimmy into a sitting position. Deciding to keep his injured leg out of the stirrup, he took a firm hold of the lamb's wool and spurred Quicksilver into a trot, following the herd in the hopes they'd lead to water. The extra exertion had seemed to make his thoughts extra fuzzy. Shortly they found a very small pond; the water was nasty, but it would keep them alive.

It was three days later when Lewis Durdon finally set eyes on his intended destination. It had been a mild shock for him to come upon the southern banks of the Great Lake Michigan after felling his lamb, his mind having been so far afield that he'd completely forgotten where he was—he had even forgotten of the lake's existence. Once he reached it, however, he basked in the chill waters, soothing his aching wound, slacking his thirst and, remarkably, clearing his head. He almost felt himself again after just a few minutes floating in the water. He'd solved the issue of dismounting by the simple expedient of riding his horse straight into the water, right up to his withers. He then swam off and steadied himself on the horn of his saddle for a time, before finally sliding back onto Quicksilver and turning him south to follow the banks around toward Chicago.

It wasn't until he had come upon the outskirts of Chicago two days later, and discovered the increased military presence, that his intended destination changed.

"Dagnabbit, Quicksilver, I could now no more go to Chicago than I could go to Detroit. I might likely be executed as a deserter in either city, just as soon as they realized where I had come from. Aw, Lordy, I can smell them a-cooking something good! Can you smell it too, boy?" Quicksilver tossed his head up and nickered. "Yes, you can—I reckon so!"

Then the smell of the cook fire was overtaken by the smell of burning tar from the watchfires. "Back to reality, boy. I guess we best keep moving along.

"Well, Quicksilver, this don't bode well for the town of Chicago, now, does it? More soldiers here tells me only one thing: that this horrible plague has indeed reached these hapless people. I can't stay here, not if'n I want to keep my heart beating in my breast. Though, truth be told, this wound on my leg seems to be doing me in all on its own. I had hoped that this here mutton would have done me well, but other than a full belly, I feel no better. The fact of the matter is, I actually feel quite worse off than I was before the lamb. Though that time in the lake was a balm, to be sure, it didn't last beyond the day."

Durdon turned his horse away from the road leading into Chicago and followed the path that circled around it. For a moment he was unsure where to go now. His whole impetus for journeying this far was to make it to Chicago to get medical attention and rest. Having reached the city, and finding no hope there, he was at a bit of a loss. Trying to put any two thoughts together was increasingly difficult.

"Well, now, Quicksilver, I'm not altogether sure where we should go from here. This was as far as I'd really expected to come. I'd no idea this accursed affliction had reached this far. You know, mayhap we should go to old Fort Armstrong. Ever since the Blackhawk War it's been deserted; maybe they left some supplies. We could set ourselves up a nice home there, and a few good nights' sleep and some fresh bandages might do for me what this lamb couldn't."

He patted the munitions cases that was situated behind him like saddlebags. He'd emptied it as he rode and, after skinning and butchering the lamb (no easy task when mounted), stored the parts in the repurposed cases. Whenever he hungered, he'd reach back, grab a chunk of uncooked lamb, and gnaw on it for a time.

"You know, Quicksilver, for as long as I can remember, I've preferred my meat cooked thoroughly, not a hint of redness or blood to be had. And yet, I find that this completely raw and uncooked lamb is some of the best-tasting meat I've ever had. Mayhap it's this odd hunger talking; mayhap it's the fever I can feel creeping up on me. You sure are fortunate that you're a horse, Quicksilver. You eat naught but grass and vegetation, a simple meal for a simple animal. Not that I think you're dimwitted, mind. I get the feeling you understand more of what I say to you than most men do. Mayhap it just seems you listen better than they do. I wouldn't mind having a simple life, like you do. Though, truth be told, you'd probably prefer to be out in the wilds, running free. Mayhap, when we reach Fort Armstrong I should turn you loose and let you be free. Would a horse who's been broken *want* to be free? Every man desires freedom, if our bloodied history is anything to go by—does the same ring true of all creatures? It is a puzzling question."

———— ((●)) ————

It took Durdon a further four days to reach a fort, although he had lost all concept of time—hours flowed by; day or night had no meaning. He slept, if it could be called sleep, in his saddle.

However, it was not Fort Armstrong but the Apple River

Fort he found. His lamb been gone for days, and his hunger was maddening. The trip was not normally so long; however, the increasing fevers storming in his head made concentrating difficult, and when not properly guided, Quicksilver was prone to wandering. His thoughts were so fragmented that nothing seemed to matter, nothing beyond the gnawing, aching *need*. He'd have startling moments where the shadows seemed to jump, the sunlight arcing in from an entirely new angle and revealing that hours had passed where he had no awareness of its passage. His whole body now ached, feeling as though his skin was being peeled from his very bones. His head was heavy, weighed down so strongly that he was hunched into a ball atop the saddle. He'd stopped talking sometime the previous day, realizing that even that task was beyond his focus.

His illness was having an effect on Quicksilver, as well. Each time he came back to himself from a bout of blackness it was to find that Quicksilver was bolting along the trail as if a pack of wolves were nipping at his hooves. It didn't take him long to realize that his beloved horse was trying to escape from him. Or, more appropriately, the *thing* he was becoming during the blackness. He now had little doubt he was turning into one of the creatures that had bitten him. It broke his heart when he noticed that there were chunks of mane missing from his steed's neck and definite bite marks in the bare patches; apparently a man could *not* bite through horseflesh, at least, not while the horse was still alive.

As these thoughts rattled around in Durdon's head, Quicksilver stepped out of the thick trees surrounding the path to reveal Apple River Fort dead ahead. Hope surged up through the chaos raging in Durdon as he feebly kicked Quicksilver into a trot, heading for the open gates of the fort. As he neared, he realized that the fort was occupied, though not by a proper regiment. It seemed other deserters had made their way here and set up something of a refuge for themselves. Quicksilver halted in the courtyard of the fort. As Durdon, who was once a fine cavalryman, straightened up, his weight shifted too far back, and he toppled over the back of his horse, twisting off Quicksilver's hindquarters as he fell. His face hit the dirt yard with a bone-crunching thud, and he receded back into the blackness for the final time, as the soldiers came to his aide.

"He's wounded!"

"Get some help over here!"

"Medic!"

"Someone grab that horse."

"He took a heavy blow to the head. I don't know how he would have survived that."

"What's that noise?"

"Roll him over, Jonah. Let's see if he's breathing."

"Would ya look at that—he's awake!"

"Is he wheezing? The sound is coming from him—maybe he broke his nose."

"He doesn't look aware of anything … Soldier. I say, soldier! Can you hear me?"

"Dear Lord, he's growling."

"What do you mean growl ... *AHHHH!*"

"Get him off, get him off!"

"God, he bit a damned chunk outta Jonah's face!"

"Shoot him! He's not letting *go*!"

"My gun isn't loaded!"

"Why the *hell* ain't it load ... *AHHHHH!*"

"Horace! *Horace!* Hold him, fellas! Don't let him bite ya!"

"He ... he got me in my side. I'm all right for now. Put him *down*!"

"I've got it. Hold him steady, boys."

"Oh my God! He ... he exploded!"

"What's that coming out of him? Dust?"

"I don't think we should have breathed that stuff in."

"Nor I. It's left an odd taste in my mouth."

"Well, it can't be helped now. We were all too close to him to do anything about it. It's not as if we knew he'd ... burst ... like that. Get Jonah and Horace to the infirmary. Then, everyone, have a wash in the river and pray another one like that don't show up."

15:

CHICAGO PLAGUED

Having left their tribe at the Indian encampment on the outskirts of northern Chicago, Howakan and Tamaha walked into the town to find the place had radically changed. True enough, Chicago was a city of change and growth, there having never been any less than four structures in the processes of erection. However, this Chicago was wholly unrecognizable. The people walking the streets were wearing strange masks covering the entirety of their faces, masks that were reminiscent of birds, with long beaks and round eyes of glass. It took Howakan a moment to recall a drawing Dr. Periwinkle had shown him that allowed him to put a name to the odd apparatus: *plague masks*. Men in the usual top hats and tailcoats, women in everyday flowered bonnets and hooped skirts, nearly every one, were wearing plague masks. There were masks made of leather, these being the most common, but also masks of cloth and masks of burnished copper. Those of cloth seemed crudely stitched, as if done in haste, while those few of burnished copper were nearly akin to a jeweled headpiece. Those sparse few without masks were still managing to cover their faces in some fashion. Cloth tied across their noses and mouths, some with their whole faces covered with just a few holes cut, so their wearers were not blinded.

The two Natives found themselves so utterly befuddled by this turn of events that Howakan realized they'd been standing in the same spot for several minutes, staring at these people as if they'd never seen a colonist before. Shaking himself from his confusion, and giving Tamaha's shoulder a jostle, he made his way to the barber's that Dr. Periwinkle now occupied. Howakan found himself worrying that, should the doctor also be wearing one of these masks, he'd have quite a challenge of finding him. Walking into a building and calling out someone's name, Howakan had learned, was considered rude in the colonists' society— though how they hoped to maintain that status quo when no one was recognizable, he did not know.

This did not end up being a problem for when they entered the barbershop, it appeared unoccupied. However, he heard the sounds of muttering and clinking glass coming through the open door at the back of the shop. Even mumbling at a distance, he could recognize the voice of his friend and fellow healer, Deggory Periwinkle. He peeked cautiously through into the back room unsure in what kind of state he would find the man. The doctor was picking up and putting down beakers and vials of varying fluids and substances. He looked harried, though healthy enough.

"Where are you? Where are you?" he repeated as he looked deep into the side and bottom of each container.

Howakan let slip with an involuntary chuckle. The sight of his old friend back to normal lifted his heart more than he thought possible.

"Howakan! It is good to see you!" Deggory said, "How are you doing? How is your tribe doing? Listen, I need to apologize. You sent a messenger down to see me, and he caught me at a particularly low point ... I hardly even remember ... "

"Easy, my friend," Howakan interrupted. "Yes. That was Tamaha. We thought you might be upset about your practice being burned down."

Tamaha now made his way from through the barbershop and leaned his head in the doorway to join the conversation. "It is no troubles, Dr. P. I am just glad you are all right now. You *are* all right now?"

"Yes, I am better than I was." He looked around his small makeshift exam room and lab and said, "Let's go to the tavern where we can sit and catch up on what has happened."

Howakan agreed. "It has been too long since we have had beer together."

Howakan was surprised, though he really shouldn't have been, when Dr. Periwinkle also donned a plague mask along with his hat and coat before they left the shop. They found a table in the corner of the nearest tavern, and the three of them settled in and ordered up some beer, and Howakan asked about the masks.

Deggory's voice was muffled but understandable through his mask. "A few weeks ago Chicago was attacked from that direction." He gestured south as they watched folks in masks walking up and down the street. "The attack was bad enough, but the aftereffects were even worse.

"The masks are the town's method of dealing with the affliction. I implored the council to implement these after so many of those who weren't outrightly killed in the attack fell ill from the dust. After examining some of it, I discovered it resembles fungal spores. We have to prevent ourselves from breathing in the spores, so we wear masks."

After a moment of thought, Howakan realized the logic was sound. If the Wentiko released dust into the air that could not be easily avoided in close quarters, the mask would prevent one from inhaling the deadly spores.

"Tell me how it's been going for you, Howakan. Has this affliction affected your people?"

"It has affected us greatly. We have lost many good people, and those of us who survived have moved to the old village here by the fort. I see that this foul disease has visited no small sorrow on your people as well."

"Yes, is has." Deggory drank his entire beer at once, stared at the empty mug for a moment, and slowly brought his thoughtful gaze up to Howakan's face. "I lost my wife and boy in the attack."

He held up his hand, halting the expected platitudes. "The thing is"—he motioned to the passing barmaid to bring another beer—"the thing is, I am not as devastated by this as I once thought I would be. Yes, I am greatly saddened to lose them, but in a sense, I had lost them already. I did not want to give up on them, and I certainly never did while they lived. But at times when they were both having bad days, it was like sharing a house with someone who was both living and dead at the same time. There is probably a word for that—I just don't know what it is right now."

The barmaid put another beer in front of him. He took another long drink and continued, "In a way, I am almost glad that it is finally over." He paused again. "It's finally over, and I'm relieved that it was not *my* incompetence that caused them to ... to ... " He left the sentence unfinished, and he finished his beer instead, motioning to the barmaid for yet another.

Howakan and Tamaha exchanged nervous glances, and Howakan put his hand over the top of Deggory's mug.

"I'm all right," Deggory assured his friend. "This one will be my last. Have you learned anything of the affliction during your proximity to it?"

The barmaid came round and left them some fresh-baked bread and cheeses as Howakan got his thoughts in order,

"There are several parts to the affliction, as you say. First is what we've come to call the Clouding; the mind becomes fogged and muddled, and it is difficult to hold a thought or keep aware. Then comes the Decay, when the skin of an afflicted starts molding and rotting away in patches. When this begins, the afflicted usually, though not always, develops an aversion to water. Next is the Hunger, a desire to *eat* that is so powerful it takes over the mind completely. Finally, the Madness, where the need for flesh drives out the mind of the afflicted for the final time, and they become Wentiko. If they are Wentiko for more than a few days without feeding, they will then have what we can only call the Bursting, where a part of their body will burst open with explosive force. If this body part is the head or chest, the

Wentiko will die; however, they *can* live on if it is just a limb or even the sides or lower parts of the torso."

Deggory had been taking notes in his ledger, perversely thrilled with this new information, regardless of the manner in which his friend had come by it. Howakan, however, was unbothered by his friend's actions. He, too, was a man of science. True, it was a vastly different science that that of the colonists, but it was still medicine. And science, their type of science, at least, was a study of medicine.

Deggory then brought him up-to-date on all of the details of what the people of Chicago had endured over the past few weeks. It was not too long after this that Deggory and Howakan were sharing old jokes and stories of better times with Tamaha; they even shared a laugh or two.

16:

NOW WHAT?

Upon the troop's arrival in Detroit, Captain Hunter called for a meeting to be held at dusk in the fort. This allowed the men a little time to tend to the wounded and to gather their wits. Smith and Chambers carried Benson to the hospital. He did not look to be faring well from the jarring journey back: he had lost a lot of blood, and his face had a deathly pallor to it. He was, however, still breathing, labored and irregular though it may be. Still, it gave his friends some small measure of hope. The bleeding from the wound just below his elbow seemed to be lessening now that he was off the horse and not being jostled about.

The doctor examined him for a moment; then he looked at the pleading faces of Chambers and Smith. "I don't know if we can save this one, but we will try. Come back in a couple hours. I'll have a better idea then."

Chambers hesitated, then nodded stiffly, took Smith by the arm, and guided him out. The two felt utterly helpless.

Outside, Chambers turned to Smith. "We still have some time, and I have no desire to stand about worrying myself into a headache—let's see if John and Nektosha are here yet."

At this, Smith brightened noticeably. "Yes, good thought. I hope they didn't have any trouble along the way."

"Agreed."

For the first time, they actually took notice of the changes in the town. The overgrown streets and the thick black smoke of burning barrels of tar gave the town of Detroit a distinct feeling of purgatory. The boarded-up windows and closed doors did nothing to lessen the feeling of dread that had settled about the town. The two were about halfway to the docks and just starting to share their stories of the battle, when Chambers was struck from the side. The huge man was almost knocked off his feet and stumbled as he leaned back trying to discern who or what had ahold of him. It was Nektosha; he had Chambers pinned in a hug so firmly that he could hardly breathe.

John was jogging up as well. "Hey! Hey! You made it! We heard you guys got hit pretty hard."

Nektosha let Chambers go and stepped back a little, embarrassed at his enthusiasm. Chambers chuckled and pulled to young man back into him, hugging him back with fervor, then moved aside to throw an arm around John's shoulders in a brief greeting as Smith shared a hug with Nektosha as well. It was positive physical contact that *all* the men were sorely needing.

When they all stepped back to a respectable distance, Chambers answered, "Yeah, Smith and I were among the lucky few. There were a lot of them, and we thought we were ready but … "

"Wait," John interrupted, "what about Benson? Did they get him? Is he … ? Did he get … ?"

Chambers held up his hands. "No. He's not dead. Well, he wasn't when we saw him last. He's at the hospital. He lost his hand, the left one, luckily, and halfway up his fore-arm. The doctor's working on him now. He asked us to give him a couple hours."

"Well, I don't know about you, but we haven't had a decent meal in a fortnight," John said, trying to get the con-versation to a lighter footing and motioning to the pub, it being one of the few businesses still in operation in town.

"That sounds like a great idea," said Chambers, the group already moving in that direction.

They were all anxious to catch up on the others' adven-tures. John told them, "The weather has already started to turn; moving anything across the north end of the lakes would likely not be possible for long."

"We could barely keep the boat from sinking," Nektosha added. "We almost turned over a few times."

Smith chimed in, "We heard no news of attacks from any one along the road, so that is something."

He and Chambers then went into detail about the at-tack at Lafayette Bridge. This had them all eager to check on Benson's condition. They stopped by the hospital on the way to the general's meeting. Quietly entering the large ward, they saw a surprising number of wounded lined up on cots, covered in blood-stained sheets.

A nurse greeted them. "May I help you?"

"We are here to see Corporal William Benson. He had lost his … " Chambers voice trailed off as he flexed his hand in front of his face.

"Oh yes, Nurse Angela is with him now."

Near the far end of the room they saw the nurse tenderly placing a wet rag on the forehead of her patient. The men quickly tiptoed over to see their comrade; the nurse looked up as they approached. With a questioning look on her face, she motioned to Benson, and they nodded.

"He's a fighter, this one," she said in a delightful Scottish accent. "He has lost a fair amount of blood. However, whoever cauterized it in the field did a proper enough job. He's got that going for him—it saved his life. We have to see if his fever breaks. If he makes it through the night, I'd say he's got a fair chance."

They all looked down at Benson. The stump of his left arm had been smartly bandaged and looked much better for it. His face, however, did not. He looked gray, weak, and old.

———((●))———

When they exited the hospital, the soldiers and officers had already started to assemble. When the four of them entered the fort, Captain Hunter and Major Shepard were standing in an upper gateway talking with a few officers before stepping out to address the soldiers and townspeople gathering below. So, Chambers, Smith, John, and Nektosha moved around the back of the crowd and found an open spot.

It was Captain Hunter who stepped up to speak. "Good evening and thank you for coming. What happened this morning was beyond description. We lost many good men today. Many more fled in the face of this new terror. This is an unconventional threat, and we learned this morning that it cannot be met with conventional means. We learned this at a great cost. This was a hard-learned lesson indeed. We must take a step back and reconsider how we deal with this. I will be going back to Washington to reevaluate our approach." Many of the soldiers started murmuring to each other.

From the back of the crowd a voice rang out, "You're leaving?! You're running off?!"

The crowd parted to reveal the accuser; it was the bespectacled man.

"What are we to do now that you have kicked the hornets' nest? They are going to come swarming back in greater numbers!"

"I will not leave Detroit without defenses. Most of the men who came with me will remain and be added to the city's defenses." The Captain continued, "For whatever reason, these things have not returned to this city after the first attack. So, I am ordering all safeguards that are in place now to stay active.

"Furthermore, the fort will be available to any and all. If anyone desires to seek shelter, you may do so inside her walls. I plan to return from Washington as soon as an acceptable strategy can be devised to combat this strange new threat." He paused, surveying the crowd. "Is Sergeant Chambers here?"

Chambers visibly jumped at this. "Here, sir! I am here."

"Good. You and your men join me in the commander's office." He then turned and disappeared into the fort.

When they entered the commander's office, they saw that a table and several chairs had been brought in, and many maps and papers were piled around it. The captain and the major were standing behind it when they came in.

"Good evening. Come in and have a seat." He returned the salutes and continued as they moved into the chairs. "First of all, I would like to commend you for your actions on the field today. I understand Corporal Benson is listed among the injured. Lost his leg, did he?" He was checking a list in front of him.

"It was his arm, sir; he lost his left hand and halfway up his arm."

"Confound it!" The major grabbed a quill and marked on the document.

"Parker!" he yelled.

A soldier came through the door and bolted to his side.

"Check this list for accuracy. We need *correct* information."

Parker took the list and was gone.

As the major regained his composure, he asked, "So, do you think he will recover?"

"We'll know better in the morning, sir," Chambers replied.

Captain Hunter nodded, shuffled some papers on the table, and grabbed a map. "It is vitally important that we know better what we are dealing with. We know that the first known contact with these things happened on Mackinac Island. You say that they came off a ship that came from Chicago."

"Yes, sir," Chambers replied.

The general continued, "We need to see if the situation on Mackinac has changed. We also now need to check on Chicago to see if this plague is there as well." He shifted his gaze over to John and Nektosha. "Now, I can't order you two to go, but ... "

"We'll do it, sir!" John interrupted, Nektosha nodding along as well.

After a brief pause, Smith leaned forward into the conversation. "You don't want us to *land* on Mackinac, sir. Do you?"

"No. Just get close and see what you can find out. Your primary mission is to investigate Mackinac and Chicago and bring back some more information. Hopefully something we can work with. Now, I'll be in Washington, so you will need to meet me there. Do you understand the importance of this mission?"

"Yes, sir!" Chambers spoke first, but they all answered in kind.

"I'll send some men to help you with provisions, you will need to leave in the morning."

"Understood, sir." Chambers and Smith saluted, and they all left the office.

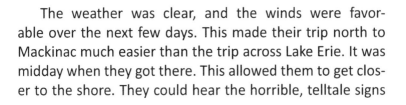

The weather was clear, and the winds were favorable over the next few days. This made their trip north to Mackinac much easier than the trip across Lake Erie. It was midday when they got there. This allowed them to get closer to the shore. They could hear the horrible, telltale signs coming from several locations on the island. They even saw a few eyes peering through the brush at their passing ship. They continued on to Chicago. Their luck with the weather held, and they made it to Chicago in less than a week after leaving Detroit.

When they arrived at Fort Dearborn, they were greeted by several muskets pointed at them and a voice calling from the wall: "Hold there!! This city is under quarantine. We are to allow no one entry."

Sergeant Chambers went and stood on the bow and yelled back, "We are aware of the situation; we have orders from Detroit." He held up a sealed envelope. "We are here on a mission to try to resolve the problem."

The soldier on the wall turned and said something to someone on the ground behind him. He returned his attention to Chambers. "Hold your position there for a moment."

Chambers nodded, looked back at John, who also nodded. Nektosha and Smith started to furl the sails, and they all waited.

The soldier on the wall engaged in another conversation behind him, then turned and shouted, "Very well, bring your craft into the first slip, stay onboard, and await further instructions. Is that understood?"

"It is," Chambers answered.

They were met by more armed guards at the fort's docks; these soldiers were wearing bird-like plague masks as part of their uniforms.

"Secure your vessel and stand ready to submit to inspection by the doctor."

"Understood," Chambers answered, as they were

already tying *The Badger*'s lines to the dock's cleats.

The doctor came on board and had them all move to the back of the boat. He then brought them up one by one to John's cabin, had them take off their clothes, and checked them over. Once they'd each submitted to this, they put their clothes back on and were sent to stand on the dock. After they were all cleared, they were taken to the commander's office. The doctor accompanied them to meet with the commander with his own report. Chambers gave the envelope to the commander, and they waited while he read the letter.

"I see," the commander said at last. "I was wondering how far this had reached. This tells me much more than I had been able to discover from here. If you want to dig deeper into what has transpired in this area, you will need to go into town. To do that, you will need protective masks, as we are trying to contain this affliction, as they are calling it, and keep it from getting any worse. We don't have a lot to spare—our patrol boats use them, as well as our men tending the watch fires. It will take us some time to gather some masks for you, so report back here in an hour."

"Yes, sir, will do," Chambers said.

The travelers took the time to go to the watch tower of the fort, so they could see the condition of Chicago. It looked to be less affected than Detroit at first, but as they studied the scene, they saw some differences. On several of the rooftops were militiamen with spy glasses and muskets scanning the outlying areas. The burning barrels of pitch were mostly concentrated along the southern edge of town. This completed a square, with the rivers and the lake forming the other three sides. Activity in the town itself appeared relatively normal.

Chambers turned to one of the guards. "What happened here? What was it like?"

The guard looked out across the town as he spoke, revealing a thick Southern drawl, "From what I been told, they came upon us from the north, from the forest over yonder." He tilted his head to the northeast. "They came up and attacked Miller's Pub. It's by the river. It was midmorning, so there wasn't hardly no one there. They went right past Wolf Tavern—we reckon it was empty at the time—and they crossed the bridge into town. Well, some folks was clearing some land up there, and they had a pretty big fire going. They didn't have no weapons on them, so they threw burning branches and such. Well, they set some of them things on fire. That set the whole bunch of them a-squalling and running off to the east into the woods over there.

"Well, the next thing we did was to blockade all those bridges up there and keep the drawbridge raised. And, figuring they don't like fire much, they put those fire barrels around over yonder. We haven't seen none of them since, but nobody is sleeping too good anyway."

Chambers considered for a moment and asked, "So, they all acted as one unit? They all stayed together?"

"Oh no, some of them didn't come down in toward here. Some of them stayed over there across the river, and they attacked some houses and farms and such; then they ran off thataway to the west."

"Well, thank you, soldier; you have been most helpful." Chambers looked at the other three to see if they had any questions; they did not.

"Hey, Sergeant? Are you going to be sending back help? We are kind of cut off here."

"Yes, soldier, that is the plan." They excused themselves and went down to see if there was any other useful information available.

"Sergeant!" A soldier near the command office was waving them back over. "We need you to try these on, to be sure they fit right." He held a pair of plague masks in his other hand.

The wearing of these masks was going to take some adjustment to be sure. They were made of leather with a large bird-beak shape over the lower half of the face and a pair of round glass disks stitched in place to see through. The beak portion was filled with shredded rags and bits of herbs.

"You have to wear these just so, or the glass will fog right up, and you won't be able to see." The soldier was explaining things as others were walking up with various other protective items.

"You need to leave no skin exposed—gloves that overlap the sleeves and a scarf around the neck. There you go. Is that head strap too tight? No? Good."

As they were getting fitted up, the commander had joined the group. "There is a doctor in town who's been working with the Indians. From what we know, they have a much better understanding of this whole mess than anyone else in town. Check with them first. You will find them working out of the barbershop in the center of town. They are the ones who advised us all to wear this protective gear."

Chambers, Smith, John, and Nektosha were suited up in

short order. Chicago was a much smaller town than Detroit, so it did not take them long to locate the red-blue-and-white-striped barber's pole by the shop's doorway. There was a portly gentleman getting a shave from the tall, thin barber. The pegs on the wall where the tailcoats and top hats were hung now had the additional duty of holding the assorted bizarre masks of the patrons as well. Though the words were not discernible, it was clear that a heated discussion was happening just beyond the closed door to the back room. It was also clear that the argument was escalating.

The four men all tightened their grips on their weapons and prepared for the worst. Nektosha glanced over at the barber, who was nonchalantly tending to his client. He was about to bring this confusing detail to the attention of his friends when there was a loud bang on the door. The four of them moved as one—they took a step back and crouched into ready positions. Then the door flew open, and there stood a somewhat gaunt man with his top hat on, next to an Indian medicine man whose foot was still in the air after kicking the door open; both of them were looking quite startled to see the four men squared off at them.

"Yeah, that door sticks. I have been meaning to get that looked after," the barber said as he swept the razor up the cheek of his client and flung a glob of shaving soap into a bowl on the floor. "These folks were sent from the fort to talk to you two."

Everyone straightened up and settled themselves for a second.

"I am Dr. Deggory Periwinkle. This is my colleague,

Medicine Man Howakan of the Winnebago tribe. We were just debating on where to go to lunch; would you like to join us?"

John spoke up first. "Yup, yup! I could eat."

"You could always eat," Nektosha replied fondly.

Deggory patted Howakan on the back. "Well, that settles that. We will go to your camp to eat, where we have space for all, but next time, it's my turn to buy, yes?"

"You've got yourself a deal." Howakan beamed.

Tamaha joined them as they gathered on logs arranged in a circle around a fire in the middle of Howakan's temporary village, which had been set up on open lots in the southwest corner of town. Howakan had his people bring out an amazing meal that would have been fit to grace the tables of even the finest restaurants in London and New York. They all talked well into the evening. They shared their stories of recent events and tried to piece together a better understanding of the nature of the affliction that was plaguing the region and had killed so many of those they held dear.

Eventually the conversation followed its natural progression to what to do next.

"We need to find a way to effectively combat it," Chambers said.

"And," Howakan added, "we need to find some way to effectively cure it or at least prevent it."

Deggory spoke up. "It is difficult for us to experiment and make progress here since I lost my lab and most of my equipment." He paused. "I've lost a lot here … With shipping being shut down, it is more difficult; we are having to make do with what we can get."

Nektosha brightened and said, "Why don't you come back with us? You can get what you need from the people in Washington. They would want to talk to you too, about what you know."

Deggory went still. He studied Nektosha for a moment, then he looked over his shoulder toward town and his home. Then he looked back at the faces now all glowing in the dancing orange light from the fire.

His eyes settled on the face of Howakan, who said, "We should sleep on this and decide in the morning. You men are welcome to stay here with us if you like," he added, looking at the rest of the party.

It was Chambers's turn to pause. He looked back and forth, considering. "I don't think we would want to impose."

"Nonsense." Howakan cut him off. "We have plenty of room here."

Nektosha and Tamaha, who had hit it off immediately as only teenaged boys can, went over to a group of Indian girls who had been whispering and trying in vain to not appear as though they were observing the two. Deggory produced a hip flask and passed it around. Eventually Smith left the others at the fire to join Nektosha, Tamaha, and the giggling group of girls.

Howakan was the first up in the morning, had the fire re-kindled, and was deep in thought when Sergeant Chambers joined him.

"Good morning, Howakan; you are up early."

"Yes, I have much to consider. No one knows this plague of the Wentiko like I do, so there is a need for me to go back to Washington with you. I am thinking on the possibilities of leaving my people here; however, our chief is not a young man any longer, and Tamaha is just becoming a man. I hadn't realized how much I had been a leader of my people. It is just something that happened along the way."

Chambers scrubbed his hands up and down his face, trying to wake himself up a bit more for this conversation. He sat on a stump beside the medicine man. "As you told us last night, you have seen your people through an awful lot of hard times lately. But they are not alone now; joining up with the city folks here has been good for both of you. They have the protection of the soldiers and the buildings for cover, and because you came here, the city now has greater numbers as well. I believe that they are glad to have your people here."

"Yes, you make a good point. I am thinking that a part of my hesitation is that I have never been truly away from my people for long, and that too makes me nervous. I can get over that soon enough, I just want to be sure that I am doing the right things for the right reasons."

Chambers nodded at him and smiled at the woman who had come to put an iron kettle on the hook over the fire. The two sat quietly as the movements and conversations from the village and surrounding town became louder than the songs and chirpings of the birds.

Deggory joined them directly, stating, "I'll need a couple of hours to gather what I need from my house and my shop. It's pretty clear that I can be of more use over there than over here."

Private Smith, Nektosha, and Tamaha were the last to

rejoin the conversation. None of them looked like they had been doing much sleeping. It was about noon when they got back to the fort and started loading *The Badger* with supplies. They decided to leave right away as the days were rapidly getting colder and shorter. They knew the risk of the lakes freezing over was getting higher. The risk of an attack from the Wentiko was increasing as well, and they simply could not afford to be delayed.

The trip north through Lake Michigan was brutal. The winds and waves were relentlessly hammering *The Badger* from the west. Howakan was not adjusting well to life on a boat, and he looked terrible. At one point, Deggory offered him his flask. Howakan pushed it away, threw Deggory a filthy look, and lurched to the rail to surrender the contents of his stomach to the waves below. The winds were howling, bitterly cold, and large chunks of ice were already forming, threatening to block the passage entirely. These ice chunks would occasionally hit the hull of *The Badger* with a crack, causing the boat to jolt and shudder. Not knowing if it was the ice or *The Badger* that was cracking was terrifying everyone. They all knew that if they went into the freezing water, none of them would survive. Nektosha made frequent trips down into the hold to bail and check for leaks, but with so much frigid water washing over the top of the deck, it was hard to tell where it was coming from.

When one of the more powerful gusts hit its peak, one of the belaying pins holding the line securing the corner of the main sail to the rail shattered like a gunshot under the tension. This sent the sail flapping and cracking in the wind. The line was whipping around the deck with an astonishing force that could easily take a man's head off.

John crouched low, wide-eyed and white-knuckled at the wheel, yelling, "Get it! GET IT!!"

Nektosha and Smith were already moving to catch the deadly, serpent-like threat. Smith eventually caught the corner of the sail, and he threw his arm around the line and slowly walked down its length, though not without a whip-crack to the back from the line for his troubles. When he finally had the end, he tied it to the rail where the belaying pin used to be. He and Dr. Periwinkle then retired briefly belowdecks to get his lash cleaned and dressed.

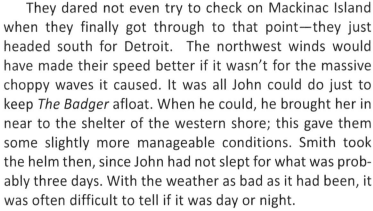

They dared not even try to check on Mackinac Island when they finally got through to that point—they just headed south for Detroit. The northwest winds would have made their speed better if it wasn't for the massive choppy waves it caused. It was all John could do just to keep *The Badger* afloat. When he could, he brought her in near to the shelter of the western shore; this gave them some slightly more manageable conditions. Smith took the helm then, since John had not slept for what was probably three days. With the weather as bad as it had been, it was often difficult to tell if it was day or night.

When they got to the sheltered docks of Detroit, they went in to tie up, so they could check the hull and recover their wits for a moment. They took this time to go to the

B. B. LeClere

hospital to check on Benson.

They found him sitting on the side of his bed. "Well, hello!" he said in a thin but cheerful voice.

He tried to stand up, but his nurse put gentle hands on his shoulders and pushed him back down. "You know better than that now."

"All right, all right." He smiled up at her.

"Hello, Benson, I'm glad to see you are doing well," Chambers said as the others crowded around to see their friend better.

"I'm getting better all the time, but they tell me it will be a while before I can leave the hospital."

Chambers looked up at the nurse. "Is there anything we can do? Is there anything you need?"

The nurse smiled and said, "No we're fine, thank you. We're taking good care of this one here."

Smith shot a look to Sergeant Chambers, who immediately got the hint. Everyone else took turns shaking Benson's remaining hand before they shuffled back out, Chambers idly noticing that most of the beds were now empty and hoping that their previous occupants had recovered rather than succumbing to whatever ailment had sent them there.

"Benson," Smith began, "I'm sor—"

"No," Benson interrupted, "Smith, you saved my life. You've no need to apologize for that."

"But," Smith tried, "your arm … "

"Smith … Douglas," Benson said firmly, getting the man's attention with the use of his given name, "I am alive because of your quick thinking. The doctors here have made that perfectly clear. If you had not done what you did, I'd have died on that field or, at the very least, on the return march. You. Saved. My. Life," he stated, enunciating each word like a hammer hitting a nail, trying to drive the idea into his compatriots' head. "Should you ever need anything of me, I am in your debt."

Waving away Smith's objections before they could be voiced, Benson continued, "As for my injury, I'm damn lucky it wasn't my right hand! I'd rather lose my off hand than my life, and besides," he leaned toward Smith conspiratorially, "I had a visit from one of those specialty doctors. They're gonna fit me with a new type of prosthetic that's got all sorts of different moving parts!"

———— ◦《◉》◦ ————

When they got back to the boat, they were happy to find that the hull was in good shape and that she was ready to ship out when they were. They truly felt that they were not yet ready, the harrowing trip down still fresh in their minds. However, they also truly had no choice, so they steeled their nerves and got back onboard.

Their trip through Lake Erie was only bearable because they had memory of their previous voyage. With the winds coming from behind them, they were now going with the waves rather than across them. Their passage to Buffalo was tolerable only by comparison.

The trip through the Erie Canal and down the Hudson River was a huge relief not only because the conditions were better but also because they were now out of the Great Lakes. The Atlantic Ocean was a welcome sight and easily carried them to the Chesapeake for the final leg of their journey.

17:

STRATEGY AND INNOVATION

Whe they got to the fort in Washington, the soldiers on the dock greeted them with high honors.
The soldiers all saluted, and the sergeant on
the dock called out, "The general told me to give you two
hours to get cleaned up and report to his office. Sergeant
Chambers, your wife told me to inform her when we sighted
you and that you are to report to her quarters immediately
..."

That was as far as he got when Sophie herself suddenly appeared, running past the sergeant on the dock, with
Tom and Victoria close at her heels. The others just stepped
around the now hugging mass and headed for the bunk
house.

They were met at the general's office by one of his
aides. "We have a pair of carriages to take you into town to
the general. Mrs. Chambers, you have the option of bringing the children or leaving them with us here at the fort."

She looked at the two, each grasping a hand of their

father. "I think my family is back together, and I would like to keep us together."

The carriages turned out to be quite grand. They had the basic design of a stagecoach but much nicer, with silk curtains on the windows and fine leather cushions on the seats. The ride too, was much smoother than anything they had experienced before.

It was, however, a short trip. They were delivered to a side door of the Capitol Building, and when Sergeant Chambers got out and realized where he was, he froze in his tracks.

"It's going to be all right, Jack," Sophie said, reaching over Victoria's head to hold his arm. "You are going to do just fine. The general really likes you. You are bringing them the answers that they want."

She looked back at the others; Howakan, Nektosha, and John were walking so close to each other that they were almost tripping on each other's feet. Dr. Periwinkle was bringing his flask to his lips with a trembling hand.

"You are making everyone nervous, Jack," Sophie chided.

She separated herself to speak to all of them. "After all that you have been through, you're going to let a few stuffed suits intimidate you?"

Howakan steadied himself and stepped out. "She is right. We are united in this. They seek our counsel, and we are here to help, that is all."

Sergeant Chambers looked into the faces of those he had come to count on over the past few months. "Yes," he said, more to himself than the others, "yes, yes, we can do this." He took a deep breath and turned, and they all went in together.

To their great relief, they were told that were not to be escorted into the great halls of Congress but, rather, to one of the remote committee rooms downstairs.

Their escort knocked on the door and poked his head in. "They are here, sir."

"Good. Send them right in."

Oddly, hearing General Macomb's familiar voice did a lot to ease the tension. Chambers looked back in time to see Howakan swatting at Deggory's hand as he tried to take another pull from his flask.

"Come in." The general was striding across the large room, and he started shaking their hands. "Good to see that you have returned in good order. Was your mission a success?"

"Yes, sir, it was." Chambers was surprised that he was not flummoxed, and his words were coming out straight.

"Great!" The general seemed a bit surprised. "Captain Hunter and the men he brought back arrived a couple days ago. He already knows much of what we will be discussing here, and we will bring him up-to-date on the rest soon.

"I would like to introduce you to Dr. Deggory Periwinkle and his colleague, Medicine Man Howakan of the Winnebago tribe. They have been in close contact with the Wentiko, as they have named them, and have been working to gain an understanding of this affliction."

The general looked over in surprise to the two healers. "Excellent! What have you been able to discover so far?"

"Well, sir," Deggory began, "we have gained a fair un-derstanding of the course and progression; however, we are still looking into the cause and cure. I brought samples of an infected arm and a leg with me."

"What did he say?!" John blurted out. "Here?"

"No, I left them on the boat."

"You mean to tell me that that stuff has been on my *Badger* this whole time?!"

"The samples are securely wrapped and crated. I would not endanger anyone by exposing them to us."

Sergeant Chambers, who was also shaken by this revelation, interrupted. "Hold on, now, you should have told us about those limbs *before* they were loaded onto *The Badger*, but this is not the time or place to settle this."

The general spoke up. "How about we introduce you to some of the others here?"

His diversion had the desired effect as everyone shifted their attention to the rest of the room. There were tables set around the outer walls, with stacks and rolls of papers on them. Several tables were in the center of the room with chairs all around, heaped with even more stacks and rolls of papers. It was clear that several conversations were in progress around the room.

General Macomb walked them around to the left to the nearest table. "This is Naval Architect Samuel Humphries. He and his team are developing not only better ways to attack from ships but also adapting shipboard weapons for use by the infantry."

They all shook hands, and the general moved them along before any conversation was able to start.

"This is our apothecary general, Joshua Lovell. He and his people will be working with you, Dr. Periwinkle and Howakan, on the affliction itself and ways to combat it."

They continued around the room. "Hard at work over here is Stephen Harrington Long. He has done extensive explorations and mapping in the areas affected, and I believe that his work in the developments in steam power will prove quite valuable as well."

One workstation remained. "Gentlemen, please meet Rufus Porter. He has developed a working model of an aerial steamer, a steam-propelled airship with the capacity to convey us over the target where we can assess and attack the enemy from above."

There, on one of his tables, was a miniature dirigible, with many unrecognizable pieces and parts arranged around it. Also on the table were many papers with calculations, a couple slide rules, calipers, and a set of scales.

Sophie had to interrupt to reprimand the children. "That is not a toy." as they instinctively tried to touch it.

General Macomb then brought everyone to the center table. "I believe, gentlemen, that the next order of business is to discuss what we know of the situation and where we are in developing the means to deal with it. Before we proceed with any plans, we will hear from Sergeant Chambers and his team about the current situation over there."

Chambers stood back up, cleared his throat, and took a beat to decide just how to arrange the information. "The situation on Mackinac remains unchanged, as far as we were able to tell. We did not dock at the island or look to the interior, but we could hear the sounds of the Wentiko from several locations, and we saw movement along the tree line. The situation in both Detroit and Chicago remains dire but was apparently stable when we were there. I don't know how long that will last." He paused and heaved a large sigh. "Getting back to them will be extremely difficult, we barely got through the straits with our lives."

The general stepped forward. "Getting back to them is just not a viable option until the winter passes. We lost hundreds of men trying to get to the battle of the Black Hawk a couple of years ago—we cannot afford to try that again. Also, we need the time we have here to prepare to meet this new threat."

Sophie gasped and hugged Jack's arm. There was a moment of stunned silence.

The general continued, "We have discussed this at great length, and it is our considered opinion that the weather will be as much of a detriment to them as to us. Our plan is to be ready as soon as the weather breaks and to aggressively move in to purge the entire area as quickly as is practicable. This will be difficult without the use of horses, but we have seen that in the face of these … What did you call them? Wentiko?"

Howakan nodded. "It is difficult to translate," he started. "I believe the closest I can come would be, something like a … a demon cannibal? Our ancient stories tell of people being possessed by evil itself to spread terror and chaos."

The general nodded. "They certainly do that, don't they." He glanced at his notes, finding his place. "With the way the horses react to the Wentiko, they are more of a liability than an asset. Not having to transport any horses will also allow for more space for additional men and equipment."

He grabbed a rolled map from the edge of the table and spread it out. Some of the men grabbed candlesticks to hold down the corners. The map showed the territory of Michigan, with Lake Michigan on one side and Lake Huron on the other.

"We will first concentrate our efforts on Mackinac Island."

He pointed at the top of the map where the two lakes met and the small island just to the east of the narrow strait. "This gives us a contained theater of operations to test our new tactics and weapons. Additionally, once we control the island, we can use this as a base of operations as we clear the surrounding area."

He swept his hand down over the Michigan territory then across Chicago. "And if things go horribly awry, we can use this as a fallback point. What we don't want to do is to flush these things into the population and spread this across the countryside. Containment will be the key. When we have secured this area, we will move our efforts to the western banks of Lake Michigan and the Chicago area. It is our thought and hope that this will clear the bulk of the problem. We then have the task of cleaning up the stragglers. We can't leave any of them alive to reinfect the populace. As you can see, we have our nation's best working on ways to bring this threat to an end. These new ideas would best be discussed later after they are more fully developed."

General Macomb paused for a moment to be sure that had everyone's full attention.

"We brought all of this here to maintain the approval of the president and those few who know the situation. It is necessary to keep all of this mess a secret, or we will panic the population. That could be as much of a problem as the problem itself. Do you understand and give me your word to tell no one of any of this?"

Only after everyone had given their word did the general's mood lighten, and everyone was loaded into carriages for the return to the fort.

It had begun to snow while they were inside and continued as they rode back to the fort. The officers and soldiers in Fort Washington had been busy indeed while they were away in the west. The fields in and around the fort were set up in workstations similar to the meeting room. It was clear that the same man was overseeing all of the operations. There was much experimentation with innovative weapons ideas. They had brought out some wheelbarrows and push carts, and they were working out the best way to carry larger weapons using manpower rather than horsepower.

"I think you would do well to see some of the new weapons we are developing." General Macomb beamed, showing a rare smile of enthusiasm.

Sophie excused herself to take the children back to their quarters. "I have already seen this, and I don't want Tom and Victoria exposed to it any more than necessary."

Even if it was only for a few minutes, Jack Chambers found it difficult to watch his family walk away.

"To move to the future, we are looking to the past for any ideas for this new type of battle," General Macomb was telling the group.

Chambers, Smith, Nektosha, Howakan, and Deggory hurried to keep up with the excited general as he strode out onto the parade grounds. "We are also looking to the navy as they are already using close-quarter weapons and tactics for ship boarding and on-deck fighting. The challenge is moving these devices through the battlefield and keeping them durable."

He pointed at sections around the field where teams of men were tinkering and studying a variety of unusual devices.

The general pointed at the various clusters of activity. "Small cannons over here, Greek fire devices with a furnace and bellows over there, steam-powered acid shooters with fire-hose-type nozzles. Rocket launchers."

One of the men from the steam-shooter cart shouted up to the general, "We are about ready to give her a go here, sir, steam only."

The general motioned for them to proceed. After some nervous chatter among themselves, one of them shouted, "Stand clear!"

A man pulled on a lever, and a cloud of steam erupted from the nozzle. Unfortunately, a sudden gust of wind blew the steam back onto the men, causing the one in front to make noises something akin to a chicken and run from the field. The man standing nearby with the steam-shooter backpack device frantically wrestled free of it, dropped it, and moved several feet away.

"It looks like we are getting closer to the answer, sir!" the man called back up.

"Very well, then—carry on," the general answered.

John was pleased to see *The Badger* was to get some patching up and some fresh paint. It was also to be fitted with four deck cannons, some new sails, and some upgrades to their crow's nest stations.

"We are looking at some innovations for the individual men as well." He was leading them into the mess hall, which was a beehive of activity as well.

The tables were covered with papers and weapons and surrounded by men pointing and mumbling about this or that. Captain Hunter was found here. He immediately detached himself from the table where he was working and came over to them.

"Good afternoon. I was glad to hear that you made it back safely. I heard that it was quite a challenge."

John stepped up to greet him. "Yup, yup. It was fierce, no mistake. But with a crew like the sergeant, Nektosha, and Smith here, I had no cause to worry. Having a doctor and medicine man on board was certainly a comfort as well. I could not have asked for better."

"Excellent! With your leave, general, I would like to show them what we have been working on in here."

"Certainly, Captain. I am needed at my office anyway, so I will leave you to it."

Captain Hunter was beaming like a child with new toys. "One of the chief changes we will be making is to equip some of the men with grenades. If we can gain the advantage of being on the offensive, these will be useful in reducing the rushing attack that was so taxing on us before. We will also be introducing the blunderbuss. This scattergun should provide more stopping power at short range.

"We are also working on ways to carry more formidable weapons through woods and other dense terrain where wheels are not practical." In the back corner of the hall, men were setting up tripods and other stands fitted with various weapons. There was a small cannon suspended by ropes from a four-legged stand, a rocket launcher on a tripod, a small catapult on a backpack, along with a few other more intimidating items.

He then walked them all out of the mess hall and up to a converted horse barn. Inside was a massive roughly cylinder-shaped object and what looked like a small ship about half the size of *The Badger*—and men swarming around both like ants on a mound. Emerging from this apparent chaos came Mr. Porter with his cigar, puffing up a storm.

"Here is the real deal. This is the gas bag," he said, pointing up at the painted cylinder. "We are making sure she is airtight. She held pressure with regular air just fine, so we are bringing her up to pressure with hydrogen now, and we are checking for leaks. The gondola, or ship section, is almost ready. If we can get some fair weather, we may be able to take her out for a tethered test in a few days or so." His excitement was almost tangible to the others.

The captain then walked them back to the general's office. General Macomb invited them all in and had them sit. He too took a chair, not his own chair behind the desk, but one of the side chairs, like the rest of them, making things much less formal and more comfortable.

"I have asked much of you all over these past months," he began, "and I will be asking more of you going forward. For now, however, we are unable to get back to the enemy for some time, and you have some well-deserved leave coming as well as some back pay."

He reached back to his desk and grabbed a stack of envelopes. "Chambers and Smith, determining your part was easy: standard pay with a bonus for exceptional service." He handed them each an envelope. "The rest of you I had to qualify as militia and figure the pay from when you started serving our cause. I added a bonus for each of you as well. Without the exemplary conduct of each of you, I daresay this affliction could have overrun us all."

He handed envelopes to Deggory, Howakan, and John; then he paused. "Nektosha, you have lost and given much to this conflict. I want to offer you special thanks. I hope that your and John's involvement continues with us after this conflict is resolved." He handed Nektosha the final envelope, along with a hearty handshake.

"Yes, sir, thank you." Nektosha's reply was choked with emotion.

"Thank you, sir" was echoed around the room by all.

The general put up his hand to quiet them. "Now, then, it will be Christmas in a few days. You all have been invited to a grand party in town, and I would like you all to look your best. Whenever you want to go into town, check in here at my office, and transportation will be arranged for you."

They all agreed to wait until morning to go into town and gathered at the general's office early the next day, eager to do something that was not directly connected to the war on the Wentiko. As they were taking shelter on the porch from the still-falling snow, to their surprise, a large sleigh came to pick them up, along with several soldiers. One of the soldiers turned out to be a fine singer. So, they all ended up joining him in singing Christmas carols all the way into town.

The town was covered in fresh white snow and full of people all dressed up and carrying packages, ducking in and out of shop after shop. All of the doorways were decorated with holly and ivy. Groups of carolers were on many of the corners ringing bells and singing merry tunes. The overall effect was intoxicating, and as their newly befriended soldiers went scurrying off, they just stood there for a long moment breathing the cool air and gazing with wonder at the sights.

It was Sophie who got them moving. "Let's meet back here at noon, and we can all have lunch together. How does that sound?"

"That'll work just fine, I reckon," John answered, only slightly less awestricken than the others.

Jack and Sophie Chambers and the two children headed off up the street.

John turned to the others. "Well, look at us; you would think we had never seen a city before."

He pointed across the street at a large variety store and said, "Let's try that one." And they disappeared into the mob of merrymakers.

When they met for lunch, Sophie had accumulated an armload of bags and packages for Jack to carry.

When Nektosha asked what they had bought, she replied, "Some Christmas presents for my new family."

John leaned in. "That would be us fellers. We better do some shopping as well."

They had a grand lunch accompanied with hot cider and hot buttered rum. They ended up staying in town until early evening. As the sleigh headed back to the fort, the coachman took them around to watch the lamplighters lighting the streetlamps on Philadelphia Avenue. The snow flurries that had been falling all day were now getting heavier—just as well that they were headed back.

The party was on Christmas Eve. Everyone showed up looking their best. Sophie was radiant in her new red-and-white dress. Victoria was also beautiful—she had a similar dress in pink—and Tom had a top hat and tails; he looked like a miniature version of Dr. Periwinkle. Sergeant Chambers and Private Smith had clean, crisp uniforms, and Howakan and Nektosha had found a leather worker who'd fitted them up with fresh buckskins. It was John who was the real shock of the evening. He showed up in a black tie and tails with a silk top hat. It even looked like he had given his beard a trim and brushing.

The Christmas ball was a grand affair held at one of the fancy hotels. They had a huge tree that was all covered in candles and ornaments. There were musicians, and all the swells were dancing with their colorful clothes. It looked like a giant quilt weaving itself across the floor. The waiters kept circling with champagne, aperitifs, and hors d'oeuvres. All of the men, even Nektosha, were rather tipsy by the time they left.

When the Chambers family got home, Jack and Sophie read to the children from Grimm's fairy tales as well as "A Visit from St. Nicholas."

Sophie had insisted that everyone was to show up for a grand breakfast at the officers' quarters where they were living. It was there that they exchanged presents. She was given a basket of soaps and oils and her husband received a pocket watch. Inside the case was a small portrait of Sophie and the children in brass. *Wherever You Go, We Are Always with You* was engraved on the back. Tom got a toy gun and a bow-and-arrow set. Victoria got a pretty doll and a new dress. John received a new spyglass, and Nektosha and Howakan each got buffalo-hide cloaks. Deggory got a bottle of his favorite whisky, and Smith got a field medic kit made up by Deggory.

⸻≫◉≪⸻

Even with the constant drills and trials, the weeks that followed ground by at an excruciatingly slow pace. Knowing the severity of the threat back west and not knowing what was happening was maddening. Up till now they had been actively working to solve the problem. The waiting was almost unbearable. The temperatures in late December and early January were bitterly, uncommonly cold, dropping to sixteen degrees below zero at one point.

In mid-January General Macomb called everyone in the fort to an assembly on the parade grounds. "The unprecedented cold we have endured over the past weeks has been daunting, to be sure. I am also reasonably sure that it has been daunting for our opposition as well. I know that we are all concerned about the situation in the west and that we are all ready to put this threat down. The decision has been made to get underway in the first days of March and hope for an early thaw. We have *The Badger* and two larger transport steam ships that we will march out to meet in Buffalo, as the larger ships will not fit in the Erie Canal. The bulk of the army and equipment will march almost due north for ten to twelve days, which is about how long it will take to sail *The Badger* up the coast to New York, up the Hudson, and west on the Erie Canal. The rider I sent to Buffalo has reported that there is no news from Detroit or Chicago and that the ships will be available, provided the lake is passable."

He stepped back, and Captain Hunter stepped up to speak. "A lot of preparation has gone into this operation, and I know we are all anxious to see how this will all work. Stay diligent with your efforts and be sure we are ready to defeat this foul threat." He raised his voice even louder. "We march in March. We march in March!"

The troops took up the chant. "We march in March! We march in March!"

A few days later, General Macomb met with Sergeant Chambers, John, Dr. Periwinkle, Howakan, and Dr. Lovell, the apothecary general. "It has been decided to have you, Dr. Periwinkle, Howakan, and Dr. Lovell, come with us and set up a laboratory on one of the ships, wherever the space is most accommodating. As apothecary general, Dr. Lovell will take the lead in this; however, your greater experience will be invaluable, Dr. Periwinkle. In my conversations with Dr. Lovell, we have determined being near the front lines to be the most expedient course. You will have access to fresh samples, and any revelations you discover will need to be shared with us immediately. You are not accustomed to marching, so John will take you on *The Badger* to Buffalo where you will transfer your equipment to one of the larger vessels. I will ask you, Sergeant Chambers, to ensure that they get whatever samples they require from the field. If there are no questions, we will proceed. Make the necessary preparations. We march in March."

It was the end of the first week in March when they finally set out. Sophie, Victoria, and Tom found their spot on the wall to send off Jack as well as the other men who had become as close as family over the past months. The field looked quite different than it had the last time the army marched out. There were no horses, and the men were arranged in smaller groups with canvas-covered carts throughout. The biggest difference was that Rufus Porter had his steam-powered airship circling overhead.

That was a grand sight in itself. It was about one hundred feet long, with the gas bag being pointed at each end. The four men aboard were in what basically amounted to a thirty-foot wicker boat with large, retractable, fin-like flaps on each side, used to assist in maneuvering. The steam engine could be heard clearly *chuff-chuffing* through the crisp, cold air, and the long pipe that stuck out the back pushed the craft along. Two of the men appeared to be fully occupied in navigating this amazing contrivance; the other two were waving to the troops and onlookers below.

Tom squeezed Sophie's hand. "There they go!"

The three of them looked over to see *The Badger* looking brand-new. Nektosha cast off the lines, and she glided out onto the Potomac River. There was a commotion on the deck, and they deployed their newly added stunsails. These were set straight out from the sides of *The Badger* at deck height and added a lot more sail area, and therefore more speed.

They turned their attention back to the parade field where the general was beginning to speak. "At last the time has come. We are embarking on a mission unlike any other; as we face a different enemy, we will be using different weapons." He gestured up to the airship; this sparked a cheer from the men in the basket, which was echoed by the troops on the ground.

"The airship will be following us after a few days—she will make better time not having terrain to navigate, and this will allow us to all arrive together. It will also allow Mr. Porter some more time for final adjustments."

The order, "Forward, march!" came from the field, and the fifes and drums started to play. Sophie started to cry.

"I told myself I wouldn't do this!" she sobbed. She forced back the tears and put on a brave face as she waved farewell to the troops, and the man she loved.

Victoria shouted out, "Go get 'em, Daddy!" eliciting a chuckle from the troops who heard her.

18:

TO RETURN AND RECLAIM

After making a great start up the coast, *The Badger* was delayed in New York for a few days as the Hudson River was still frozen and not yet open to navigation. Dr. Lovell treated them to accommodations in one of the hotels near the water. They were too keen to get going, so they did not do much exploring of the city, but they did appreciate being out of the weather for a time. They knew that they were going to be exposed to the elements, and more soon enough, so being served a hot meal in a nice restaurant did not go unappreciated. They topped up their water and food supplies before they castoff and headed up the Hudson River. Traffic on the river and canal was heavy with many vessels reestablishing their supply routes after the winter's isolation. It turned out that they needn't worry about the delays caused in New York, as Lake Erie too was just opening to navigation when they got there. They met up with the rest of the army, who had been waiting there for a couple of days. Captain Hunter had ordered the men to take up residence on the two large ships, *The Daniel Webster* and the newer and larger *Michigan*. He did not allow any of them leave to go into town, for secrecy's sake.

On the orders from Captain Hunter, the "men of science"—Dr. Periwinkle, Howakan, and Dr. Lovel—transferred themselves and all of their equipment from *The Badger* over to the steamship *Michigan*. Sergeant Chambers and Private Smith rejoined John and Nektosha on *The Badger* and brought a naval cannoneer and three sharp shooters as well. The captain set up a field command center on *The Daniel Webster*; this one had just been rebuilt after suffering a midwinter fire.

In two days, they were able to arrive in Detroit. It had been agreed that the nimbler *Badger* would make the first approaches, then signal back to the two larger ships when they were sure it was safe for them to approach. As they had done at Mackinac before, *The Badger* came in parallel to the dock to watch for normal activity.

They were greeted with eager waves from the workers on shore. They still followed protocol and docked *The Badger*, made contact with the men on Merchants Wharf, and gave the hand signal that it was safe to approach.

They were still watching the two larger ships being secured to the Kings Warf's cleats when they heard a familiar voice: "Welcome back! I've been looking forward to seeing you again." Corporal Benson was there, in full uniform, and briskly walking up to greet them.

"Hello! Hello!" Nektosha was first to close the distance and gave the soldier a hug before he took a step back, thinking that might not be the right thing to do.

Benson held his hands up—he appeared to have two perfectly normal hands, nestled in cream-colored kid leather gloves. "Good to see you too, Nektosha!" He stepped forward and returned the hug.

The rest of the group caught up then, wanting to see Benson and his new hand. However, at that moment, the steam zeppelin was making its arrival, and everyone and everything in the city stopped as it came sailing overhead and tilted its wings forward and angled its nose down to reduce its height. Soon it was low enough to drop an anchor from the stern onto the parade field near the fort. The grappling-hook-type device eventually found a grip in the partially frozen soil, and they used that to leverage the airship lower, so two men could jump off with lines. They quickly pulled the lines out forward and angled in different directions and hammered long spikes into the ground. When these points were set, they pulled in the slack and brought the gondola to near ground level where several more lines were anchored and adjusted.

Corporal Benson turned his attention back to Sergeant Chambers and the others. "It appears we have much to talk about."

"We do indeed!" said Smith, taking Benson's elbow and gently raising his new hand for examination.

Benson excitedly started telling his old friends about his new appendage.

They were interrupted by a soldier who suddenly appeared at their side. "The captain would like you to meet him on his steamboat as soon as you can, Sergeant."

"Right away, soldier. Thank you."

As they were walking, Benson was explaining his new hand. "It's mechanical and adjustable. I can do almost anything with it! It has knobs on it, so I can move the fingers. I will have to show you later," he said as they were approaching the steamship *The Daniel Webster*. The guard escorted them in and to the stern of the ship.

"Good afternoon!" the captain said as they saluted and entered into the small dining area that was converted to a war field office. "I trust you have used the time on your voyage across the Erie to get your cannoneer and shooters situated and accustomed with *The Badger*."

"We have, sir," Sergeant Chambers replied. "They seem to be good men, thank you, sir … Also, sir, this is Corporal Benson. He appears to be fit, and we would like him to join us on *The Badger*, if it would be all right with you, that is, sir."

Chambers could feel himself getting flustered again; he stopped talking and tried to retreat a step. In doing so, he stepped on Nektosha's foot. When he spun to catch himself, his arm caught Nektosha on the chin, causing them both to almost fall over each other. They ended up grabbing ahold of each other for balance. This left them hugging and grinning like schoolboys at the captain for a second. They then realized what they must look like and bolted upright, shuffling away from one another.

"*This* is the corporal Benson I have heard about?" the captain asked with a barely concealed chuckle, trying to regain control over himself and the meeting.

"Yes, sir," Benson said, coming to attention and saluting.

"I thought you had lost a hand or a leg or something?"

"Yes, sir, this one here." The corporal held up his left hand. Seeing the look on Captain Hunter's face, Benson wasted no time in removing the glove, showing off his new metal hand. The captain's eyes grew wide as he studied the intricate knobs and gears.

"Allow me to show you, sir," Benson offered. He held his new hand palm up over the captain's table and started turning two knobs at the wrist. As he turned the knobs, his fingers flexed open and closed. One knob controlled the thumb and pointer, and the other knob controlled the other three fingers.

"They tell me it's based off a design built for a German knight in the 1500s, Gotz von Berlichigen, I think was his name, though I'm probably mangling the pronunciation horribly. It has the strength to hold a sword and the dexterity to hold a quill. It's not the same as my real hand of course, sir, but it is so much better than I thought I would end up with."

They all studied the hand for a long moment before the captain looked up. "It can hold a quill, you say. Are you left-handed, Corporal?"

"Not anymore, sir."

This brought a rare chuckle from the Captain.

"Well, that is splendid. And you think yourself to be fit for action, do you?"

"Yes! Yes, sir, I do."

"Well, that's good enough for me. Consider it done. Now, let's get things back on track." With that, the captain's demeanor changed and became more businesslike.

"Now, I called you all in here to review the plan. It looks

like the weather is cooperating for the time being. So, haste is in order. You and your men are to be the first landing party; you've had the most experience on the island and know the enemy. You will land on the southwest corner of the island, at Biddle's Point. Once you are sure that it is clear, you are to work your way over to the docks, clear and survey the area, so we can bring in the larger ships. Then we will be able to land the larger force. The entire force will move out unit by unit and clear the southern coast. When that is accomplished, we will move north and occupy the fort. From there we can conduct operations to clear the entire island. As you will be leading much of the attacks, I feel you and your team should be equipped with some of these."

He moved over to a stack of crates and opened the top one, moved some packing straw, and pulled out a case that he then opened to reveal a most unusual pistol. "These were just made by Samuel Colt, who's just started Colt's Patent Firearms Manufacturing Company; he calls this one a Patterson Repeater. It is able to fire five shots without reloading. This cylinder here can then be removed and replaced with this loaded secondary cylinder, to give you another five shots. That's ten barely interrupted shots before cover is needed to actually reload the weapon. That process is further expedited by the use of this innovative powder horn that can fill all five chambers of the cylinder at once. In our testing runs we have found that, once you're accustomed to the mechanics of the weapon, it should take you less than a minute to reload both cylinders and have the weapon ready again for firing."

He closed the repeater back in its box, stowed it back

in the crate, and hefted it. Spinning about, he handed it off to Chambers. "These are for you and your men. Distribute them as you see fit, Sergeant. I want you men to have every advantage we can muster on that godforsaken island."

He stepped back and turned to face the other men. "Unless there are any questions, we are done here. We will sail at sunrise. Be sure to have everything in order."

Just as they were leaving, the captain suddenly called them back. "I've had a thought. Benson, I heard you were handling the pottery-lamp grenades when your team burned the ships in the harbor, correct?"

"Yes, sir. It was really Sergeant Chambers's idea, sir. I was just the one throwing ... "

"That will do nicely." The captain continued, "I want someone in the airship who knows what he is looking for, someone who has an idea how these Wentiko look and act. Are you all right with that?"

"Yes, sir" was clearly the only reply the captain was going to want to hear.

"You stay here then." Captain Hunter looked over to the guard at the door. "Have Mr. Porter summoned here at once, please."

Sergeant Chambers reached into the new crate and handed one of the repeater cases to Corporal Benson, clapping his hand on his shoulder he looked into Benson's eyes and said, "You be careful up there."

When Rufus Porter arrived, his ever-present cigar was being worked so hard it looked like a campfire dancing around on his face. He was clearly stressed and deep in thought, trying to anticipate what the captain had in store, but he would not question the captain's authority, especially in front of others, at this critical moment.

"Good afternoon, Mr. Porter. I trust the preparations with your aircraft are going smoothly?"

"Smooth as silk, sir. What can I do for you?"

"I'm going to have you switch one of your crew with this man here. Benson has handled these grenades before and has firsthand knowledge of the enemy as well as the lay of the land on Mackinac Island. Are there any questions?" Captain Hunter leaned into Porter's smoke-shrouded face ready to counter any resistance.

"Actually, sir. That suits me just fine. One of my crew has been getting more and more skittish as we get down to the point of this thing." Porter looked at Corporal Benson, who reflexively stood at attention. "You're not likely to go all faint at the thought of this, are you, boy?"

"No, sir! In fact, I've got a debt to collect that needs paying." Benson pulled off his glove and showed Porter his artificial hand.

The inventor was immediately fascinated. "Well, would you look at that?!" Without so much as a "by your leave," he took Benson's mechanical hand in both of his own and started twisting it side to side to get a better look. He quickly found the control knobs and started opening and closing the fingers. "Fascinating! And the workmanship is just superb."

The captain interrupted, "He says he has great control with it."

"I can see that. Yes, this is terrific." Porter then studied Benson's face, trying to get a quick assessment of the man before him, "Yes, sir, he will do nicely, General." He shook Captain Hunter's hand and returned his attention to Benson. "You had better come with me. There is much to show you and not much time."

He turned back at the door. "Sir, what should I do with the other man?"

"Send him here; we'll put him to work on one of the ships where he's less likely to panic and mess something up."

"Understood, sir. Will do … and thank you."

As the two of them left *The Daniel Webster*, Porter was already telling Benson about the wonders of his airship.

"It is a lot like sitting in a small boat, but it's a lot more stable. Your position will be in the front as spotter and grenadier. You got good eyesight?" Benson nodded. "I will be in the rear with the engine controls and primary steering. We will have two men in the middle working the flaps to assist with steering and stability. She will comfortably hold four more, but we are only going to have four of us and use the extra weight allowance for weapons. General Macomb was thinking all we will be able to do is be spotters, but I think we have a chance to really show the capabilities of my new pride and joy. I'm glad to get someone with some years in service; I think Hunter originally sent me soldiers he didn't have good use for. Now that we brought her here from Washington, and he has seen her fly, I believe he is more confident about the whole thing."

The captain was standing at the top deck's rail watching Porter and Benson chattering excitedly as they cut through the bustle of activity. This sight brought the captain feelings of confidence for the way things were coming together, and nervousness for what tomorrow would bring.

———◦((◉))◦———

As the sky began to show the first colors of predawn light, the harbor was already alive with activity. It seemed that everyone in Detroit had turned out to help prepare the ships for their all-important mission. *The Badger*, the two large steamboats, and the zeppelin were each like a beehive of activity as supplies and weapons were checked and re-checked, townspeople and soldiers alike running back and forth with last-minute thoughts.

Captain Hunter appeared on the top deck of the command ship, had a man blow a loud, shrill note on a bosun's whistle, and the bustle of activity ground to a halt as all eyes turned to the captain.

"We will cast off in one hour and make our best time to Mackinac. I will need to see all unit leaders here aboard *The Daniel Webster* in fifteen minutes to go over last-minute preparations and to answer any questions. That is all. Fair seas and following winds to you, men."

The commotion was renewed immediately. The unit leaders could be heard shouting instructions to their groups before heading to the command ship. Soon dozens of men were crowded around the general's command deck and crowding up to the table, some shaking hands, some wishing each other luck.

General Macomb tapped on the table with the butt of his pistol a few times, and the crowd fell silent. "To facilitate quick and efficient communication among ground, sea, and air units, a scaled-back flag system has been set up. A black flag meant the enemy had been spotted. A red flag was the signal to attack or advance. A white flag is the signal to cease or retreat. These would be fixed to a staff or musket and angled to indicate the direction of intent. So, if there is a battle to be joined, a red flag should be waved and pointed in the direction of the battle. If a retreat is in order, then a white flag should be waved and pointed in the direction of the retreat. Each of you be sure to get a set of flags before you leave here.

"The first unit to land will be led by Sergeant Chambers. They will go in by longboat and canoe to reduce noise and visibility. They are to secure the harbor. If possible, we will bring the larger ships in and dock them, and the rest of our forces will move in directly from the ships. Otherwise, we will have to tinder everything in on the longboats and this will complicate things considerably, especially with regards to the equipment and larger weapons. We will hold the larger ships near the mouth of the harbor and wait for your signal."

Chambers gave a curt nod of understanding. One of the captain's attendants was already distributing large squares of black, red, and white cloth.

19:

RETURN TO MACKINAC

The *Badger*, as previously planned, was not to enter the harbor. It was not known whether the charred remnants of the ships they'd destroyed were still floating in the slips. Damaged timber and bits of flotsam resting just beneath the waterline could be silently waiting to rip a hole through their hulls like they were so much tissue paper. The airship, however, would be able to scout ahead for them and relay some directions to the most ideal anchorage.

The sergeant's team was quick to launch once John had moved *The Badger* close to the shore,

taking John's canoe and several longboats to head for the accursed island. Chambers and the soldiers, making the tenuous trip to secure the beach, were silent; only the gentle splashes of the paddles in the water could be heard. The tension in these boats seemed to be adding undue weight to the crafts.

Chambers was tamping down hard on his emotions,

keeping a stone-cold façade as his fear and apprehension roiled just beneath the surface. He had not wanted to return to this place, and the memories, and the men, he'd left behind. The screams of his fellow soldiers—some of them had been good friends and all of them good men—still woke him in the night. He tried in vain to push the memories and nightmares from his mind. How they'd thrust him into wakefulness with a hoarse gasp and an out-flung hand, reaching for a weapon that wasn't there, trembling and almost crying like a child still in swaddling clothes. Each time he woke from these terrors, he knew that regaining any modicum of restfulness was futile, and he would often find a quiet spot away from whomever he was with, be it his wife or his men, and try in vain to calm his racing heart before the dawn.

Smith was likewise anxious, though his efforts to hide it were much less successful, and he sat trembling slightly in the canoe, recalling far too easily the happenings of his last venture aboard this very craft. A single arrow, fired by a boy barely out of his schooling years, had meant the difference between life or death. As a soldier, he'd had his fair share of close calls, some closer than others. Never before, though, had he truly stared death in the face and had death stare back at him with eyes full of hunger and rage. He remembered the creature had been wearing a fine white shirt and black coat; both were smeared with blood and gore. What had once been a normal, everyday gentleman had become a ravenous demon-creature, hellbent on devouring his flesh, if it had only managed to pull him up another two feet. That arrow, that boy, and those two feet were honest to God miracles, as far as Douglas Smith was concerned, and he was sure he didn't have many more miracles coming his way.

John was faring no better than the soldiers, though he was able to calm himself somewhat in the knowledge, cowardly it may be, that the soldiers were going first. This was not something he'd ever been trained or prepared to do. He was a trapper, a man who worked at a distance with iron traps and rope snares, not up close and in the fray. His quarry was, more often than not, already dead by the time he got to it. He killed from afar and without witness. These Wentiko were something he was ill suited and ill prepared to combat against. His thoughts often strayed to the day he heard that shot in the abandoned fort. If he'd not heard it, or not investigated it, he wouldn't be here now. Of course, he might be worse off, afflicted himself, or the meal of one. He'd also have never known Chambers, Smith, Benson, or Nektosha. He was able to surprise himself and hold the line when they were attacked on the dock in Detroit, Nektosha by his side. It was a nightmare that featured frequently in both his sleeping and waking hours; but for Nektosha alone, he'd do it all again. Trapping was a solitary lifestyle—he'd never married, let alone had a child of his own—but the young Indian had grown on him to a point that he missed him dearly when he was away. He worried immeasurably about what the boy was paddling into.

Back on the command ship, Deggory, Howakan, and Lovell were almost eager to be on a canoe themselves, though their orders were to wait. Their scientific minds were alit at the possibility of examining the Wentiko and discovering ways to combat this threat, eager to do their part. Howakan was, of course, almost relieved; his memories of having fought the Wentiko before lingered in the back of his mind like a wolf in shadow. However, his excitement at possibly dissecting one far outweighed his nerves, especially as he had the security of the soldiers' presence with him this time.

Lovell had never encountered an afflicted, Wentiko or not, and was therefore naïve to the threat they posed. He'd heard the stories, true enough; however, he could not properly quantify the fears of others in his analytical mind. As a near genius, he suffered the shared downfall of all exceptionally smart men: an almost total lack of empathy. He understood that these men had witnessed horrors he could not comprehend, but he could not put himself in their shoes and feel their fear with them, not without having the experience himself. The three men stood at the rail in intense silence, watching as *The Badger* and the canoes moved slowly toward the troubled shore.

Deggory, for his part, had not yet come face-to-face with a true Wentiko, nor with anyone afflicted, excepted the decayed remains Howakan had brought. He had deluded himself into thinking that it was a lesser monster than portrayed. The others knew an awakening was soon to arrive for the doctor and allowed him his delusions for now, as they kept him calm … and off the bottle.

The canoes scraped to a halt on the beach, jarring the men back into the moment, and the group disembarked, got into formation, and set off into the interior of the island. Chambers, Smith, and Nektosha had been first off and were on high alert, their ears straining for the slightest rustle of leaves or snap of a twig, their eyes raking the foliage for any sign of movement in the trees. It was difficult to see well as their plague masks restricted view at the best of times and the goggles were now fogging up with the excitement and exertion. They were heading for the main docks. However, they were having to cut across some rough ground and dense foliage to reach it; their planned path was to take them through the more sparsely wooded point to the harbor. At the overly cautious pace the soldiers set, it seemed to take them hours to make the trek. Most of the party had removed their masks, so they could see, hear, and breathe properly.

———◄(◉)►———

The unit moved in a single line snaking its way through the trees. The high tension eased slightly when they cleared the trees and could see across open ground to the fort and the harbor. The abandoned fort was just as they'd left it, a bit more overgrown perhaps, but obviously unused.

Sergeant Chambers motioned for the soldiers to come in close. He said in a loud whisper, "We better clear the fort first to reduce the odds of these things coming at our backs when we are busy at the harbor." He held up a hand for emphasis. "Keep quiet and be on your guard."

As he let his men over the open ground, he focused all his senses on the fort—any movement, any sound could make all the difference. As he got to the fort's gate, he motioned for the men to spread out and search the interior.

After a few minutes, the men had spread around the perimeter and looked into the open doorways.

One of the men said just loud enough to be heard across the courtyard, "It looks like there is nothing here."

The man next to him made an attempt to ease the tension. "Maybe they went on holiday."

That's when it happened. Three Wentiko burst from a watchtower doorway and grabbed the two men with a savage fury that stunned everyone. One faltering heartbeat passed before the muskets erupted, and all five bodies dropped to the ground.

"Take cover and reload!" Sargent Chambers yelled as he ran for an open doorway; his hand was already reaching for his powder flask.

He had instinctively already added the powder ball and wadding to the barrel and tamped the load down. He primed the pan of his musket and scanned the courtyard

A face appeared in the window in front of him. He launched himself back to see Nektosha already climbing through the opening.

"Hey! Good!" Chambers whispered and reached over for a quick handshake. He gave a quick look around through the window. "We are in the guardhouse. We are near the center of the south wall—this is the lowest point in the fort. This won't do. We need to get to high ground, so we can see what's going on. We need to get to the east blockhouse."

Chambers looked Nektosha in the eyes and saw iron determination looking back at him. He gave a nod and a smile, he then turned back to the open door quickly scanned the area and sprinted up the hill to the blockhouse. He barely slowed at the threshold and charged up the steps, all too aware of the noise his boots were making as he ascended. When they got to the top, there was a second's pause as they both realized that this was the same blockhouse they escaped from in the first attack. Chambers shook his head to clear his thoughts. He then pointed at Nektosha and then to the window facing out, and he went to the window facing in.

He looked back over his shoulder. "We have to get the main force in here. If those things show up in mass, we won't be able to hold them off."

They then heard the unmistakable hissing of the airship overhead. They both thrust their heads out the window and looked up.

"It looks like you are in the clear for now, as best as we can tell." Benson was leaning far over the front, obviously anchored to the airship at a point the two in the fort couldn't see. That was all he could say before the balloon passed over and banked away.

Chambers gave another quick look around the fort and motioned for Nektosha to follow, and he headed down the stairs. He noticed when he got to the door that Nektosha made no noise on the stairs, and his admiration for the young man grew.

He saw many of the soldiers peeking out from whatever cover they had taken. He motioned for them to follow him and pointed toward the docks. Some dubious at first, they each came out of hiding and fell in behind at a run as they headed down the hill to the docks.

They were about halfway there when the airship flew over.

Benson was yelling over the front. "We went to the harbor and looked, and the ships are … "

That was all they heard before the chuffing steam engine overtook the conversation. Chambers turned to see if anyone else heard what was being said, when he realized that they had bigger problems. A large pack of Wentiko was approaching through the side of the fort.

"Form ranks!" Chambers yelled, instantly realizing that his words did not escape the spun cotton filter in his mask. He pulled his mask away and roared the order again, sliding his musket from his back and moving to cover the men in the rear, who were quickly fanning out into formation. These men were well trained and had been handpicked for this mission. They moved into position with precision and skill.

"Ready! Aim! Fire!!" The muskets fired almost as one, and many of the creatures fell, but many still continued. The two men with the Greek fire backpacks advanced on either side. They sparked the wicks and began to spray fire toward the oncoming hoard. The man with the steam shooter took a step forward in the center and sent a cloud of acidic steam toward the approaching enemy. Chambers and the men strained to look past the fire, smoke, and steam. Their eyes were watering and vision blurring from all that had just been sent into the air in front of them, and they were anxious to see how the Wentiko would react to this.

The pack seemed to falter; something like fear shown in many of their still human faces. While they were focusing, the second pack attacked from the side and hit the men with a shock. The men had not had time to reload. They all reacted instantly. They brought their bayonets up and counterattacked with a mechanical precision of motion born of countless hours of training. There was no time to regroup or space to do anything else. All they could do was to keep stabbing into the faces and chests of the ravenous enemy. The two forces were closing in, constricting the abilities of the soldiers.

"The fire is going out!" came a cry from one of the men with backpacks. "We are running out of fuel!" The first pack was pushing forward again.

"Fall back! Fall back! We need some space!"

The unit began moving quickly backward. Not only did this give them some room to operate, but in following them, the two packs merged into one, so now they were only fighting on one front.

Chambers looked to Private Smith, who was now at his side. Smith had drawn his pistol and used it to pierce the chest of one of the more aggressive attackers.

"Oh! The repeaters!" Chambers said aloud as he drew his as well. Together they shot into the leading faces of the advancing hoard. As those in front fell, those behind them stumbled over the bodies, and the ravaging mass started to thin and falter. The soldiers did not need an order; they extended their bayonets and charged back into the madness.

The few feral creatures that remained did not stand a chance. The soldiers more than matched the fury of the attackers, some of whom continued to fight even though they were still in flames, and then it was over.

When Chambers looked up, Smith was walking away. It was soon clear that he was walking over to tend to the two fallen soldiers, those that had been caught unawares in the fort. They were both badly wounded with both gouges and bruises from the Wentiko, and though neither was dead, one was very close.

"Just lie still," he was saying as he pulled some precut bandages from the kit Deggory had given him.

Chambers reached Smith's side and gently laid a hand on his arm. "No, Douglas. You know as well as I that there's nothing to be done."

Impotent rage filled Smith's face for a brief moment as he stared at the bandage in his hand. Before the answer to his rage could form in his mind …

"There is more!" Nektosha called out, appearing behind them as if by magic.

Pointing across the dying men into the woods to the north, a faint noise could be heard, an odd stirring in the shadows. For a brief moment, no one moved. Then suddenly, *everyone* was on the move. It looked like the entire tree line had come to life and was running at them.

"To the docks!" Chamber's roared, though the rest of the force was already well ahead of them and headed out of the fort and down the hill.

It seemed to every man as if they were running in slow motion. With all the gear they were carrying, the panic setting into their minds, and their feet slipping and sliding on the sloping ground that was still wet with morning dew, they could sense more than hear that they were steadily being overtaken by the monstrous hoard. Those in the front turned to check on the rest of the party, causing a ripple effect of turning heads and clumsy footing. A handful of soldiers found uneven ground at this moment and fell into each other. Nektosha was the first to stop to help them up. It was then that the world seemed to explode.

The ground around and behind them heaved into the air all at once; all anyone could hear was a high-pitched ringing in their ears. Then it happened again. Mud and sod splattered the faces and bodies of the warriors. Some of them fell and lay still on the ground.

"The cannons! It's the cannons!!" Chambers yelled, though his voice was lost in the chaos.

The Badger and *The Daniel Webster* had both entered the harbor area and were firing over their heads.

This allowed them time to gather themselves and run to the docks. When they got there, John had positioned *The Badger* at the end of the longest pier, and *The Daniel Webster* was tying off to *The Badger*. Planks were being laid across, and men started to stream from the large ship across the smaller one and up the dock to join Chambers's struggling squad.

Chambers cried out, "Turn and set! Form ranks!"

Halting their retreat and refocusing themselves, the men turned and formed a wall of bayonets. For the first time, they got a real look at the huge wave of screaming, howling rage charging down on them.

"Fire!" came the shout from the deck of the *Webster*.

The world erupted again. This time instead of rending the

ground in between the soldiers and the afflicted, the mass at the front of the charging pack was struck. Bodies flew into the air, looking for an instant like leaves in the wind. Then the men from the ship sprinted past Chambers and his men, forming a new rank in front of them. Their weapons were fresh for the fight, and they fired a wall of lead into the remaining marauders, sending many to the ground while many more turned and fled back into the woods; some small sense of self-preservation was apparently still present in their afflicted minds. Those few that did not immediately flee were soon dispatched by the quickly forming army, as the second rank fired, and then they all charged with their bayonets to finish those that remained.

Typically, when an army routs an opponent, there is whooping and cheering, pats on the back, and glad-handing all around. Not this time. These men had finally seen the horror that they had been training for months to fight. Though they had been talking about little else for some time, no words could describe the living nightmare they had just experienced.

As the soldiers moved through the battlefield ending the screams and guttural wails of the wounded, everything faded to a sickly quiet. After a few very long seconds, the chuffing of Porter's airship could be heard. All eyes turned to the welcome interruption. Benson was leaning over the bow; he had a black flag over a white flag in one hand, and he was pointing to the north with the other.

"They're running!" was all he could say as the steam zeppelin traveled across the field, moving as much sideways as forward in the stiff wind.

However, that was all the troops needed to hear. Captain Hunter charged to the rail, his orders being echoed across the troops by his subordinate officers.

"All soldiers, get ashore! Get the other ship in here! Reload the cannons! As soon as those men are off, reposition *The Daniel Webster* to the other pier."

Moving as quickly as they could across the hastily laid planks, the men all assembled in the field in front of the harbor docks. The captain quickly organized the men to brace for the next wave; they got to their positions and held. They stood in frozen silence for many long minutes, each man hoping they were ready for the next onslaught ... that did not come.

When the men were ashore and the nerves had settled for a moment, Captain Hunter stood with his back to the fort and the rest of the island and said, "I need three platoons to begin sweeping around the coast to the west, as well as three platoons to do the same to the east. Six platoons will match pace and cover the center. The rest of the men will stay here and protect the docks and the ships. Chambers, your men will lead the advance to the west. Sergeant Sawyer, your men will lead the advance to the east. I will lead the company up the center. The airship is having trouble with the switching winds, so try to maintain contact across to the other units. We don't want anyone getting cut off. Be thorough—we do not need any surprises from behind."

Chambers led his men in the direction of the mission church, following the path they'd taken when they'd escaped. The majority of what they had seen on the island appeared untouched from the time that Chambers and his men had evacuated those many months ago. They could see from a distance that the same could not be said for the mission church. The windows had been boarded, the door barred, and the surrounding area cleared of brush and tree alike. Someone was taking refuge within, or they had been at one time. Chambers had stopped their party on the edge of the forest, not willing to lead his people out of the cover of the trees before he could ascertain whether the building was still inhabited or not. Or by what.

"Fan out, keep to the trees, surround the church. Every second man, keep your eyes to the woods. We could face attack from any direction," Chambers ordered.

He and Nektosha made the first approach to the front of the chapel turned fortress. The kept their weapons ready to shoot, Chambers working to move with the silence that seemed to be natural for Nektosha. It took a bit of time for them to find a peephole. Chambers took a few heartbeats to rally his courage, only to be rewarded with blackness from inside. He turned to the men on the perimeter; he pointed two fingers at two of the largest soldiers and then at the door. He then motioned for Nektoshe to stand ready at the other side of the door.

The men hit the door at a run, and the barrier was sundered on impact. The assailants scrambled back to brace for whatever might come out of the darkness.

They heard a weak voice from within: "Sergeant ... is that you?"

"What? Who goes there?"

"Private Jenkins, sir." The private who had been too fat to escape through the window on the day of the first attack was now much reduced, his uniform hanging on him like a boy dressed in his father's coat.

"Leeroy? Is that you?"

"Yes, Sergeant. There are others here as well."

Seven in all were holed up in the church: four adults, including Private Jenkins, and three children. None of them were in good shape. They all looked starved, dehydrated, and just plain exhausted.

"We have some ships at the docks; they can get you food and water and tend to your wounds. Wait! Are any if you infected?"

"No, sir. We are all clear."

"You can go with these men; they'll take you to safety." He pointed to the two soldiers who had destroyed the door. "Take them to the docks and catch up with us as soon as you can."

The two saluted and moved into the church to help carry the children, as the surviving adults were barely strong enough to stand themselves. Private Jenkins moved to shake the men's hands, ending with Sergeant Chambers. He pressed a small leather-bound book into his other hand. Chambers looked at it curiously for a moment, then back to Jenkins.

"It's a recordkeeping of sorts, of our time here, how we survived, and what we've discovered about the demons. Read it—it may help you."

Chambers nodded and stowed the book in his pack before gently ushering Jenkins to join the other survivors headed for the docks.

"We were starting to lose hope," one of the women was saying as they were led away.

"All right men, form up." Chambers was wasting no time. "You men, cover the coast and the tree line. We will cover the middle, and the other platoon will move toward the interior. We need to catch up and make contact with Hunter's men. Move out!"

They had only traveled a few minutes when they were hailed from the woods. It was a runner from Macomb's company.

"They routed some small group on the other beach, but all clear otherwise. How's by you?"

"We found some survivors in the church. We sent them back to the ships."

One of the men could be heard saying, "They looked pretty rough."

"Keep your voices down!" another man said.

With the size of the island and the number of men, communication was not as much of a problem as they had initially feared. Apparently, most of the surviving Wintiko had been taken out in the initial rush. Those that remained ended up being herded up the island to the northern shoreline where they were dispatched handily by the soldiers.

20:

THE MICHIGAN CAMPAIGN

O nce all of the forces had converged on the northern shore of Mackinac Island, the captain ordered an assembly, and the piper sounded the call. The men quickly fell into formation.

"Well done, men! We cleared this island much more handily than I had expected. However, make no mistake— this is a very small step in a much larger war. We will need to inspect each of you to be sure no one was injured or infected. Further, having now seen some of the difficulties our troops are having with the terrain and heavier gear, I am considering some alternate strategies for the main assault of the Mishka-Michigan peninsula.

"We will employ the same tactics as we return to the south end of this island. I want to be sure that there is no chance of infection left on the island. Take your time— check every thicket and rabbit hole. I will call assembly at the docks after I have considered our next move."

The soldiers dutifully checked every possible nook and

cranny on the patrol back, and the island was eventually declared clear. The oil lamps in Captain Hunter's planning room burned well past midnight, and often raised voices could be heard arguing passionately over some point or another. Try as they might, the soldiers at the watch fires could not make out what was being said.

It was just after dawn when the call to assemble rang out through the crisp clear morning. The soldiers were directed to form up by the docks.

General Macomb called out to his troops, "Good morning! We have decided to approach the mainland from the north with our main force. We will use the topography of the land to allow us to section this campaign into more manageable fields of endeavor. As many of you are no doubt now aware, this is very unlike fighting an organized force, as we are accustomed to—there is no central core or base to attack. Resistance can come from anywhere at any time and in any size. We will use the rivers to contain the fields of action and hopefully limit the numbers in any one conflict. We will work to drive them back onto themselves or into the sea if we can.

"However, having seen the difficulties of moving through the woods with the new weapons, I am changing the original point of attack. We have seen how these things can swarm unexpectedly; we have also seen that they are much less prone to retreat. Make no mistake—if we get overwhelmed, it could be the end not only for our forces but for the entire countryside.

"We need to take this in steps so we do not miss anything, so we need to isolate the northern tip of the

Mishka-Michigan mainland and move everything toward the north.

"Our landing point will be Grand Traverse Bay. We move across to the southeast to Sandy River, and we will follow that out to Sandy Bay. This will define our first line. Once we have cleared everything north of that line, we then will proceed and clear the west coast down to the next river and establish our line there. We will then move the line south, river by river, until we reach the southern area before reaching the most populated regions, where we will reassess the situation and our strategies."

Even though the battle-hardened captain was speaking in a calm, confident manner, the men could not miss nervous apprehension peeking through his typically iron façade. He was also giving all of the plan details to everyone. This was not his usual way of doing things. This could be taken as an indication that he felt that he may not survive the campaign, and it made the men nervous.

"We will prepare the ships tonight and plan to form up and begin in the morning. The terrain is unfamiliar and undeveloped. We need to make as much of the first day as we can. I am not too eager to spend many nights in the middle of the Wentiko." He paused, clearly trying to rid himself of that thought.

"Mr. Porter!" he called out suddenly. "Can you get that airship figured out or what?"

"Yes, sir," Rufus Porter said as the men cleared out around him, leaving him the lone man in a pool of emptiness within the ranks, "I apologize for today. We decided the only prudent course of action was to leave the battle and make adjustments. We have reduced the size of the wings and fins, as well as adding more ballast to the ship. This should add stability. The switching winds out here are a greater challenge than I had anticipated."

The captain leveled a hard gaze at the man to gauge how confident he was in what he was saying, "Good man, Porter; we will need every advantage we can get." After a brief pause, he added, "Also see what your team can do about making these new weapons easier to move around, and more effective. We need to be able to cover ground more efficiently and do more damage before fuel runs out."

"We will get right on that, sir," Porter replied, relieved that his airship's lack of effectiveness hadn't cost him his credibility.

"Further, we need you doctors to figure out precisely what this hell is and where it comes from. If we can't figure out how to stop or cure this madness, this will all be for naught."

Dr. Lovell stepped forward, looking gaunt and tired. "We were able to gather some fresher specimens, but with the liberal use of flamethrowers, there is not much useful material left to work with … We will do what we can." The last statement was in response to stern glare from the captain.

Captain Hunter returned his attention to the assembled troops. "Return to your ships. We will sail out as soon as we can to allow us time to set up properly in the bay. We don't know what we will find there.

John, I will have you take *The Badger* in first to scout for suitable landing sites."

"Yup, yup, Captain, I was thinking the same thing." John

made quick eye contact with Sergeant Chambers, Nektosha, Smith, and the infantrymen assigned to them. All nodded confirmation. They were ready to go.

Even before all the soldiers had finished loading themselves and their gear back onto the two larger ships, the crew of *The Badger* was already securing the last of the supplies, and Nektosha was up on the yardarm releasing the mainsail. Though the weather was relatively calm, the trip was not restful, for anyone.

The ships were like beehives. Everyone was buzzing around, excited about the early success, talking about how they did and how they were going to get them the next time. The captain finally had to send some officers around to order the soldiers to douse the lights to try and get some rest.

The next morning *The Badger* had already been into the Great Traverse Bay and found a likely docking location, as deep into the bay as they felt would be safe to take the larger ships. As they escorted the ships into the spot, they dropped the sounding line often to be sure depth was sufficient for the ships to make it in and out without running aground. The powerful steam engines could most likely get them off of any mud bank, but they did not want to take any chances. They finally found a spot where both of the ships could anchor and run a gangplank to the bank.

As the ships were being secured to the shore, Rufus Porter, Benson, and a couple men left the cluster of work tables that had been set up around the airship that had been tethered in a clearing nearby and made their tedious way through the organized chaos on the captain's ship.

"Sir? Sir!" Porter was anxious to redeem himself. "We have something to show you!" He was holding large canvas sack in front of him for the captain to see. "We have reduced the size of the flame pumps and the steam pumps by half. And reduced the diameter of the nozzle greatly. This gives a more focused stream and uses less fuel so it can more easily be carried by a single man on foot.

"In the first design, we were trying to hit them as a whole group, but targeting individuals allows for a much smaller system. Benson here was a great help. It turns out he is quite handy. Oh! Um … no offense intended, William."

Benson laughed. "None taken, sir." Benson was already strapping on the backpack and buckling the small bellows to his wrist just above his mechanical hand.

Porter moved quickly and used his ever-present cigar and a splash from a flask of whale oil to light the small pile of coals in the bottom chamber of the backpack.

"Now you see, Captain—he is able to draw the steam from the chamber and control the stream with ease. Once it heats up, I believe we will be able to show those nasty freaks a thing or two with this."

"Excellent," the Captain exclaimed. "How many do we have?"

"Oh." Porter flushed slightly. "Well, sir, this is the pro-totype, the only one for now. We will have to check with your ship's cooks and engineers to get some copper pots and hoses and such. The flame pumps are already one-man weapons; we just need to get the men to carry more fuel and use less of it. The smaller nozzle will make that easier."

Captain Hunter pondered for a long moment. "See how

many you can get done in a day. We will delay our advance, so we can have them ready. I will send some men to help you."

"Yes, sir!" Mr. Porter pulled his team aside. He was talking and pointing in a most emphatic manner for a moment. Then each of them hurried off on their own missions.

21:

THE ADVANCE

After one day, Porter, Benson, and their team managed to cobble together seven additional steam guns. Due to these results, Captain Hunter divided the troops into eight companies with one steam gun bellows and one flamethrower pump each. He also reorganized the companies so that each could function equally and independently.

The captain walked to the front of these eight companies, noting the nervousness on some of the men's faces and, worse, the arrogance on others. The men were all already in formation, ready to march out, but there was a buzz of noise permeating the ranks, a low hum of whispering and murmured voices as the men talked among themselves, if for nothing else but to fill the oppressive silence.

"All right, men!" The captain's voice pierced the tension of the gathered men and ended the murmuring and fidgeting. "We have taken an extra day to better prepare for this campaign, I trust that each of you have used the time for just that same purpose. We have redefined our organization somewhat; however, our tactics will be much the same.

"We will again have Chambers and his team in front as scouts, while the other companies will be in close communication, following right behind them. We will be marching in single file, so it will be imperative that we remain keenly aware of our flanks, and also be mindful of the company before and behind your own. As we will be defining our first line of separation, we will be marking our trail as we go.

"We will again do without the drums and try to move with as much stealth as we can. We would rather hear them before they hear us. Keep a keen eye out, and you can be sure, we will win this day!"

He then took a deep breath before bellowing out his order: "Forward, march!" This was echoed throughout the companies, though it was unnecessary, as all the men had been standing in silent anticipation.

Porter's steamship roared into the sky. Even though the wings and fins were now smaller, it somehow looked bigger and more impressive with its sleeker design, and a few men took a second or two as they marched to marvel at its ingenuity and beauty.

Chambers, Nektosha, Smith, and the twenty handpicked men assigned to them led the army east into the interior of the Mishka-Michigan territory. They had marched for about an hour before they encountered the first pack of Wentiko. There may have been twenty, though it was difficult to tell. They were crowded together looking like the twisted roots of an old oak tree and moving in a writhing mass like a barrel of eels.

However, Captain Hunter's plan worked remarkably well.

The second company, led by the captain, came up quickly to one side, with the third company immediately taking up the other. The men's months of training showed with the first rank taking a knee and firing their already prepared weapons, then promptly starting reloading as the second rank stepped between them and fired, then the third rank. The first rank, now reloaded, rose to fire again. It almost looked like a country dance. By the time the soldiers' minds emerged from the response that had been so hard-trained into them that it was an automatic sequence of actions, the pack of vile afflicted had fallen.

The captain was quick to call, "Hold!" striding forward and turning to the men and holding up a hand to forestall any further action or any cheers that may erupt.

"Quiet now, men. We have made enough noise for the moment. We will hold here for a moment and reload. I want to see if any others come as a result of the commotion."

After reloading, the men stood in silence for a moment. With a wave and a nod from the captain, Sergeant Chambers led his team forward, and the others fell into formation behind them. They made their way to the Cheboygan River and had to follow it to the south for a couple of miles to find a suitable crossing point. They then continued their trek southeast toward Sandy River.

The second encounter did not go as well. The attack struck without warning near the middle of the column, and several men fell before they could react. Many of the surrounding men were so startled that they overreacted, tangling up the response, the men frantically backstepping from the middle, hindering the actions of those in their way.

Then, at the worst moment, there was another attack toward the back of the line and from the other side. One of the soldiers bearing a flamethrower pump completely lost his head and fired into the heart of the fray, unintentionally setting three soldiers alight, who then were obliged to engage their attention in extinguishing themselves. This further disrupted the troop's fighting ability. The captain was now at the front and nose to nose with the mottled horrid faces of the disgusting creatures. He attempted to step back, putting some space between himself and the foaming, spittle-spraying mouths of the Wentiko. He was pinned into the branches of a tree. Just as he was thinking he was done for, the side of the lead beast's head exploded just as the one next to it had an arrow pierce its temple, the point coming out its opposite ear. He could see their expressions change as they fell before him. The smell of burning flesh filled his senses. He brought his musket butt up sharply to catch a third one under the chin with such force he saw its neck crack. He pushed himself off from the tree and bayoneted another in the chest. The sound of musket fire echoed from the trees. There was a period of chaos and pandemonium as the soldiers scrambled to form some semblance of a defensive posture while fending off the ravenous attacks.

The soldiers quickly rallied and began focusing on the centers of the two writhing masses, both much larger than anything they had encountered before. They appeared to be gaining the advantage and driving back the two onslaughts, when the third pack hit from the rear.

The screams of man and beast drowned out the crackling roar of musket fire for a moment. Soldiers and creatures alike were fighting like wild beasts, bayonets ripping the limbs from the Wentiko and teeth of the crazed once-human creatures rending the flesh of the soldiers.

The airship soared over the fray. Benson began deftly dropping grenades around the outside perimeter of the battle, destroying many of the less aggressive monsters in the backs and centers of their packs. This created a distraction as well and a momentary lull in the ferocity of the attack.

"FORM UP AND PUSH!" The voice of Sergeant Chambers thundered over the chaos.

The men pushed themselves into a rough formation, bayonets forming a thorny wall upon which many crazed Wentikos impaled themselves, being pushed from behind by the others. More creatures succumbed to thrusts to their heads from the second rank of soldiers. The men then began to make an organized push, trampling over the bodies of the fallen creatures. As the beasts were being driven backward, many lost their footing in the foliage lining the path and fell back onto the ones trying to charge in from behind them.

"KEEP PUSHING FORWARD!" Chambers's voice was heard again over the battle.

"Let none escape!" the captain's voice was strained almost to the limit, having been in the center of the mob, his orders almost lost to the cacophony surrounding him.

The waves of hell that had threatened to overwhelm the company began to fall and then dissipated to a few individuals. The men surged forward and were on the remaining creatures with a ferocity, quickly destroying the last remains of the horde.

Relief and shock flooded through the men, causing more than one to paint the surrounding foliage with that morning's rations. They were relieved that they were alive and shocked that they'd almost died; those who had been so cocky that morning were the worse off for it now. The survivors took stock of the situation they were left with. Twelve men were dead. Nine more were wounded; four of these were considered at risk of infection. All nine wounded had to be escorted back to the ships. After a quick count, it was determined that three more men were missing and presumed to have fled.

When they examined the fallen Wentiko, they found that most of them were once Indians. They were determined to be of the Ottawa people, based on their location and the remnants of their clothing.

The captain gathered the survivors together and spoke slowly, clearly, and as loudly as he dared. "We set out with two hundred men; we just lost 10 percent of our force, and some very fine soldiers they were. We cannot win if we cannot do better. And winning is our only option. If we fail, the whole country will fall, and possibly the whole of mankind. We will have to do better. We will put twenty paces between the companies to allow a better opportunity to react to an attack and gain positional advantage. We cannot get bottled up like that again. The howling that warned us of previous attacks did not happen this time. Muskets are to be carried in hand, not on the shoulder, with the bayonets facing straight out on all sides of each company."

His voice dropped in volume and rose in intensity. "Go now! Form up! We don't want to be caught bunched together like this."

As they began to march forward again, the airship crossed overhead and Benson made another pinpoint drop, nearly hitting Nektosha on the head. This caused the entire company to snap into full alert. It was a small ballast rock with a note tied to it. The captain saw the drop and joined them as they opened it.

We know what to look for now! We saw the last attack happen from up here. We hope to be able to give you some warning. Mr. Porter says we should not stay too close, so we do not draw them to you. Rather, we will try to spot them and direct you to them.

Captain Hunter, Sergeant Chambers, and Nektosha read the note; together, they all looked up to the circling airship and nodded their approval.

The way that Porter, Benson, and crew decided to let them know where the Wentiko where located was quite excellent. They indicated the location by dropping a grenade or two into the heart of the pack. Often the pack would be all but finished when the infantrymen arrived.

Eventually they successfully found Sandy River and followed it to the bay. Captain Hunter gathered the men. "This is where we split up. We are running damn short on men, so we have to make some adjustments.

"Chambers, you take your men and backtrack to the Cheboygan River. I need to be sure our flank is secure, and I am betting that you and your men can handle the job better than anyone.

"I will signal Porter and his steamship that they are to stay with the main force while we flush these buggers out to the north. We will have them fly down to you and let you know when we reach the north end of the river, and we will then clear the eastern side and meet back at the ships."

Captain Hunter swept a pointed finger across his troops, pointed straight up, drew a circle in the air, and pointed northward, and the men fell into formation as they marched off. Each man wore a face of grim determination as their past arrogance was now wiped from their expressions.

Sergeant Chambers, Private Smith, Nektosha, and the twenty men assigned to them saluted and wished them luck as they passed.

Chambers watched the departure for only a moment before turning to address his men. "We will use a similar tactic as we did on our march over here. We will form squads of five men and keep these squads about twenty paces apart. At even a thought of anything that might be trouble, speak out, and we will all stop until we figure out if there is a threat." He paused for a moment. "I feel like someone is watching us here, so let's move out."

They followed the tree line along the Sandy River back to the northwest. Several times the hushed call of "Hold. Hold!" was raised. Once for a startled raccoon that had managed to escape the devastation of the ravaging horde only to meet its end on the bayonet of one of the soldiers. Most of the time the disturbance came from across the river, and whatever made the noise could be heard retreating into the underbrush.

The marked trail led them back to where they had crossed the big river. There was an almost tangible moment of relief as they emerged from the trees and could see clear, empty space around them.

"We will take a ten-minute pause here before we move back to the gap between the rivers. I believe that is the point that may be breached and needs most to be defended."

Several men nodded and mumbled in agreement, and the men fell out of formation. Some went to fill their canteens, some sat on the riverbank, some went to relieve themselves in the woods. It was one of these men who was the first to fall.

He did not even have a chance to cry out. The only sound that gave away the attack was a dull thud and the sick sound of rending flesh. A wall of Wentiko came from the shadows of the tree line and charged the soldiers.

Many of the soldiers were already standing guard, none completely at ease in the open, and fired into the advance. This had a definite effect, but it was clear that it would not be enough.

Sergeant Chambers quickly surveyed the situation, and his thunderous voice cried out above the howls of the afflicted. "Fall back! Fall back!! Get away from the trees!"

The men formed a line along the water's edge. Some of the men had no muskets, as they had been left on the beach; some of the soldiers were already being eaten on that same beach. The remaining men were quickly driven into the rushing, cold water of the river. They retreated until they were hip deep, except for one man, who hesitated, turning to grab his weapon from the ground. He was grabbed by a few of the creatures and savagely eaten while the rest of the men impotently watched. The crazed marauders stopped at the water's edge, their wild eyes fixed on their intended prey. The men could not retreat any farther—the river was too deep and swift, and with the weight of their gear and boots, they would quickly sink. They could not reload their muskets in the water either. The wind was in their faces, so the steam and flame weapons would do no good. They could smell the diseased creatures, mixed with the gore and bile of their own fallen comrades, and do nothing but stand there.

22:

A TALK WITH PRIVATE JENKINS

In an effort to get a clearer picture, it was decided to interview the survivors who had been trapped on Mackinac. Dr. Lovel, Dr. Periwinkle, and Howakan were appointed to conduct these interviews. They decided that the best information would come from Private Leeroy Jenkins, and they were not wrong. He, however, as a result of his ordeal, was a changed man. Speaking of it was difficult for him, to say the least. They first had to find him. He had refused to go to the interior of the ship, always staying on the top deck near the rail and always seeming as if he were ready to jump off at any moment.

They decided to walk him off the ship all together and talk to him at a quiet spot up the shore. This helped, but it still took some time and coaxing to get him talking. His demeanor became remarkably darker when he finally decided to speak of what had happened.

"It … It was sh-sh-shortly after the f-f-first attacks there was, um … this calm after the st-storm."

He tried to laugh and failed; his mouth had gone dry. Deggory offered him his flask, but Howakan quietly pushed it away.

"We de-decided to ssssee what … what was hap-happening. There was just a handful of us. We um … we went to see how many of th-those those thhhhings … " The interview ground to a halt as Private Jenkins stopped talking and just stared at his boots.

"Leeroy, is it?" asked Howakan. "Yes, Leeroy, take a moment." He dipped a rag in a puddle and placed it on the soldier's forehead. This definitely helped, and his focus seemed to sharpen.

"You are here with us, and we are here with you. Try to detach yourself from the situation. Try telling us as if it happened to someone else. Take a few deep breaths and try again to tell us what happened."

After staring into each of their faces for a moment, Private Jenkins continued his story.

"We wanted to … to see what we were up against, and if there were any other survivors." He took the rag from Howakan and wiped his own face and began wringing the rag in his hands. "We fought back a few small groups of those things. God, what ARE those things?"

"We call them Wentiko, and we are working to determine what they are exactly," Dr. Lovell told him as Howakan took another cloth and dabbed the cold sweat from Leeroy's brow.

Dr. Periwinkle remembered that he had his flask in his hand and with a trembling hand took a small sip from it.

Jenkins continued, "We found the ship. We found the

ship that brought them here." He shuddered and began breathing heavier. "It was terrible. Most of the top part was just burnt up. We searched the whole thing. Most of the ship was empty, but not the hold. Oh God, NOT THE HOLD."

Another pause. "We went down into the hold, and there was a bunch of those things. I don't know how many ... They were quiet at first, just sitting around. Then somebody, I think it was Barney, just yelled out *my* name and charged in ... like a madman, or a man possessed. He ... he woke them all up!!! It was crazy. I ... I ... I d-d-don't know how long we fought, but we just *fought*. They kept coming. and we kept fighting, throwing everything we had at them, and they kept coming. Then, when it was over, we stood there and stared at each other for a while. I remember we cheered a bit ... just because we were alive, I guess.

"Then we reckoned to search the rest of the ship. We found one survivor. He was a cook's mate. He said he saw it all coming. He saw things, the people, they were all getting really odd, acting strangely, so he locked himself into the pantry. He said it started with the cook when he got bit by a nasty rat. He saw it happen. He said the rat was diseased ... and worse. It was all covered in patches of white and yellow fuzz, and it had foam on its face, and there was a smell of sulfur or something."

Deggory made some kind of wheezing noise from the back of his throat. The two other learned men paused and turned to look. Dr. Periwinkle had turned white as a ghost and was staring wide-eyed into a tree trunk; he downed his entire flask in one go, attempting to steady his nerves.

Jenkins continued his story. "The kid told me that the

rat's face just exploded all over the cook's."

Dr. Deggory Periwinkle's legs just gave out, and he fell with an audible impact to his knees. "Oh my God. Oh my God, no." He just kept repeating, "No, No, No, No." Deggory's ears were ringing. His eyes could not focus. He got to his feet and stumbled toward the trees; he could feel his ability for conscious thought slipping away.

⸺ ⸺ ◈ ⸺ ⸺

When Deggory came to, he had to fight for awareness for a long time; he felt very heavy, and one side of his face was colder than the other. He found he was shivering uncontrollably, and he was squeezing something soft and grainy in his hand. Over and over his hand opened and closed, squeezing, releasing, squeezing again. He had to force himself to open his eyes. He discovered his hand was just in front of his face. Dirt. He was lying in wet dirt and clawing at the mud with his hand. What had happened to him? What had brought him to this? He could feel his consciousness slipping away again; his ears were ringing, and the blackness was closing in, and he fought with a will to stay awake.

"I am a doctor. I am Dr. Deggory Periwinkle. I cannot let myself be defeated like this. I must recover from this and return to my office. My office? No, wait ... Where am I? What has happened to me?"

He forced his eyes open. "I am in the woods. I can see that. I must get up."

He willed his heavy arms and legs to move. After some

great effort and nausea, he was on all fours. He then brought one foot under himself and pushed himself upright, relying heavily on a nearby branch. It took a long while for him to stabilize his body and his mind.

He looked around. "There is nothing familiar, trees, bushes ... There is not much light either," he said to himself. It was with a growing sense of alarm that he realized he didn't know if it was dusk or dawn. He didn't know when the last time was he ate or drank. Another battle with nausea and he was almost felled like a tree.

"Walk, just walk. I need to eat. I need to get back to ... to ... I need to figure out where I am."

As he walked, he realized it was getting darker, which at least answered that question. He was unable to recall anything about what had brought him to this point. He was keenly aware, however, that he did not want to be alone in the woods at night.

He had no idea how many hours he walked, or in what direction, before he passed out again.

⟫⟩(⟨(◖)⟩)⟨⟪

When he came to, he was looking into the face of Dr. Lovell.

"Yes." He thought out loud, "I know this man. Dr. Lovell from Washington."

Dr. Lovell yelled, almost directly in his face, "He is awake!"

He heard conversation from the other room ... only then

realizing he was in a room, in a bed. He could recognize his friend Howakan's voice

"I am coming."

"Hello, Deggory! How are you feeling?"

Deggory was slow to respond; he did not know—he could barely feel—anything. When he finally spoke, it was only to ask, "Hey, who gave you the black eye?"

Howakan gave a warm smile. "You did, my friend, just before you ran away."

"What?! Why would I do that?"

Dr. Lovell answered, "It is a classic hysterical response, a form of shock. Exacerbated by drinking an excessive amount of whisky on an empty stomach. So, we will talk no more for now; first, you must eat." His tone held no allowance for argument.

Some warm chicken broth was brought in, and it was not until he started eating that Deggory realized how hungry he was.

"Slowly," said Howakan, who was now sitting in a chair beside the bed.

As Deggory felt the warmth of the soup spread through his body, he started to remember where he was and what had brought him to this point; by now though, he was too tired to react. He was too weak to panic. Too hungry to do anything but eat his soup. The clinking of his spoon against the bowl seemed to be the only sound there was.

After Howakan had brought him a couple more bowls of soup and some fresh bread, he finally talked.

"So, this whole mess, all of this … "

"Was *not* your fault," Howakan interrupted. A long

silence followed, only broken by a faint creaking as some waves rocked the ship.

Howakan leaned over and put his hand on Diggory's shoulder. "While you were missing, we went through your papers to see if we could find a clue to explain what had happened to you."

"We found your research. The rats ..." Howakan gently increased the strength of his hold on his friend's shoulder. "The rats must have been carrying some disease, maybe rabies. Dr. Lovell and I agree that your work was sound. It shows great promise. This started with whatever the two rats already had."

Howakan was speaking very carefully and methodically. It was clear that he had planned out what he was going to say and how he was going to say it.

Deggory closed his eyes and slowly handed the empty soup bowl back to Howakan.

"Have you found a way to fix it?" Deggory asked weakly.

"No, we are going to need your help with that. There are some gaps in the information. It would help to know which treatment that specimen received." Dr. Lovell was leaning in the doorway.

"I need to get up."

"You need to rest!" they answered together.

Dr. Lovell then said, "You were almost dead when we found you."

Deggory stared into each of their faces then asked, "Can you bring me my papers here, so I can start puzzling this out?"

"I will be right back." Dr. Lovell smiled and turned, and his footsteps could be heard fading down the passageway.

Deggory sat himself up in bed, though he chafed at still being confined therein, and opened the much-used log book of Private Jenkins that Dr. Lovell had pressed into his hand when he'd brought Deggory's research papers. The log book had been passed to Dr. Lovell by Sergeant Chambers. The private had seemed adamant that they read the ledger immediately, and Deggory was curious as to what within could be so important. Opening to the first page yielded a mess of scribbled-out lines and ink blots that were completely illegible. The second was more of the same. The third, however, began:

Log entry 1: September 17, 1834

I'm not sure why I'm writing this. I guess it needs to be documented; this is an unusual new threat, these demons. That's what Private Clinton called them, and I can't say he was far off the mark. I am Private Leeroy Jenkins and I ~~am~~ was stationed at the Fort on Mackinac Island. I'd been right by the northwest blockhouse when these demons came rushing through the main gate. I heard Sergeant Chambers tell the men standing around him to run, and I joined them. Unfortunately, the way out was too narrow for me to go through, so I had to run for the storehouse gate, meeting Private Eric Clinton and his wife, Allie, at the top of the storehouse stairwell on my way. We locked ourselves in there real tight for a while. When we finally opened the door, however, we discovered that the fort was now deserted. Not a soul, living or damned, remained in the area. It was eerie, and though I still had a bone-deep desire to flee, that the Clintons shared, we still went back into the storehouse and collected as much food and munitions as we could easily carry. While there, we were met by young Cadet Oliver Murphy, who gathered his own provisions before joining us. We made for the mission church and, upon arriving, found it likewise deserted. We were able to rig up some fortifications with the pews, and I pray the demons do not find us.

Log entry 2: September 22, 1834

We were able to rescue a family of Indians today. We'd had to go back to the fort to get more supplies; what we had barely lasted us these past five days. It was fortunate that it was on our way to the fort that we happened upon the party of Indians fighting off a pair of demons. They'd appeared to have already lost three members of their party as we arrived and were swiftly losing the battle against the horrid creatures. This was due in no small part to the fact that the three men were having to protect the three women, one of them heavy with child. We were able to shoot the two demons before they became aware of our presence and brought the Indians with us to the fort for supplies, and thence back here, to the mission church. I say it was fortunate that we encountered them on the way to the fort as one of the gentlemen had a sled with him. The sled had been carrying his injured father; however, he was ... the demons had ...

Yes, well, we were able to use the empty sled to tote far more provisions back to the mission church than expected. With each person also carrying a pack of supplies themselves, we were able to bring along enough to last us a good while. There are veritable mountains of dried foodstuffs and munitions still at the fort; however, we've too few men available to us to be able to stay at the fort without risk, even with the addition of our Indian friends. The mission church has a solid wood door that is easily fortified, and the bell tower acts as an excellent lookout station.

Log entry 3: September 27, 1834

We are now stranded on this island. The ships in the harbor were all burned to the waterline last night. We could easily see the flames from the mission church, though we couldn't risk going out at night to discover their purpose. Today we found every boat in the harbor destroyed. I fear all is lost.

Log entry 4: October 15, 1834

It is getting colder—in the coming days, we will have to make several forays to the fort to gather enough supplies to last us the winter. This is dangerous, of course—the longer we are out in the wilds, the more likely for demons to find us. However, the supplies are needed. Zintkala finally had her baby, and we had to fight off five demons who heard mother's and child's birthing cries and tried to attack. Our fortifications held up well, though we lost a goodly amount of ammunition to the trees and scrub around the mission church. The men and I are going out tomorrow to clear out the area in a wide berth around the church, so as to eliminate the cover for the demons. The women will be focused solely on the new babe, ensuring that its every need is taken care of immediately. Newborns cry often and loud, something we cannot afford to occur when the men are otherwise occupied. This child is like to be spoiled rotten, but we'd all rather it spoiled than in the belly of a demon, and us along with it.

Log entry 5: October 17, 1834

The clearing is completed. It was back-breaking labor, and one of the trees proved particularly troublesome, as felling trees while maintaining silence is no easy feat. Thinking back on the attack on the day of little Wahya's birth, the demons do appear to have some rudimentary intelligence. A few of those who were once soldiers were still holding their rifles, though they used them more like clubs than any sort of useful weapon, beating them upon the walls and door of the mission church. They also would not just attack mindlessly from the woods. They used the scrub and trees for cover, darting in and bolting out before we could get a shot off. The bell tower proved a godsend as Cadet Murphy, a crack shot if ever I saw one, was able to fell four of the five from on high. The last was shot by Ma-Cha with an arrow through the eye socket, not something I'd ever wanted to witness, especially at such a close range. We'd also had to wait for most of the day to clear the bodies, as every one of them had burst open upon death and emitted this mist dust, that we all knew to stay far away from. I could not say how we knew to stay away; some deep internal voice screamed from the back of our minds to not go near.

Log entry 6: October 20, 1834

I've noticed more curiosities of the demons. We were at the fort, on our third trip gathering the winter supplies. I was in the lookout post this time, as we rotate the duty of lookout, and witnessed the demons tracking a deer. They worked together, as a pack of wolves might work to fell the same deer. The animal was able to escape, and when it did so, the demons set to shrieking at each other. However, they did not attack one another as I expected them to. It seems they understand, on some level, their own mortality. It is quite interesting, and were I of a scientific mind, I'd rather like to examine it further. If I was guaranteed not to die in my observations.

Log entry 7: October 31, 1834

Today was All Hallows' Eve, traditionally a day when the spirits of the dead are said to walk among the living. Given that these demons have been walking for far longer than that, I'm inclined to believe that the veil between worlds is not so much thin as nonexistent. Oddly enough, we saw no demons today. It has happened before—we'd go days without seeing a single one, though today seems all the more ominous for it. Still, we carved turnips and pumpkins into jack o' lanterns and set them in the bell tower to ward off any additional evil spirits.

Log entry 8: February 13, 1835

Oh, dear Lord! My thoughts are racing through my head like a herd of buffalo! This is amazingly terrible, dangerously fortunate, wonderfully perilous. I feel I could run seven times round the island. All right, Leeroy, get yourself together, lad. I need to get this written down before all these thoughts make their way out of my head. We caught one! We caught a demon! Alive!! Two of our Indian friends, Ma-Cha and Cho-Ho, were exploring the lookout post. It's nothing more than a small tower near the beach, but it made for a reliable vantage point. They were trying to discover if it could be used to signal passing ships, as the ice of the lakes was starting to crack. While there, they were set upon by a demon, and managed to trap the thing inside the tower! They rigged the door closed with rope and a brace of timbers and assure me that it is secure. I'm not sure what we're going to do with the demon, but we can at least safely study the creature to figure out how best to fight others. Things may be finally taking a turn for the better!

23:

MOCCASINS ON THE SHORE

"Dam, sir!" one of the soldiers shouted over the howling Wentiko and rushing river.

"Damn is right," Chambers replied.

"No, sir, a dam! Ahead!" The soldier pointed upriver where a sizeable part of a beaver dam had broken free and was floating right toward them.

Chambers looked over and saw it. "Inconceivable! Use your butts!"

"What, sir?!"

Chambers scoffed at himself, then shouted, "Your musket butts! Push the dam away with the butts of your muskets."

"Yes, sir!"

The retreat into the river had left the men standing in a relatively straight line. So, when the mass of logs and branches hit the first, it carried him back into the next and so on until four men were sliding down river toward the rest. Then five, then six men. Finally, there was enough men fighting the forces to gain some slight advantage and start to move the mass sideways spinning out into the river.

However, in the struggle, Nektosha and one of the soldiers had become ensnared in the branches and were now a part of the tangle that was floating down the river.

"Get on top of it!" Nektosha yelled as he fought to keep his head above water.

The soldier let go of his musket, reached up, and started to pull himself higher. The shift in weight caused the dam to roll, plunging Nektosha underwater again. Fortunately, the soldier saw this and moved back down into the river. He then worked his way around to the opposite side, balancing the spinning mass.

"I think I'm set; let's try again."

As they moved up, the already broken dam fell apart and became nothing more than a bunch of floating logs and branches.

"Swim for the shore," Nektosha called as he pushed off from the log he was holding and swam back toward the riverbank.

As soon as he was in shallow enough water to stand, the young brave stood up and looked for the soldier. He had a good-size branch under his arms and was kicking his way to the bank.

Nektosha could see that he would reach the bank quite a ways downriver from where he was. He could also see that they had already drifted around a bend and were out of sight and sound of the soldiers and the howling mass of Wentiko. He swiftly turned and waded up to dry land. He then ran down to meet the soldier and help him get safely ashore.

They quickly and quietly made sure they were not injured and took an assessment of their situation.

"We need to go back and see if we can help the others," Nektosha said as the soldier collapsed to sit on the bank and emptied the water from his boots.

"I lost my musket." The soldier was checking himself. "It had my bayonet on it, and all of my powder is wet anyway."

"I still have this," Nektosha said, pulling his bow from across his shoulder and checking the string. "Good, and, let me see, three arrows and my knife. We can use my knife to make a spear for you, so we both have weapons. It is still not a lot though."

As he turned to go, he nearly turned his ankle on a rock.

"Rocks! Yes, we can use the rocks!" the soldier exclaimed. He started to grab fist-size rocks from the riverbank. He quickly realized he would not be able to carry more than a few. He paused only for a moment; then he dropped the rocks and started taking off his jacket. "I can make a pouch out of this!" he said, regaining some hope.

"Good, you work on that, and I will make a spear"

After just a few minutes, they had buttoned the jacket around the new stout spear, filled the body cavity with rocks, and were carrying it between them up the tree line.

Where possible the traveled side by side so they could talk.

"We will want to get behind the enemy so we can divide their attention." Nektosha was clearly trying to think like Sergeant Chambers. "It looks like there's a good place to cut in up there."

The two did not end up talking much; they knew what

they were going to do and that the likely outcome was not good. They could hear the scuffling and whooping in front of them, and they slowed their movement so they would not be heard and turned to angle their approach so that they would come up from directly behind the enemy. The smell of the horde was disgusting, like rotten meat and human waste.

"Wow." The soldier coughed, trying to avoid breathing through his nose. "Well, we know we are coming in from downwind—that's a good thing."

Nektosha nodded in agreement.

As they got close, they would stop and listen from time to time to be sure there were no others wandering separate from the pack. They found a likely spot to set up behind a large fallen tree that offered at least some cover. They placed the bundle on the ground and unbuttoned the jacket to spare the noise of pouring the rocks out of it.

Nektosha leaned his bow against the tree. "We can use the rocks first, try to hit the ones on the far side, maybe we can cause some confusion."

They stared at each other for a second.

"Here we go," the soldier said with a hard resolve in his voice.

They threw at the same time; the rocks arced over the clear space between them. The soldier's rock flew over the whole pack, landing with a splat just at the water's edge. Nekoosa's rock hit one of the ones in the middle in the middle of the back. It screamed and collapsed. This gave them the moment of confusion they were hoping for. As the wild monsters looked vacantly at the rock that had landed in front of them and their fallen member, the next rocks were already in the air. This time the brave and the soldier had found their range and the one who was front center turned to look just in time to have his chest implode from Nektosha's rock. Another had the side of his head crushed in at the same time.

"One more rock is all we're going to get."

They both already had a rock in hand, and they threw together at the Wentiko closest to them. The pack had turned and was quickly closing the distance between them. They grabbed the spear and the bow, and Nektosha started moving backward as he nocked his arrow. He pierced the chest of one of them, but it did not appear to notice that it had been shot.

As Nektosha was nocking his second arrow, he got tangled in the twisted roots and fell with a *whump* on his back. The wind had been knocked out of him. He could not breathe! He could only make an odd *huunnh* sound when he tried. He looked over just in time to see the soldier get his face bitten into by one of those things. Both the soldier's hands were being held in the vice-like grip of the disgusting creature. They looked like some macabre version of a kissing couple. His panic doubled. He looked up to see the crazed eyes of a wild man bearing down on him.

Then its head flew off to the side. The headless body dropped to the ground to reveal Douglas Smith's bloodied but smiling face looking down at him. A wall of flame erupted behind him as a couple more screaming Wentiko were silenced.

Smith extended a hand and pulled Nektosha to his feet.

This helped him get his breathing back in order again.

"Well done! Well done indeed!" It was Sergeant Chambers. "You broke the siege. Once you two turned them around, we were able to close in and regain solid ground."

Nektosha looked over at his fallen comrade, sadness in his eyes.

"Jaxon did not make it. I'm truly sorry, son, but he fought bravely, and he will be remembered as a hero."

They had to turn their backs and walk away.

"We need to assess our situation. Check all of your weapons get them in working order. Check your powder to see if it is still useable. Do this as quietly as possible and keep your eyes and ears open."

They formed up for the march back down the path. They did not march far before Sergeant Chambers ordered a rest period. The men were exhausted and would be of no good use in a fight. The remains of the company set up a quick camp; half stood watch while half tried to rest, sleeping with their loaded muskets beside them, and they just lay down in full uniform and gear.

This ended just before dawn by a flock of birds that had been startled into flight from a nearby tree. Every man was so skittish that they jumped into ready positions almost instantly. After a tense moment, Chambers used hand signals to deploy the company in three groups into the woods to investigate. After a few minutes, they were reasonably sure that there was no threat to them at the moment. Chambers signaled for the men to return to the clearing where they had slept.

Only nine of the remaining twenty-two men had dry

powder. Nektosha was able to recover some arrows from the site of the earlier retreat into the river; he now had five arrows available. The powder was redistributed among all the soldiers. The flame gun and the steam gun were still functional and needed only minor repairs.

"We need to track back along the line again and hope that a pack like that did not slip through to the back of the main force." Chambers could see the fatigue and the resolve of the men under his charge. "Men, I know this is the toughest thing we have ever done. It is probably the toughest thing that anyone has ever done, but we have to do it. And I have to say I could not have found any better men to have at my side through this."

"Yes, sir!" came from many at once along with a quiet "Hurrah!" of approval.

The men quickly fell into the formation that had become so familiar; the company headed back down the line.

They had marched about half a day when they heard a familiar sound coming from the north. The whooping and screaming of another pack that was clearly headed right for them. The forest was thinner here, so they could see them coming. The galloping mass of rage was even larger than the pack that had driven them into the river. They were running deftly through the trees at an amazing speed. The large pack compressed in on itself as the front runners slowed and straightened up.

"FIRE!" Chambers's yell echoed through the trees.

Having had some warning this time, the company had moved quickly into formation, and when the hellish horde came into range, they were met with a full volley of musket fire followed by a wall of steam and flame. Gun smoke, steam, and oil fumes filled the air, obstructing all view of the enemy.

Chambers did not wait. "Charge! Charge! Charge!"

Without hesitation, the men extended their muskets, leaned forward, and advanced into the sulfurous cloud. The mass of Wentiko met a line of bayonets as solid as a stone wall. Then the soldiers saw flashes behind the pack and heard several deep booms. The steam gun and the flame gun closed in from the ends of the pack, further confining the movements of the Wentiko. The infantry drove resolutely into the first line; the enemy was contained and dispatched, and the end of the battle was achieved.

It was only then that they heard the *chuffing* of the airship as it dived down to pass directly overhead.

Rufus Porter shouted, "Well done, men! Great stroke of luck that we … " *Chuff*, *chuff*, *chuff* … and the airship climbed and banked and disappeared over the treetops.

"Reload and fall in on the trail, men," Chambers said as loud as he dared. "Keep a keen eye on our perimeter."

The airship circled around again, and Chambers had to dance out of the way to avoid being hit by the message rock Benson threw down.

Chambers read the note aloud, as many of the men gathered in close to hear.

"I was saying it was a great stroke of luck that we ran into you! We had separated this pack from the battle in the north and were herding them away, hopefully into a river or something. That was not working until we drove them into you. Again, I say well done to you and your men!"

He looked up to see the airshipmen nodding and smiling.

"Look out!" Benson called, as the airship drifted over head, and another rock was dropped, this time landing several feet from the crowd of soldiers. The rock was quickly passed to Sergeant Chambers.

"The news from the main force is good. they have all but completed the task of clearing the area. They are finding that many of the Wentiko were previously slain, apparently by the Native population. If you have matters in hand here, we are going to see if we can find these Natives and have them join us, for our best interest and theirs. Keep up the fine work!"

After reading this, Chambers looked at the faces of his men, and they were all nodding confidently.

Chambers looked up, saluted, and waved the airship away. Only a few hours had passed before Captain Hunter and the rest of the men met back up with Chambers and his company. The march back to the ships seemed incredibly short indeed. They encountered no more Wentiko, and spirits were high. Sergeant Chambers had been ordered to march alongside the captain so he could give a report of his recent activity. He was glad of this, as it gave him a chance to hear details of what they had encountered.

After giving his report, Chambers asked, "Sir, how did things go for you?"

"Better than expected, Porter had that flying steamship working like clockwork, most of the time. He was able to spot most of the enemy early enough for us to dictate the conditions of the encounter. We did lose a few men, but far less than I had feared. The natives had already done a fine job of thinning out the packs. We were able to move the other end of our line much farther south than we had originally planned."

"Great news, sir." Chambers was brightening up. "Benson dropped us a note that said that they were flying out to recruit those Natives."

"Yes, we can see by their results that they would be a valuable addition. Though we do not have a clear picture of their numbers, we need every bit of help we can get. I had hoped to recruit more militia by now, but most of the population have either fled or are dead."

Sergeant Chambers and John were included in the planning meeting that night.

"We have again done well, men. The new weapons and revised tactics have served us well. We also cannot undervalue our unknown allies in the Native population. Without them taking the fight out of the enemy before our arrival, I fear we might be having an entirely different conversation. However, we must push on. We will move the ships overnight to the southern end of Lake Michigan and advance to the east to form a new southern line to Detroit where, I pray, we can gather some more men."

The captain paused, looking at the moment not like the commander in charge but like a tired soldier with too few options. "John. I need you to take *The Badger* around to Detroit and meet us there. If you get there before us, I ask you to rally the people there and get us some more fighters. I will leave Sawyer and his men to guard the existing line instead of Chambers, as they have seen less hard action and are fresher men for it."

It took a full day for the ships to steam to the southern shore of the lake. This allowed the men to spend a full day and two nights on the ships. The great benefit of getting clean, dry clothes, a hot meal, and two solid nights' sleep on a real bunk renewed the men like nothing else could. The ships were still getting docked when the sun came up, and this allowed a little extra time in the morning for a hearty breakfast before the captain called assembly.

"Stay ready, men; we will drive them hard, but we can expect to take a minimum of three days to reach our first goal of Detroit. Be sure your weapons are loaded and at the ready at all times."

The call to march was echoed through the ranks, and the men moved out.

The trek across to Detroit was considerably easier than the earlier cross-country march. Having clearer roads meant that the men could move easier and that there were far fewer places for the Wentiko to hide. When the few that were encountered came charging from the brush, the men in the front ranks would usually dispatch them before the men in the back knew that there was an issue. After two days on the road, the captain called a halt as he heard the familiar chuffing of Rufus Porter's airship approaching just over the treetops.

A message rock was dropped at Captain Hunter's feet.

"We found the Native population. They said that they can send thirty warriors to help. They are running down the coast of Lake Huron and should be in Detroit soon."

24:

MUCH-NEEDED ALLIES

John did indeed reach Detroit before the troops and was able to get the word moving through the town that the army was coming and that more men were needed for the cause. When the company arrived, twenty men and fifteen women were ready to take up arms and march. Another twenty men and twelve women were to guard the city, around which a well-constructed system of defense had been built up. They had barricaded all the streets from building to building and fortified all of the doors and windows on the perimeter structures.

"We need to reprovision and be ready to move out in the morning." Captain Hunter hastily sorted the men into work groups, assigning a task to each group. "You men get food and water. You men get ammunition, flint, and powder, and you get us some carts. We have better roads now and I mean to use them." The weary men turned and set about their assigned tasks.

Captain Hunter grabbed Sergeant Chambers's elbow

before he could take off. "I want to talk to find out what went on while we were away. Go find the governor and bring him to the fort."

Captain Hunter and Major Shepard were seated at the planning table when Sergeant Chambers came in. "Sir, the governor was lost in an attack in early June."

"Yes. Thank you, Sergeant. The major was just telling me about that."

The captain got right to business. "We will tell you how things are going with this war and answer any questions momentarily, but first I need to know what has transpired here since we left."

Major Shepard stood up in a deliberate fashion as he organized his thoughts. "The first few weeks we secured ourselves in the buildings and meant to defend the town in this way. The attacks were sporadic in nature as you can well imagine. We lost the governor almost straightaway. Fewer of these monsters were advancing at a time after that first assault.

"We realized that we were severely hobbled in our ability to function as a community with our movement so restricted. So, we set about the business of establishing a greater perimeter. It was decided to use the materials available in town rather than risk sending men out to gather more.

"When winter came, and the snows began to fall, the attacks dropped off considerably. We sent a few parties out to the nearby farms for food and seeds and whatever they could get. We debated for some time about venturing out to try to gather other survivors, but it was decided to be an unwise risk. It was also determined that any survivors would be more likely to find us here than we would be to find them out there. So far only two families have been taken in. One family of four and one family of seven."

As the major sat, the captain stood. "We had hoped that there would be more men here to join us. We are nowhere at the strength we need for this endeavor."

He looked over and saw Chambers was visibly uncomfortable in the official meeting situation. "Sergeant, you know what we have been up to. Go check on the preparations and make sure things are going well."

Chambers was clearly relieved. He quickly stood, saluted, and walked out.

He saw John and Nektosha walking into the fort. "Halloo!" John shouted as he approached. "Boy, am I glad to see you all made it through safe and sound. Nektosha was telling me about your problem at the river. I don't know whether I am glad I missed it or sorry I was not there to help."

Chambers was beaming to be back in the company of his friends. "Well, you and *The Badger* would have been a big help."

"Yup, yup!" John replied, giving Nektosha a slap on the back.

Nektosha held up a hand. "Hush, wait." He pointed off and up. "There, the airship."

"I hope they are bringing good news and more men," Chambers said as he paused a moment to gauge where Mr. Porter was headed to land.

"More men?" John asked. Nektosha told him about the

note as they hurried back to the fort's parade grounds to help get the flying ship settled.

They were barely on the ground for two minutes before Benson excused himself. "Um, medical supplies. Yes, at the hospital." He went almost running to the hospital. He did not get halfway there before Angela, the nurse who had helped him heal and figure out his mechanical hand, rushed into his arms. The two held each other for a long moment as everything else in the world ceased to exist for them.

Rufus Porter told Chambers, "The Indians are approaching the city now."

Chambers shook his hand vigorously, thanked him, and sent him into the meeting with the general, the governor, and the major. "We should go meet our reinforcements." The three of them headed through town to meet up with the Indians just as they were being let through the barricade.

"Good afternoon!" Chambers called out as they approached. "I am Sergeant Jack Chambers. This is Nektosha, and this is John Tucker." They shook hands all around, and the clear leader of the newcomers spoke.

"Greetings, I am Misko Makwa of the Ottawa people. I have been more or less keeping us organized out there."

"Great to meet you, Misko Makwa."

"Just call me Makwa please"

The sergeant smiled. "Will do. Most folks just call me Chambers. I need to get you into the planning meeting with the captain and the major." Chambers kept talking as he set a brisk pace toward the fort. "Your men can get some food down that way; they have set up some tables at the council house. Hey, John, could you go with them and see about getting some food sent up to the fort."

"Yup, uup!" The trapper and nearly thirty large Indian men peeled off toward the smell of hot stew and fresh-baked bread.

When Chambers and Nektosha introduced Makwa to the members of the meeting, the captain nodded and smiled, then held out his hand.

"Find a seat, Makwa—I will be right back." He then pointed at Chambers and gestured for him to follow him out the door.

Once outside, he asked Nektosha to excuse them as he wanted to talk.

Sergeant Chambers began to get nervous, rummaging around in his mind for what he may have done wrong.

"Jack." The captain was addressing him by his first name—how bad was this going to be? "On the field, you are possibly the best leader I have ever seen. But when you get into a meeting, your backbone melts like so much butter. You have *got* to get past this. I am telling you you have to get in there and to conduct yourself accordingly. Is that understood?"

"Yes, sir."

Chambers followed the captain into the meeting and took a seat off to the side where he would not feel like the center of attention.

Captain Hunter promptly refocused the meeting, "We should get straight to the point here. Makwa, your people have shown impressive results in dealing with this menace. What tactics are you using?"

"We have been treating this like a hunt. We set up

hunting parties of seven or so. We sometimes would have one man go out and make much noise to draw them out; then he runs back to us and we attack."

He paused as the captain was visibly processing this revelation.

"We also made baited traps with fresh meat. We just wait to see if they come; then we attack."

"Yes, yes ... " the captain interrupted. "This makes sense. We have been doing something like that but staying close together. Except for Sergeant Chambers, right, Jack?"

Chambers took a breath to steady his nerves. "Yes, sir. With the exception of getting taken by surprise, things went well for us. We had gathered everyone together at that moment. If we had been in smaller groups, I believe we may have done much better. I do think keeping the groups close is necessary for when we encounter the larger packs."

"Exactly!" the captain exclaimed with a nod and a smile. Chambers felt much of his tension drop away.

Captain Hunter looked optimistic for the first time in a long time, "Makwa, I ask that a couple of your men join each of the hunting parties we are going to set up so that they can show us how you use these baiting tactics as we go." Makwa nodded in agreement.

"Good, gentlemen, now I think we should go and get some food."

"I had John go to send some plates up here, sir." Chambers's words stopped the men in their tracks.

"Excellent! Thank you!"

Everyone retook their seats and cleared a spot in front of them.

The captain began detailing the finer points of the plan. "We will send one party up each coast to meet up with Sawyer and his men. They can then all push to the south as we push to the north. We will use Mr. Porter's airship to keep the parties in touch with each other. We will meet back at the ships—"

There was a knocking at the door. It was John and some of the local women loaded down with too much food. "Good. John, I am glad you are here. I need you to take *The Badger* around and meet us at the ships, They are docked at the southeast point of Lake Michigan."

"Yes, sir. I will sail in the morning. Is there anyone you want to send with me?"

"Just keep the men I have assigned to you. We need everyone else for the hunt. Keep an eye on the coast in case you can spot something we missed."

With that, John nodded and backed out of the room, and the ladies started dispensing the hearty feast.

25:

APPLE RIVER FORT

The Chippewa hunting parties had already cleared a great deal of the surrounding area over the course of the winter, so it only took a few weeks to cover and clear the rest of the territory. They were able to do this with the loss of very few men. Most of them died due to illness and dysentery.

When they arrived at the ships, they were greeted with great anticipation, and the men were just as glad to be back in a familiar environment.

Dr. Lovell and Howakan quickly pulled the captain into a private meeting and explained what they had discovered about the Wentiko plague. Once they were sure that the captain's response was not going to accuse and fault Dr. Periwinkle, they sent for him to join the meeting as well.

As Deggory entered the room, the captain was already speaking. "So, can we then find a cure for this?"

Dr. Lovell answered, "Not yet but having a solid idea of what it is tells us what it is not. We can eliminate a great deal of pointless experimentation and focus on the mix of things we know to be present." He paused, wanting to see Captain Hunter's reaction.

Captain Hunter just nodded and turned to Deggory. "Doctor, I understand what your part in this is, and I also understand how unforeseen factors took this situation beyond your control. I think it is best that this information goes no further than this room. We simply need to find a solution."

"Would it help to bring you a live specimen?"

"No!" Howakan shouted, standing so quickly that his chair fell backward. "I tried something like that back when this started. It did not go well. It infected half of my people."

"Fair enough. If there are no other questions, get back to work and get me a solution."

When the steamships arrived in Chicago, John had already docked *The Badger* and had his crew standing by to help secure the lines of the USS *Michigan* and then the USS *Daniel Webster*.

"Deggory! Deggory!" John was calling out to the ship. "Is Dr. Periwinkle there?"

"I am here." Deggory was standing at a rail watching the first mass of soldiers clear the gangplank.

"You have got to come here, quick."

Deggory faltered for a moment. He was planning to avoid the ghosts of his hometown as much as he could. There were just too many painful memories, and too much guilt.

He saw the urgency in John's face and reluctantly headed for the dock.

"It is your man James, sir. Here he comes now."

When James approached, Deggory smiled. The sight of his employee and friend was an unexpected and needed boon. He extended a handshake that turned into an embrace.

"Well, sir, you said to take care of things when you were gone. I was not sure what you meant by that, so I reckoned to take care of just about everything for you. First of all, I went through the boxes of belongings that was not burnt from your old lab and found some more of your notes. They must have been under something as they survived in surprisingly good condition." James handed him a carefully wrapped bundle of papers. "As for the house, sir, I figured maybe you was talking about protecting it. So, I went out among the farms and such and got us some help."

"He got you a seventy-five-man militia, Deggory!" John blurted out, unable to contain himself for another second.

"Well, seventy-three, anyway," James corrected.

Deggory was gobsmacked. "Holy mackerel! We need to tell the captain."

Captain Hunter was even more excited than Deggory and John at the news. "Excellent! I will be adding them into our squads as soon as we get situated here. Have your man meet me in my office on the ship."

Howakan was very glad to hear about the recovered research and to see that his people had fared well in his absence. Tomaha had done a fine job as a leader of their tribe.

It was decided to leave the handful of men from the Winnebago tribe with their people to help guard Chicago along with a few of Jim's Militia, as they had come to be known.

Deggory, Howakan, and Dr. Lovell were eager to sift through the recovered notes, but Tomaha insisted on hosting a grand meal at his camp and would not take no for an answer. Many of the townsfolk showed up, and the food, drink and good humor lasted well into the night. The captain allowed the men, and himself, an extra hour of sleep before calling assembly the next morning.

Deggory and Howakan, who had clearly not slept, met him on his way off the ship. "Sir, we may have something here." He was shaking a stack of papers, as if the captain would be able to look at them and see what he was talking about. "We are going to meet back up with Dr. Lovell at the lab and run some more tests."

The captain looked into the faces of the two bedraggled men. "Good! Get to it, then." He turned to one of the soldiers following him. "Call assembly. We dare not delay any longer."

"Today we are going to head north—we will clear the area to and around Lake Winnebago. Then we will move to the west to the Mississippi and clear everything else as we head back south. There is a contingency of men secretly moving war supplies through Apple River Fort. We may be able to get some additional men to join us there."

With the newly added men from Jim's Militia and the more mobile hunting parties, they were able to cover the vast area between in just a couple of weeks. Many remarked at how few of the Wentiko they were finding. The talk around the cook fires at night was that they might be nearly done. When they got to Apple River Fort, they found no soldiers, and the walls and towers were unmanned, and the gates stood open.

Captain Hunter shrugged, "They may have gone out on a patrol. Well, at least we can take some shelter here and use this defensible position to gather and plan our next move. Get the men inside."

It was a small fort with an old cabin and a smaller building on one end and a single blockhouse tower on the other. It was just a local defense built for the Black Hawk War, being just over ten miles from the Mississippi River. The small fort was getting quite crowded as more of the soldiers, Indians, and militia continued to file in.

Captain Hunter stood on a small lookout platform and called for quiet.

When all the voices stopped, the men by the blockhouse heard some soft noises from the doorway. When they turned to look, a small girl walked out of the darkness.

"I thought you checked in there."

"The wee thing must have been hiding behind the barrels." Her hair was tousled, and she was wrapped in a pink blanket. She was covered in a fine black dust. With her head down, the men thought she must be very frightened from all the commotion.

"Hey, little miss, there's nothing to fear now. We have come to rescue you."

When the girl looked up, her face was a mottled, rotted mess. The growl she let out belied her tiny frame. In a reflex move, the soldier closest to her pulled up his flamethrower and doused her. She ignited instantly with a bright flash and let out a shrill shriek. She fled back into the darkness of the powder magazine.

BOOM!!!! The fort exploded. Half of the men standing in the courtyard fell. Many were never to rise again. The fireball that filled the courtyard also rose up and engulfed the airship.

Benson had been watching from his spot in the bow and fortunately had clamped his artificial hand to the rail. The other two men in the gondola were not so lucky and were thrown out and fell some forty feet to their deaths.

"Get us down!" he shouted at Mr. Porter.

"I'm working on it!" Porter yelled back. With the loss of the weight of two men, the airship had ascended rapidly. "We lost a wing as well. See if you can get over there and work the other one." Porter had braced a foot on the rail and was pulling the tiller over so far it looked as if he too might fall overboard.

As he stretched to reach the wing lever in the center of the craft, Benson could feel the heat coming through his boots. "We're on fire!"

"The grenades!"

"Arrrrgh!" Benson grabbed the burning box with his free hand and threw it over the rail just as the hydrogen air bag ignited.

The airship followed the crate of bombs as each became a tumbling mass of smoke and flames, with several of the grenades exploding on the way down.

The entire conflagration impacted the earth in a thick patch of woods a few hundred yards from the fort, sending up another grand plume of flame and smoke.

Sergeant Jack Chambers was slow to stand up, carefully checking himself for injuries. He pulled a large sliver of wood from his left forearm and clamped his hand to the wound to slow the bleeding. He looked next to him as Nektosha was just getting to his feet. He had a cut across his right cheek that was also bleeding freely.

They looked at each other for a moment. Nektosha was speaking, but Chambers's ears were ringing to much make any sense of it. The air was thick with acrid, sulfuric smoke that stung the eyes and made it even more difficult to see. The two groggily staggered around and tried to assess the situation. They could see many of the men struggling to stand up and looking around.

Nektosha pulled on Chambers's sleeve. The sergeant winced and turned. "The captain." Chambers could just make out what the brave was telling him.

"Yes ... Where?"

Nektosha just pointed to where Captain Hunter was up on one knee staring across the devastation.

It was at that moment that they were able to discern the screeching and whooping of rampaging Wentiko. Though it was difficult to tell with his head full of smoke and high-pitched ringing, it sounded like a lot of them.

"Get up!" he shouted over the field of mutilated soldiers. "Get UP! They are coming!" His own voice sounded distant inside his head. "To arms! To arms!"

A few at the far end of the fort responded at first, but

as they caught on, the men heaved themselves into motion and readied their weapons and gear as they stepped over the dead and dying to face the nightmare that was descending on them.

They picked their way to the newly formed breach in the defenses. "Form ranks!" Chambers heard Sawyer shouting from the far side of the fort.

"Yes," he thought. "Form ranks!" he echoed.

The soldiers carried out their duty admirably. Despite the fact that many were coping with serious wounds, they lined up behind the debris that a moment ago had been the northern fortification looking to see what was coming.

As they recovered from the shock, the soldiers got back into proper fighting postures. The captain called out, "It sounds like we have some time. Clear out the courtyard and barricade the breach. Get me some lookouts on the roofs. We need to know when and where they are coming from."

The guard tower was still standing. Most of the force of the blast had been channeled out the open door. The wall beside the door and most of the men that were standing near it were now destroyed.

Chambers suddenly looked at Nektosha. "Have you seen Smith? He is usually already tending to the wounded." The two of them looked frantically for their comrade.

"Bring the wounded in here!" They heard his familiar voice calling out from inside the larger cabin.

The shrieking cries of the Wentiko were getting closer.

Chambers and Nektosha turned their attention from moving the bodies of the fallen to the vacant corner of the tiny fort. This was the spot where the captain was standing just before the blast. Other soldiers were carefully stacking the logs that had made up the wall forming a zigzag barricade.

"Here they come! Oh my God!" There was clearly a dose of panic in the voice of the lookout. "There are hundreds of them!"

The men who were moving the logs quickly shoved the sharpened ends of some of the shattered logs through the hastily built fence to further slow the rush of the impending attack. The attack came from the north, the side with the two cabins. The Wentiko quickly swarmed around all sides of the fort like ants on a berry.

All of the soldiers fired into the mass, but the effect against such an overwhelming number was not even noticeable.

"WE NEED HELP OVER HERE!!" It was one of the men at the fence. They were stabbing wildly with their bayonets and taking out many of them, but there were so many behind them that it was clear that this would prove a futile effort, and they would be overrun.

The lookouts turned from their rooftop perches and fired several muskets into the front of the writhing mass. This too had but a little effect. The other walls of the fort could be heard creaking from the pressure of so many accursed bodies massing against them.

Over all of this they heard something unexpected. Was it thunder? No, there was a rhythm. It was drums! Many large drums beating together. There was something else too. Horns, battle horns ringing through the air.

The attacking horde had a decrease in its frantic fury.

The horns and drumming were increasing in volume rapidly. "What in the world IS THAT!" the lookout cried out. The attacking creatures started craning their heads from side to side, and the ferocity of their attack waned even more.

Then everyone was startled when a huge arrow pierced through three Wentiko near the front of their attack. Many more had regular-size arrows appear in their heads and torsos.

It was a massive army of Indians mounted on what looked like large wagons propelled by massive painted sails. The drums and horns were now incredibly loud and they were not stopping as several of these sail-powered war wagons circled behind the Wentiko pack which was now clearly dazed and nearly ineffective. The soldiers in the fort were greatly bolstered by this turn of events and surged back onto the offense. Flamethrowers and steam guns wreaked their devastation on the front of the pack.

Each of the wagons had one or two of the giant ballistas mounted at the bow. Yes, Chambers realized, the wagons were shaped like ships.

The pressing on the outer walls eased and stopped. This allowed the men inside to focus their firepower on the main attack at the breach. Many of the Indians were leaping from the war wagons and attacking the pack from the rear with long spears. The Wentiko, now surrounded, flailed with savage fury, but their end was now inevitable. When the battle was at last at an end, the drums and horns stopped, and everyone stood for a second in silence; then many cheered a few wept in relief. They had all thought that they would die that day.

Captain Hunter made his way to the front to address the Indian army. "Thank you!" His voice was choked with emotion. "You saved us. Thank you. I am Captain Hunter of the U.S. Army."

Their leader stepped forward from the tiller of one of the war wagons. He was a huge man with bright warpaint and a mohawk shaped into a horn. "I am glad we arrived in time to do some good. I am Arusa of the Chatiks Si Chatiks. Your people refer to us as the Pawnee."

26:

THE JOURNEY HOME

He hopped from the prow of his wind wagon and exchanged a long, sincere handshake with the captain.

Chambers and Nektosha walked up and shook the hands of a couple of the spearmen nearby, and they were not alone as soon everyone was shaking hands, and the soldiers marveled at the overland ships.

Arusa spoke over the greetings and platitudes. "Your men have paid a dear price for this victory. You have many wounded. Do you have a place nearby where they can be tended to? We can help you carry them."

Captain Hunter surveyed the area, assessing the damage. "Yes, thank you! This was a hard day indeed. After the explosion, we have set up an aid station in that cabin." He raised his voice to address the whole company. "Move those that are unable to walk onto these ..."

He looked to Arusa.

"Wind wagons."

"Yes, wind wagons." "Load them onto the wind wagons, and we need some men to help tend to them. We also need to keep a watch out for more of those … " He stopped mid-sentence. His gaze shot skyward in alarm. "The airship! Porter and his crew!"

He had realized the airship was not able to be seen nor heard. He looked around and saw a column of smoke in the distance. "You two go check on … " he said as he pointed to a couple of militiamen nearby.

He had not yet finished his sentence when Sergeant Chambers and Nektosha sprinted past them. "Follow them. Go!" The men took off after them.

They found Porter and Benson high up in a tree with their repeating pistols in their hands. Both were shaken up, scraped, and bruised but not seriously injured. Once they had accounted for everyone and administered aid to the wounded, everyone was then occupied with burying the dead. They had lost seventeen men overall. It was not as bad as they had feared, but there was a lot of wounded, and many of the injuries were severe.

Captain Hunter told Arusa, "Chicago is about three days to due east of here. Can you travel with us that far?"

"Yes, we were hoping that someone was fighting these things on this side of the river. We should go and share information, so we can work together to stop these things."

Even with the great number of wounded, the captain was able to find a spot on the wagon with the chieftain. He was eager to talk to him and get news from him. "We thought we had cleared these things out. We had not seen a pack of any size for some time. We had never seen one as big as this. You say you have been fighting the Wentiko on the other side of the Mississippi?"

Arusa smiled. "Wentiko? That term fits nicely. Yes, we have. We had a large problem on the other side of the Mississippi River. Many villages were lost entirely as they drove out to the west. We learned early that horses were too frightened of them, so we needed another way.

"We went to our elders for counsel, and they recalled hearing of the sail-powered wagons. We had also seen that these devils … Wentiko … became confused by loud, rhythmic noise. We took to the hunt, and we believe we have driven them from the west. However, we knew that if they were over here, they would return again.

"If, as you say, you have driven them from your lands as well, then we may in fact have the situation under control."

"So, Arusa, tell me, how did your elders know about these wind wagons?"

"The story goes back a long time on these. Our ancestors had befriended some of the conquistadors from Spain, and they told us stories of these. They are at their best on the open plains of our homeland. With some practice and modifications, we have been able to manage them in many terrains and conditions."

"Well done!" the captain exclaimed as the wagon creaked and wobbled down the road.

"Those weapons you have developed are quite impressive as well, General."

"Thank you. I was fortunate to have a great team. Did you get to see the airship?"

"That is what got us headed your way; unfortunately, I

did not get a good look at it before it exploded."

"Well, Porter said that was a prototype. I have no doubt that he is already planning the next model."

The whole town of Chicago turned out when they returned. Everyone came out to see the war wagons and welcome the return of the soldiers.

"We need to get the injured men to Detroit. The medical facilities are better able to deal with them. We will have Drs. Lovel and Periwinkle and Howakan with us. They can give the men a better chance once we get them on the steamships."

"We must return to the hunting of these Wentiko, as you have named them. That is a good name for them." Arusa was reaching to shake the captain's hand.

"It is good to know you are fighting this with us." The captain took the chieftain's hand in both of his. "I will send out some fresh troops to join you soon. I cannot thank you enough for your timely assistance."

The ships were quickly loaded, and they got underway for Detroit.

During the voyage to Detroit, Dr. Lovell took a moment away from tending to the wounded to meet with the captain.

"It will take more time and testing, but it appears to be a mix of afflictions and that the principal component is rabies. The only answer for that is death. However, this plague seems to be accelerated by the odd fungus. So, we are working on a way to combat that part of it."

"I was hoping for better news, sir. Keep at it. If we can stop it from spreading, that may be enough."

When they got to Detroit, the wounded men were moved to the hospital for care. The rest of the men were ordered to stay on the ships in the interest of time. The exception was Benson, who was allowed to stay with Angela and help in the men's recovery.

They sailed back to Washington, the ships were under full steam, and *The Badger* deployed as much sail as John felt possible.

When they docked at the fort in Washington, General Macomb came to the docks to greet them. After a short conversation, he sent orders for all the men to assemble on the parade field in two hours.

This allowed just enough time for the men to get their gear off the ship and into the bunkhouses and to greet the loved ones waiting for their return.

Jack Chambers, Sophie, Thomas, and Victoria embraced for a long time without saying a word before they all erupted in simultaneous chatter.

"How are you?"

"Look how you have grown!"

"Tell me what happened."

"Did you get them good, Daddy?"

When the men assembled on the field, there was a flat wagon that was set up as a podium. Then President Jackson himself stepped up to address them.

"What you have accomplished over the past few months is nothing short of heroic. You have done this great nation, and I daresay the world, a service that cannot be repaid." He paused.

"However, if word of the horrors you faced were to

spread to the general populace, the resulting panic would leave this nation in a state of ruin from which we would not likely recover.

"So, I must ask each of you not to speak of this to anyone. I am sending word out to the west for them to do the same. We will find other causes to fault for the devastation caused by those afflicted by this plague, these"—he leaned over to one of his aides—"Wentiko, as you call them. I thank you in advance for your cooperation in this."

General Macomb stepped up as the president stepped down. "I need the following men to come forward." He produced a folded paper from his pocket.

"John Tucker, Nektosha, Dr. Deggory Periwinkle, and Howakan." When they stood in front of the wagon, the general spoke again.

"Though you men are not in the military, you dropped everything and sacrificed much in the service of this nation, and you have our thanks and recognition. Since this operation has been declared clandestine, no public accolades can be forthcoming. All of us gathered here know what you have done, and we thank you."

Thunderous applause and cheers rose from the large crowd. He leaned down to speak just to them. "However, if any of you are agreeable, we would gladly offer you gainful positions as we reforge the new frontier." He shook each of their hands.

"Jack Chambers, Alexander Sawyer, William Benson, and Douglas Smith."

"Private Douglas Smith, I am hereby promoting you to sergeant and assigning you work with Dr. Lovell for additional training and equipping to establish medical assistance for soldiers in the field.

"Sergeant Alexander Sawyer, you are hereby promoted to the rank of captain and assigned to Fort Dearborne in Chicago, where you will ally with Arusa. You will work with him and the Pawnee to ensure that this menace has been suppressed.

"Sergeant Jack Chambers, I am hereby promoting you to the rank of captain; this is necessary because I am assigning you to Fort Mackinac to oversee the rebuilding of that key location, to be used to oversee the safety of the Michigan territory.

"William Benson is not here; however, he will be promoted to sergeant and assigned a post in Detroit. I understand he has a girl there."

The general shook their hands and announced, "I will be meeting with the rest of you soon. You have all done a great job. Dismissed." Another round of cheers swelled from the ranks.

Captain Chambers walked over to his wife and children, who were clearly thrilled at the idea of going home together.

He was almost accosted by Nektosha and John, who said, "You are not going without us, are you?"

"I was hoping you would come."

Captain Chambers looked through the crowd and spotted Howakan and Deggory talking to Dr. Lovell. He excused himself and weaved his way over to them.

"What about you two? Will you come join us on Mackinac?"

Howakan looked at the new captain through old eyes. "We have some work to do here still. We may come visit soon."

Dr. Lovell joined the conversation. "I see no reason why you two could not continue your work on Mackinac. I will plan to visit you soon."

Captain Chambers was getting excited at how things were shaping up. "Yes. That would be excellent."

He went and rejoined his family, who were already making plans to build their new home.

Captain Sawyer wasted no time getting his company assembled and out to Chicago. When he arrived in Fort Dearborn, he was informed that Arusa of the Plains Indians needed to speak with him as soon as possible. He gathered a few men and went searching. Using smoke signals, he was able to meet up with him at the restored Apple River Fort.

"It is good to see you again." Arusa was gracious and had a hot meal ready for them when he arrived.

"I have troubling news, my new friend. Some of my scouts have reported that they have discovered a few buffalo across the river that have the same affliction." He paused for a long moment to let the potential consequences of this be realized by the captain and his men. "Those that were found were put down.

I have sent a hunting party out to see if there are more, and they are late in their returning."

It was a few weeks later when *The Badger* sailed into Mackinac Harbor, accompanied by the USS *Daniel Webster* carrying a company of soldiers assigned to Captain

Chambers and eager to rebuild the fort and harbor.

It was a few weeks after that that Tomaha and the rest of the Winnebago tribe joined Howakan and the others on the island as well.

CPSIA information can be obtained
at www.ICGtesting.com
Printed in the USA
LVHW030237100320
649433LV00004B/502

9 781977 219565